Strictly Family

The Twin Find

Ruth Cardello

Author Contact

website: RuthCardello.com
email: ruthcardello@gmail.com
Facebook: facebook.com/ruthcardello
Instagram: authorruthcardello
TikTok: @author.ruthcardello
Bookbub: ruth-cardello

Copyright

Note to my readers

You can read more about Jesse Rehoboth in *Strictly Business (The Switch Book 1)* and his twin **Scott Millville in Out of Love (The Switch Book 2)**. I'm having so much fun writing these twin books and delving into the backstory of how they were all separated. Stay in the know for all releases by signing up for my newsletter: Go here.
ruthcardello.com/newsletter

CHAPTER ONE

Ashlee

I HAD TO pee, but nothing could have dragged me from my car as I waited for Thane Rehoboth to emerge from his office building. My phone vibrated, causing me to jump and I swore under my breath before answering. If I didn't, my sister would only call back. "This isn't really a good time," I said in a low voice, even though there was no one around to hear me.

"Sage wants to say good night," she said. "And I'm still hoping I can talk you out of this before you get yourself arrested."

"Is Sage beside you?"

"No, Harry is reading her a bedtime story. It's a school night, Ashlee. You were supposed to be back hours ago."

I sighed. "I'm sorry. I thought I would be. All of this would have been easier if they'd let me in to talk to him. Or if the man worked regular hours. The parking lot is pretty much empty. It's eight o'clock. Who works that late?"

"A lot of people," Joanie answered. "Come home. For all

you know, he intends to work until midnight."

"No," I said with determination. "If I leave now, I may not have the courage to do this again."

"Which sounds like a sign that you shouldn't be doing it at all."

She was right, but that didn't change how much I didn't want to close the door on this idea. Still, she'd done more for me than I could ever repay. "If you need me to go home, I will. I wasn't thinking about how this would affect your kids."

"My kids are fine," she said gently. "And so is Sage. We're fine. There's very little difference between putting three or four kids to bed. It's you I'm worried about. This is crazy."

"Isn't that what everyone said when you offered to be a surrogate for me? People focused on all the possible ways it could go wrong, but look how it turned out. I have Sage and you have my eternal gratitude."

She chuckled. "Oh, no you don't. Don't soften me up with my favorite niece like that, thinking I won't give it to you straight. You're taking this too far."

Sage was her only niece. Normally the favorite label would have made me smile, but I was a bundle of nerves. "You were there. You heard Sage. She wants to know about her father."

"One DNA match does not mean Sage has a father. Men who donate to sperm banks anonymously want to remain just that—anonymous."

"He doesn't have to tell anyone about her. He doesn't even need to get to know her. I'd be happy with any tidbit of a story he could give me that I could one day pass on to her. He obviously didn't do it for the money. Did he want to ensure his line would continue? He might not want to tell me, but what if he does? I have to take the chance."

"Oh, Ashlee, I wish I believed that. You and I both know that some part of you is hoping for more. You have this fantasy that he'll want to meet her and be part of her life. The man jizzed in a cup then signed paperwork to ensure his information wasn't linked to whatever came from that deposit. He doesn't want to know about Sage or any other children he might be connected to."

"There aren't more. I was able to squeeze that much information out of the secretary at the clinic."

"By implying your child's life depended on getting the name of the donor—which she didn't give you—so she probably didn't even believe you."

"She believed me. I saw her open the online files to check. The donor's name wasn't listed, but she had the history of his donation. If there were others, she would have told me. We bonded. And I didn't lie to her. I told her it was imperative that I track down the father for health reasons. That's true. Family health records are important."

After a moment, Joanie said, "I know you want to give Sage a piece of her father and I understand, but is pouncing on him in his workplace parking lot like a stalker really the best way to contact him?"

"I've tried to make appointments to meet him. He's too busy for normal people."

"Normal?" Joanie asked with light sarcasm. "Is that what we're calling you now?"

I made a little growl deep in my throat. "I need to do this, Joanie. If there is the tiniest chance he would even consider writing her a letter or sending her a birthday card—"

"He won't, Ashlee. You're setting yourself up for disappointment. And you need to acknowledge the possibility that he won't be happy that you found him."

"I know."

"Do you? You're not dealing with Joe Schmoe who works at the local grocery store. The Rehoboths are big news now that their company is part of the Bellerwood space station. That's why he has no time for you. He's busy being rich and becoming a household name. You'll be lucky if he doesn't call the police."

I didn't have a good argument against that because once again she wasn't wrong. I was crossing a line, but I couldn't look Sage in the eye if I didn't at least give her a chance to know him. A few months earlier, at our annual Father's Day dinner with my parents, my sister, her husband, and their children, Sage had asked questions I'd hoped wouldn't surface for years.

"Do I have a daddy?"

"Does my daddy love me?"

It had been heartbreaking. I told her that her life is full of people who love her. When she pressed, I told her that her daddy hadn't been in a place where he could have children, so he gave me the gift of her. He'd loved her enough to make sure she had a good mommy and cousins to chase around.

It wasn't the best explanation, but it was what I came up with in the pressure of the moment. At first it appeased her, but a week later she circled back with more questions. Was her daddy alive? Did he have other children? Did I have a picture of him?

I lovingly deflected the questions until she stopped asking, but I knew this wouldn't be the last time she wondered about him. I wanted something to give her that was real—anything. Yes, I understood being a sperm donor was very different from being a father. Thane might want nothing to do with me, Sage, or even the knowledge that she existed.

But what if he did?

What if a small part of him wondered if he'd sired a child?

A person could change their mind on a matter. Maybe all he'd want was to see a photo of her and nothing more. Maybe he wouldn't want even that. I'd be content if he told me the answer to a question I was sure she'd ask me when she was older: Why? I wanted to tell her the truth and I wanted it to be beautiful.

If he said he didn't want anything to do with her, I'd

respect that. No one ever had to know that we'd met, but I had to open that door just a crack... I couldn't leave without something to go back with. "One more hour. If he doesn't come out by then, I'll..."

"Wait another hour," she finished. "I'm worried about how this will go, but I do understand. I would do anything for my children, and it broke my heart to hear Sage ask if she has a daddy. Call me in an hour even if he hasn't come out yet. The kids will all be in bed and we can stay on the phone until you see him."

And this was why I had always, and would always, consider my sister my best friend. No one knew me as well or supported me as completely. "How much babysitting will I owe you for this?" I asked.

"Depends on whether or not I have to bail you out of jail," she said without missing a beat. "Luckily for you, Mike just got home so there'll be someone to watch the kids if I have to."

I chuckled. "Let me say good night to Sage." After clearing my throat, I added, "And thank you."

"Be careful, Ashlee," she said in a low tone before her voice rose a few octaves. "Sage, it's Mommy on the phone."

At almost four years old, Sage was torn between wanting to talk to me and not wanting her cousin to stop reading to her. "Mommy, I'm having a sleepover."

"Yes, you are," I said with a smile. She was the single best decision I'd ever made. "Are you being good?"

"Not as bad as the boys," she answered cheerfully. "Alfie shot Josh in the face with his Nerf gun so now all the guns are outside toys. Auntie Joanie doesn't care if people get shot in the face outside."

Trying not to laugh, I said, "I'm sure she does, honey. It's never a good idea to shoot anyone. Tell Alfie it's better to shoot at targets."

"I told him that," she said with the confidence of an only child who spent far too much time talking to adults. "He said I'm not the boss of him."

Oh boy. "Okay, so maybe it's better if we let Auntie Joanie remind him of the rules."

"Harry told him I *am* the boss because I'm a girl and that means he can't punch me. I like Harry. Alfie said he could punch me if no one was looking so I kicked him in the leg."

"Sage Diane Pryer, we do not kick our cousins."

"Not even when they say they're going to hit us?"

"Not even then. Ask Alfie to come over and put me on speakerphone."

"He's not going to be happy."

"Sage."

"Okay." She called her cousin over.

"Am I in trouble?" Alfie asked. He would be if his mother found out what he'd said to Sage, but that wasn't where I hoped this was going.

"Not yet. Sage wants to say something to you."

"I do?" Sage asked, all innocence.

"Sage," I said firmly. "You know what you need to say to Alfie."

"I'm sorry I kicked you, Alfie."

It wasn't the most enthusiastic apology ever spoken, but I accepted it and hoped Alfie did as well. "Now, Alfie, please tell Sage that you would never hit her."

"I would never hit her," Alfie agreed. "All I said was that I could."

"Alfie, how old are you?"

"Almost nine."

"Then you know that saying something like that to someone half your size can scare them."

Alfie protested, "She wasn't scared when she kicked me. She was angry."

"She won't kick you again. Sage, tell him you won't do it again. You know better. Family is a gift. It's something not everyone has, and it's something to treasure. I love all of you and I am never prouder than when I see you taking care of each other."

"I won't kick you again, Alfie," Sage said, this time sounding sincere.

In the background, Josh, Joanie's middle child, spoke up. "Alfie failed a math test today and I laughed when he told Mom. I'm sorry, Alfie."

"That's why Alfie shot him," Harry, Joanie's youngest, said, "I was the only good one."

"I'm *good*," Sage said.

"Not today," Josh countered. "You kicked Alfie."

"Mom—" Sage started, but I cut her off.

"It sounds like it's time for all of you to go to bed. Can you hand the phone back to Auntie Joanie?"

"I love you, Mommy," Sage said. "Where are you?"

"I love you too, honey. Just getting some business done. Go to bed. When you wake up I'll either be in the spare bedroom sleeping or having coffee with Auntie Joanie."

A moment later, Joanie was back on the phone. "It wasn't actually as bad of an evening as they made it sound. Most of the time they were playing nicely."

I grimaced. "I know. I feel bad about adding Sage to the mix on a school night, though . . ."

"Sage is welcome here any night or every night. You know that. And the boys love her like a sister . . ." She chuckled. "Which is a blessing and curse all at once. I hope when they grow up they remain as close as we are."

My heart warmed. "They will. We used to argue like that. Mom and Dad always made sure we made up and apologized. All we can do is do the same and pray for their crazy little Nerf-gun-shooting, leg-kicking souls."

"Oh, I pray . . . mostly for patience." I could hear the smile in her voice. "But they're worth it."

"Did Alfie really fail a math test? That's not like him."

"He didn't fail. He got the extra credit part wrong. You know how hard he takes things like that. He considers that failing."

"Oldest child syndrome. You used to have that."

"Used to? I alphabetized my spice rack today. Why? I have no idea."

"How would you and Mike feel about going on a romantic weekend this month?"

"Really? That would be amazing."

"Just say when."

"Mike," Joanie called out. "Ashlee said she'll watch the kids any weekend we want to escape." A moment later she added, "He said you're now his favorite sister-in-law."

"I'm his only sister-in-law."

In a more serious tone, she said, "I told him where you are, and he's looking up the address. He doesn't want you there by yourself."

I gasped. "Tell him not to come."

"I'm not sure I can stop him. He's worried about you too."

I let out a breath. There was no way I could let him get involved. Mike was a gentle giant with a heart of gold, the type who'd let the police arrest him for an idea I was beginning to think wasn't one of my best. "You were right, Joanie. This is crazy. And the fact that Thane Rehoboth is still in his office is a sign that I shouldn't do this . . ."

"Are you sure?" Joanie asked slowly.

I nodded even though she couldn't see me. "Sage has a wonderful family already. We're enough. I'm enough. She doesn't need a story or a card from a man who has given her nothing more than his DNA."

"So, you're coming home?"

"Yes."

"I'm so sorry, Ashlee. I wanted this for you as much as you did."

"I know you did."

"I just didn't want to see you hurt."

"Well, you don't have to worry about that anymore."

"Do you want me to stay on the phone? I can have Mike put the kids down."

"No, you go. I'll call when I'm almost there."

"Okay." To Mike, she said, "Stand down, she's leaving now to come here."

"See you in a little bit," I said, then spontaneously added, "and tell Mike I love him for wanting to protect me."

"She loves you, Mike," Joanie said with a laugh. "He rolled his eyes, which I think in man language means he loves you too. Drive safely."

"I will."

After ending the call, just as I was about to start the car, I was reminded by my bladder there was a second matter that required my attention. The foyer of the office building was still lit. Would they allow someone to use their bathroom?

I hoped so.

CHAPTER TWO

Thane

EVERYONE IN MY office was long gone when I slammed my hand down on my desk and stood. It was dark out, but I often stayed late. The weight of my family's company was fully on my shoulders and failure wasn't an option.

Walt Bellerwood was quite possibly the most frustrating, irrational, narcissistic man I'd ever had the misfortune of working with. Over a year ago, when my brother and I had been approached by Bellerwood to design and install a life support system for a recreational space station, we'd known that taking on the project would change our lives.

I'd assumed it would be in a good way.

Pinching the bridge of my nose, I took a deep breath. What Bellerwood was demanding and what he'd contracted us to produce were now two very different things. Our system was performing as designed. A scaled-down version had been tested and retested in the upper atmosphere. There was no reason to believe it wouldn't perform as reliably on a larger scale.

The issue was that Bellerwood was making last minute and, I would argue, unrealistic changes to the station's energy core. He wanted his station to be self-sustaining and that meant someone needed to pull a renewable fuel source out of their ass.

Bellerwood would have won the race to space had he been satisfied with using what was currently available, but he not only wanted to be first, he needed to be the best. I sighed and walked to the window of my office. It was a philosophy I'd been raised to value and one I normally supported, but Bellerwood took it to the extreme.

By putting the completion of his space station on hold until we solved his fueling issue, he was essentially holding my company hostage. And so far, there wasn't a fucking thing I could do about it.

A screen on my desk beeped. I glanced over and groaned. Fantastic. My father had taken my lack of responding to his last two calls as a sign that he should contact me via the company's system. "Accept," I growled in resignation.

As soon as my father's face appeared, his voice boomed through the room. "Do I need to call our lawyers or will my son tell me how today went?"

Still standing I moved closer to my desk so he could see me. "It went as expected. Bellerwood isn't budging. Today he strongly suggested that I temporarily move in with Scott and Monica to help them resolve the volatility issue with their bean paste. He won't give up on the idea that it could be stabilized. The entire project has stalled, and he's laying the fault for that on my shoulders. Mine. I'm not a chemist nor am I a marriage counselor—"

"I wasn't aware that Scott and Monica were having issues."

"They're not. Bellerwood is delusional." About so many things. Several months earlier, just for a moment, he'd had me thinking I might also have a twin. I was beginning to believe that Bellerwood deliberately messed with people's minds so he could remain in control. It was proving an effective strategy even with me. Until recently, most would have described me as stoically determined to succeed. My brother Jesse had always accused me of being a bit of a snob because I held myself above the drama. Lately? I was drowning in shit that made no sense to me. I sat and crossed my legs at the ankle, not surprised at all that I was wearing two different socks. Lack of sleep, stress, and no solution in sight did that to a man. "Yes, Scott has engineered something that may one day be developed into a new fuel source, but right now it'd be like trying to power a kite with dynamite."

"I'll talk to Walt."

"This isn't your issue, Dad. I'll figure it out."

"Jesse—"

"Is a nervous wreck since Crystal was put on bedrest. He'll come back around after the baby is born." I took a deep breath and raised a hand before my father had time to respond. "I understand why this is hard for Jesse. He likes to be in control and he can't control this. You don't have to defend him, I get it."

"I wasn't going to defend him. I was going to remind you that this is not a weight you need to carry on your own. I'm retired, not dead. Jesse is preoccupied, but if he knew how Bellerwood is changing the terms—"

"He'd what? Take it to the courts? Threaten him? Normally I'd have no issue with doing either myself, but Bellerwood has become . . ."

"Family."

I ran a hand through my hair. As the father-in-law of my adopted brother's twin . . . "Life was a whole lot easier before Jesse found out he had a twin."

My father couldn't argue that it hadn't been, so he didn't. "And yet, I've never seen Jesse so happy. Scott, too. When I first met him I had low expectations of Scott's intellect, but he's brilliant—if a little on the odd side. Have you tried speaking to Monica about her father? Perhaps she could talk some sense into him."

"Say that last part to yourself again, Dad, and tell me if it sounds remotely realistic."

He pursed his lips. "You're in a tough spot."

I glanced at the ceiling then back. "Even if I thought she could sway him, I wouldn't ask Monica to get involved. Her relationship with her father is still fragile. I respect that." None of the recent chaos had changed what I believed was most important—Rehoboths put nothing before family. As someone who'd been adopted as well, that core belief had given me the strength to weather any storm. No matter what happened, Ethan Rehoboth was my father and Jesse was my brother. Perhaps not by blood, but by what mattered more . . . intention.

Responsibility.

Loyalty.

Family.

When Jesse found Scott and decided to honor their relationship, Scott became a brother to me as well. And Scott's wife, Bellerwood's daughter, my sister.

It was a mess, but one I was taking on as I did every issue—head-on. I met my father's gaze. "Bellerwood will come around. We're simply playing a multi-billion-dollar game of chicken. Eventually he'll realize a space station that has to be refueled periodically is better than no space station."

"Or you'll resolve the bean fuel issue."

I laughed without humor. "Or that."

After clearing his throat, my father said, "I didn't call about Bellerwood. It's my understanding that the lawyers met with the Steele woman this morning."

"They did."

"And?"

"And she dropped the paternity case."

"Because the child isn't yours," my father said with less

certainty than I would have preferred.

"Exactly. I went to dinner with the woman. Dinner. One time. Nothing happened. So unless a woman can get pregnant from scarfing food off my plate, I am one hundred percent certain the child isn't mine."

"Did you have a DNA test done?"

"I never had sex with her. We didn't even touch lips."

"Because she stole food off your plate."

"Does it matter why as long as it didn't happen?"

"You're so damn picky."

"I get that from you."

He laughed at that. "You do. And I'm not sorry. People need boundaries."

With a hint of a smile, I conceded, "The DNA test was negative."

"Aha. So you did have one done."

"To close the case, not because I had any doubts. I suppose I should be grateful she claimed our imaginary coupling was consensual." I frowned. "I had a healthy, reasonably happy sex life before we agreed to work with Bellerwood. Now that our name has become linked with his, I might as well walk around with a target on my forehead. Women used to want me, now all they see are dollar signs and a meal ticket. If one more woman comes out of the woodwork claiming I'm her baby's daddy—"

"You'll do the right thing and have a test done before you send her to the lawyers."

I sighed. "Unless I've never had sex with her. I reserve the right to tell all gold-digging psychopaths to shove off."

He expelled a huff. "I suppose that's fair." After a pause, he added, "It's past eight. Have you had dinner yet?"

I blinked a few times as I tried to remember if I had. "I'm not hungry."

"If you're going to conquer the world, it's best not to do it on an empty stomach. I'm on my way over. I'll call you when I'm on the street."

"That's not necessary, Dad."

"My son had a difficult day. Are you telling me that seeing me and having a good meal won't help you feel better?"

I rubbed a hand over my face. "No, I would never say that." My father hadn't built a successful HVAC business by being meek. Jesse and I hadn't grown it that way either. None of us backed down and we lived by the code that we were stronger together. "Thanks, Dad. I'll wrap things up here and come down."

"This will all work out, Thane. You always find a way to win."

I nodded and ended the call.

Bellerwood's game could financially ruin us. The idea of starting over wasn't something I feared, but my father was right . . . winning mattered. At least, it always had.

But what did that look like when it involved family?

I shut down my computer and locked my office. Dinner with Dad would hopefully help me figure that out.

CHAPTER THREE

Ashlee

I STOPPED BY the security desk to thank the man who'd allowed me to use the facilities despite the fact that it was against the rules. He looked to be in his early twenties, likely either still in college or fresh from graduating from one. Although being in a relationship with someone wasn't on my current list of goals, it was nice to know I hadn't completely lost my touch when it came to swaying a man with charm and a big smile.

Dating was very different when one had a child. It wasn't that I couldn't attract male attention, but my list of nonnegotiables had grown so long that it was often easier to simply not date.

I didn't want a drinker.

He needed to be local or be okay with moving to where I was because it was important to me that Sage grew up around her cousins.

No smoking. Not around my child.

No gambling. I was working too hard to build a secure

future for Sage and me to tolerate someone who might threaten that.

He couldn't have a temper.

Had to love children.

A good sense of humor was a must.

To even consider getting serious with someone, he had to have the capacity to love Sage as if she were his own. I'd been dating someone for a year when Joanie came to me and offered to be a surrogate. Her pregnancies had been relatively easy, but her baby-making was ready to close up soon. Endometriosis, one large cyst, and a few surgeries in my mid-teens had made it impossible for me to carry a baby myself. If I wanted one that was biologically mine, she preferred for me to have it while hers were young enough to be raised along with my child. She also, understandably, couldn't leave that offer open for some unspecified future time.

I'd laughed, cried, laughed again . . . then spent days debating if I was ready to be a mother. I was twenty-five, had a stable job, but I wasn't married. Did I need to be? Statistically, children did better in two parent households, but my child wouldn't lack adult role models or family. My parents were both young enough to be active and attentive grandparents.

When I'd mentioned what I was considering to the man I was dating, he'd said he didn't know if he could love someone else's child. We broke up that night and it was a decision I've never regretted.

Nothing mattered more to me than my family, and I'd either find a man who felt the same way or I'd be celibate until Sage graduated from high school. I shuddered and shook off that depressing thought.

The security guard smiled at me. "Now don't go telling anyone I broke the rules for you," he said with a wink.

"I won't." I shot him a bright smile. "Thanks again."

When I turned to leave, he said, "Hey, if you ever want to meet for a drink, you know where I am."

I considered flirting with him a little, simply to make myself feel better, but instead I said, "I have to get home to my daughter."

His eyes rounded a little and his smile wavered. The poor guy looked like he was unraveling a complex moral puzzle.

This time I winked. "It's okay. I'm too old for you anyway, but just so you know . . . when you meet the right one it won't matter if she comes with a whole litter of little ones. Or, at least, it shouldn't. Thanks again for bending the rules for me."

He nodded with a spark of admiration in his eyes and leaned forward. "I wasn't judging. It's just that I still live with my parents . . ."

I chuckled. "Enjoy that stage and every one that follows. Don't rush to get your own phone plan. I still miss my parents' unlimited data."

This time he laughed along like we were friends. "Right?"

"Have a good night," I said with humor before I turned and walked away. Yes, I was a single mother working hard to support myself and my daughter, but life was good. Not being in a relationship hadn't made my life any less wonderful.

Was that how I needed to look at Sage having a connection to her biological father? It mattered on a holiday when everyone was celebrating having a father, but did she need one? Had I tracked down Thane Rehoboth for my daughter or to appease unnecessary guilt?

Sage wanted a father, but she also wanted to find a way to shrink down zoo animals to keep them in the bottom drawer of her bureau. I wasn't researching the viability of shrink rays because doing so wasn't realistic.

Wasn't chasing down a man who'd anonymously donated sperm to ask him if he wanted to hear about his daughter just as crazy? Mr. Rehoboth, thank you for hiding out in your office. You saved both of us from what could have been quite the awkward encounter.

I reached for the door only to have a male hand beat me to it. "Let me get that for you." His deep voice sent a confusing warmth through me.

My eyes slowly worked their way up his muscular, suited torso to meet his intense gaze. "Thank you." My voice betrayed how affected I was by this sudden wall of testosterone looming above me.

I may have watched too many romantic comedies, but I

could have sworn time froze. We stood there simply looking into each other's eyes for a long moment I was certain I'd remember for the rest of my life.

Holy hell, he was gorgeous.

Every inch of him decadently lickable. Since when did a complete stranger have the power to turn me on? My lips parted as I reminded myself that I was taking a sabbatical from men.

And sex.

Okay, it was way too easy to imagine the two of us naked and tangled with each other in front of a fireplace. I shook my head, swallowed hard, blinked several times—then swayed back onto my heels when I recognized him.

His hand left the door and clasped my upper arm to steady me. "Are you okay?"

"Mr. Rehoboth? *Thane* Rehoboth?" I asked breathlessly as images I'd seen of him flooded my head and answered my own question. There was no doubt in my mind that he was the man I'd been waiting to meet.

"Yes." His hand dropped away from my arm.

"If I could have a moment of your time."

"Make an appointment with my secretary," he said in a cold voice as his expression hardened.

"I've tried," I said in a rush. That he'd appeared when I'd given up and was ready to go home had to mean I'd been right to come. "That's why I'm here."

"Ms. . . ."

"Pryer. Ashlee Pryer."

"Ms. Pryer, if you're here to ask me about my business, I have no comment. If you're here for any other reason . . ." He looked me over from my printed canvas shoes up my jean-clad legs, to briefly take in my science themed T-shirt that said: *You matter until you multiply yourself by the speed of light squared—then you energy.* "I'm not interested," he finished.

Ouch. I sucked in a breath. Okay, so the attraction wasn't mutual, but that wasn't why I was there. "Please." I dug through my purse for the paperwork that would prove what I was about to say. "This is about your daughter."

He rose to his full height and if looks could kill I would have been D.E.A.D. "I don't have a daughter."

Pulling an envelope from my purse, I waved it between us. "You do. Here's the DNA report to prove it. She's—"

He was through the door and slamming it closed between us before I had a chance to finish. Shit, I'd done that badly. I chased after him.

"Mr. Rehoboth!"

He kept walking. "Get the hell away from me."

Not the response I was hoping for, but I hadn't exactly given him a great first impression. "I don't want anything from you. Not for me. Not for her. I just want to show you a photo of her."

He stopped, spun on his heel and I nearly barreled into him. "Do not come one step closer to me. For future reference, every inch of this parking lot is under constant camera surveillance—sound included. I don't know you. I don't want to know you. I'm asking you to leave the premises voluntarily. If you don't go, I'll be forced to have you physically removed. However, at no time have I or will I touch you so if you're hoping to get something on film you won't."

Wow, he had trust issues. Still, I couldn't waste what might be my one opportunity to show him a photo of Sage. I stashed the envelope in my purse and pulled out my phone, turning it so he could see it. "Look, she has your eyes. My nose. But your ears."

His face reddened and between gritted teeth, he said, "I don't drink, so if your hope is to convince me that we hooked up one night, I'm sorry to disappoint you—I remember the faces and names of every woman I've ever fucked." His nostrils flared. "And as I've said—I don't know you."

There was nothing about having him lean toward me in a threatening manner that should have been sexy, but my body rebelliously came alive beneath his glare. Oh, shit. I need to have sex with someone soon because nothing like this had ever happened to me. I do not find myself inappropriately attracted to men who clearly want nothing to do with me. Celibacy must be rotting my brain. "You're right we've never . . . you and I . . . Sage is from . . ." I stopped because I wasn't making any sense. "You know that thing you did that you probably want to forget you did? Well, I used that to make Sage."

He shook his head. "Are you on drugs?"

"No." I put my phone away and took a deep breath. God, in my head this had been so much easier. "I know I shouldn't be here. You wanted it to be anonymous, but DNA matching is so good right now and—"

"Lady, you're fucking crazy and I'm beginning to feel sorry for you, but that doesn't mean I have time for this. Do you want me to call someone to come get you? I can do that much."

"I'm not on drugs." I rubbed a hand over my eyes. "I wouldn't be here but when Sage started asking if she has a father . . . if you're not comfortable with writing her a letter or a card, could you at least tell me what your reason was for making a donation at the clinic."

"The clinic?"

"The fertility clinic. You made an anonymous sperm donation—"

He leaned in again, deliciously angry and growled. "Do I look like a man who would donate anything to a fertility clinic?"

I swallowed hard, my mouth opening and closing without a sound coming out.

He straightened. "I had a hell of a lot more respect for women before you all started coming up with these crazy plans to entrap me."

"Entrap you?" I waved a hand through the air. "I'm not here to trap anyone. You don't have to be part of Sage's life."

"Good because you are obviously mentally unstable and confused. Let me say this as clearly as I can . . . I have never been to a fertility clinic. I have no idea what you're talking about and no interest in hearing more about it. You're beautiful. If you get some professional help, I doubt you'll have a problem finding a man willing to overlook a little crazy to be with you and the daughter I'm not convinced exists. Goodbye, Ms. Pryer."

Embarrassment brought a smile to my lips. This would not be an easy story to tell Joanie. She'd been right about how badly it would go and that would make the night difficult to live down. He wasn't calling the police, though, which I counted as a win.

Had I not just decided that my daughter didn't need him I would have been devastated, but she'd be okay. How many uptight, angry, slightly paranoid workaholics did a child need? My guess was none. By denying her, he was likely doing us a favor.

Still, I couldn't leave things the way they were. My intention had never been to upset him or leave him feeling guilty about how he'd reacted to the news I'd laid at his feet. He wasn't the one breaking the rules, I was. "Hey, I'm sorry. Don't feel bad about this. Knowing about where your DNA went and what it produced wasn't part of what you signed up for. I respect that. I took a chance coming here. I knew you probably wouldn't want to hear about her, but I had to take a shot. At the very least I'd hoped you'd give me answers to questions she'll ask me one day. But it's okay if you don't want to. You don't owe us anything."

"Because I never went to a clinic and am in no way involved."

I took out the paperwork again. "Except that you did and you are," I said gently and held out the envelope to him, but he didn't reach for it.

As if speaking to a child, he said firmly, "You're wrong."

It was a step better than being called crazy. I nodded and tucked the envelope into my pocket. "Wrong to be here, yes. And that's okay too. Nothing is more important to me than my family and this will be one of those stories we'll tell for years that simply confirms that. Good night, Mr. Rehoboth."

CHAPTER FOUR

Thane

I STOOD IN the middle of the empty parking lot wondering what the hell had just happened. I'd come out after my father called with the intention of retrieving the pair of glasses he'd left in my car. He claimed he didn't need them to read a menu, but that was his pride talking. He couldn't read anything without them but was also unable to remember where he left them, so he owned several pairs.

Instead of immediately going to my car, I stood there watching the beautiful, but looney as the day was long, woman climb into a little tan car. Of all the women who'd tried to manipulate me into a relationship lately, her story was at least unique.

A sperm bank? Me? Never.

Her mental instability was a shame because inside the building, for just a moment, I'd thought she might be worth asking out. She was dressed far too casually to be my type, but there was no denying she had a hot little body and the kind of beauty that would make any man stand a little straighter.

She even smelled good. Natural instead of perfumed.

It was only when she opened her mouth that it had all gone downhill. What the fuck was wrong with women? I was all about them being equals and living their lives however they wanted to, but when had they become stalkers?

A man liked a little chase now and then. I could appreciate a bold approach. Bold, not psychotic.

And what the hell was the forgiveness she'd offered at the end? Deliberate gaslighting or a manifestation of mental issues? I had no idea, but thankfully she'd left without me having to call security to have her removed.

She glanced back at me as she drove across the parking lot and dodged a pole at the last second. My breath caught in my throat. God had played a prank on humanity by putting a whole lot of trouble in a woman that beautiful. How many broken men had she left in her wake? My guess was a lot.

As she pulled out onto the road, I noticed the envelope she'd tried to give me was lying on the pavement. Shaking my head, I walked toward it, picked it up, and was debating what to do with it when my phone beeped with a text.

I'm in front of the building.

On my way. I texted back, stuffing the envelope into the breast pocket of my jacket before making my way to my car and retrieving my father's glasses.

The sound of a crash echoing from a distance had me halting briefly as I strode away from my car. I sent a quick text. **Dad, you okay?**

I'm fine, but someone isn't. A truck ran a red light and plowed right through a tan sedan.

My pace quickened. No. It couldn't be the same person. **Call 911.**

My driver is on the phone with them.

On instinct, I ran to the front of the building. My father and a man I didn't know were beside the car I just watched leave my parking lot. It was on the sidewalk now, slightly wrapped around a pole. The truck that had hit it was still in the middle of the road with some damage to its front.

I immediately went to the driver's side and my chest tightened as I took in the blood on the glass. A front airbag had deployed, but that hadn't saved her from smashing her head against the side window. I went around to the passenger's side, opened the door and bent inside.

"Ms. Pryer."

She didn't respond.

"Ashlee," I said louder. Her head turned toward me and she blinked slowly, looking as if she was just about to lose consciousness. "Try not to move," I ordered.

"Sage," she said in desperation. "I can't die; I have Sage."

"You're not going to die," I swore without having any idea what her condition was.

She closed her eyes. "My phone. Tell my sister to come. Joanie. Call Joanie."

Her phone was in the cupholder between us. I wanted to help her out of the vehicle, but didn't want to hurt her and sirens announced help would be there in a moment. I told myself to leave this and the phone call she'd requested to them, but I couldn't.

She wasn't my responsibility.

The accident wasn't my fault.

The wisest course of action would be to walk away now while I was uninvolved in the situation. Still, if she really did have a child, and God, if there was a chance she might not live, her request for someone to call her sister should be honored.

I grabbed her phone, staying partially inside the vehicle. While reassuring Ashlee that she was not alone, I swiped her phone and was surprised when it opened. Who doesn't lock their phone? I pushed that thought away and chose her most recent call. As soon as a woman answered, I said, "You don't know me, but your sister has been in an accident. An ambulance is pulling up. She'll be taken to a hospital where I'm sure someone will contact you, but she asked me to ask you to come."

"Oh, my God," the woman said shakily. "Mike, Ashlee has been in an accident. I don't know." To me, she asked, "Why are you calling me and not her? How bad was the accident?"

"I didn't see the accident happen, but my father did. Someone ran a red light. Ashlee appears to be unconscious right now, but I'm not an EMT. In fact, they're here now, so I'll give them the phone."

"No, don't go. Stay on. I have to know what's going on and they need to help her. Please don't hang up."

How could I after that? "I won't." I moved out of the way of the paramedics. A police officer asked me what I'd witnessed. He spoke to me then my father before stepping away to speak to the driver of the truck. I kept Joanie on the phone, updating her on what was happening.

A fire engine arrived. In a coordinated effort, Ashlee was removed from the vehicle and put on a stretcher. She woke temporarily, asking for Joanie. I walked closer and held out the phone with the speakerphone on. "She's here, Ashlee. She can hear you."

"I'm on my way," Joanie declared in a thick voice. "All I need to know is where you're being taken."

I looked to the paramedic. He said, "Mass General."

"No," I said. I couldn't explain my need for her to have better than the general hospital or why I felt at all invested in her survival. "Baldwin Memorial has a private wing. It's closer and I'll cover the costs."

My father put a hand on my shoulder. "Do you know her, son?"

I shook my head. "No, but . . ."

I'd forgotten Joanie was still on the phone until she said, "Mr. Rehoboth?"

My father and I answered in unison, "Yes."

"She told you about Sage?" Joanie asked.

"Who's Sage?" my father demanded.

"I told her you wouldn't want to know about her," Joanie said, getting the words out between sobs. "But if you're still there she was right. Oh, I'm so glad she was right."

"Who's Sage?" my father barked out the question again.

I waved him off. "It's not what you think." I met my father's gaze. "Don't ask me what I'm doing because I don't know. It's just important that she's okay."

My father nodded. "Understood."

I gave Joanie directions to Baldwin Memorial then ended my call with her to contact the hospital to make arrangements for Ashlee's arrival. The police officer told me he'd be in touch. I told him I wasn't a person of contact. He took my information anyway.

A moment later I was in the backseat of my father's car, instructing the driver to take us to the hospital. I'd make sure Ashlee was alive and admitted to a room, then I'd close the door on meeting her and everything we'd said that night—until the bill came in.

Neither my father nor I spoke for part of the ride. He broke the silence first. "You didn't tell me you were dating anyone."

"I'm not."

"So, is she an employee?"

"God, I hope not."

"Who is Sage?"

"Her daughter."

"*Her* daughter?"

"Yes. Hers. Only hers. Not mine." It was then that I remembered the envelope in my pocket. I took it out and tossed it to him. "No matter what this says."

He opened the envelope then looked pointedly at me until I handed him the glasses I'd retrieved from my car. After putting them on, he studied the paper. "It looks official enough."

"What?"

"The DNA test that matches you with nearly a hundred percent to one Sage Diane Pryer."

"It's a fake."

"Could be. You were never with the woman?"

"I met her for the first time tonight."

"You're sure?"

"I'm sure, Dad."

"Did she claim she'd ever been with you?"

I let out a long breath. What a fucking surreal night. "No, she claimed I'd donated sperm to some clinic and that this Sage child was the result of that."

"*Have* you ever done that?"

I pinned my father with a long look. "Seriously?"

"Okay, so she's either misled or a liar. Why are we rushing off to the hospital like she's family?"

Turning her phone around in my hand, I shrugged and slumped a little. "I don't know." I opened her phone with a swipe and went to her photos. I scrolled through them, telling myself I was looking for something incriminating, but all I saw was a woman who clearly loved children. There were many of her taking selfies with the young girl she'd claimed was my daughter. So, so many more of that little girl with three young boys. There were birthday parties with an older couple who looked enough like her that I guessed were her parents. A group photo had a woman who was likely named Joanie standing next to Ashlee and with a man who had one hand on the shoulder of one of the boys as if warning him to settle down. This was her family. They looked so happy—so normal. Scrolling more brought up pictures of Ashlee at a table of children doing what appeared to be a colorful science experiment. They were all laughing. Nothing I found supported my impression of her as unstable.

I brought up a photo of the little girl Ashlee claimed was mine. "This is her daughter, Sage."

My father took the phone. "She looks a lot like you did at that age. Not exactly like you, but she has your eyes. And your ears in some of the photos."

"She's not mine, Dad."

"I'm not saying she is, just saying she looks like she could be."

I took the phone back from him and pocketed it. "If I tell you something it stays in this car."

"Of course."

"Bellerwood claimed I had a twin."

"I thought you had dismissed that as nonsense."

"I did." I reclaimed the DNA test and studied it, before returning it to the envelope and putting it in my pocket beside Ashlee's phone. "I found no mention of a twin in any of the paperwork you had. There was so much going on, I can't say I looked further than that."

"Jesse's paperwork didn't mention a twin either. So, this child isn't yours, but—"

"But what if I do have a twin? What if this kid is biologically my niece? I couldn't let her lose her mother."

"Because you know how much that hurts."

"I don't waste a moment or a thought on the woman who walked away from me and Jesse."

"And the woman who birthed you?"

"She didn't want me either so why would I?"

My father sat back and sighed. "If that test is real and you actually have a twin—"

I sat back as well, mirroring his stance. "Yes?"

"This Ashlee Pryer could be the mother of your niece."

I groaned. "Could this year get any worse?"

He removed his glasses and placed them in the center cupholder where I was certain he'd forget them. "Worse? That's not at all how I see this. Your family might be expanding and that means mine is as well. I have a grandchild. A little girl. Sage. That's a beautiful name."

"We don't know if any of this is true, Dad."

"Is Grandfather too formal? I don't see myself as a Grampa. I suppose we'll have time to sort it out. Sage can help me decide before Jesse's baby joins us."

"Dad, one step at a time."

"Papa? No, that's not good either."

I looked out the window at the blur of buildings, but that didn't stop my father from continuing. "No daughter-in-law of mine will be in a shared hospital room. You did book Ashlee into a private suite, correct?"

"She's not a daughter-in-law, Dad. The jury is still out about if she's even being honest with us. What we discussed about her daughter possibly being related stays between you and me."

"Of course. Pops?"

I groaned and covered my eyes with one hand. This hadn't been him until Jesse had found Crystal. He'd always claimed women weren't to be trusted. Lately, I was struggling to recognize my family. We had no real proof that Ashlee was anything but a liar, but the more I learned about her, the more I thought she wasn't.

The text that came through from Joanie was a welcome reprieve. I told her we were approaching the hospital, would coordinate checking Ashlee in, then would hand off her phone as soon as Joanie arrived.

She thanked me, then asked if there was a place for her family to gather since her parents were coming with her. I said there would be a family room attached to the suite Ashlee would end up in, but I didn't know what Ashlee would require before that or if they'd have her in an ICU or not.

She wrote: **This must all be so weird for you, but thank you for taking care of my sister. We'll change the bill over to our name when we arrive.**

I glanced at my father. "They want to pay for her hospital bill. Do you think they have any idea how expensive it's going to be?"

"Probably not, but I like them already just for offering."

"Me too," I said slowly. I'd become used to people wanting something from me, but these people didn't appear to. What had Ashlee claimed? That she'd settle for something to tell her daughter one day when she asked about her father?

Sadly, I wouldn't be able to give her that since I wasn't yet sure who he was.

I typed back. **I'm covering the bill. It's settled.**

She didn't respond, which was probably for the best because I was flying by the seat of my pants through this. We pulled up to the private emergency room entrance and the driver came around to let us out.

As we walked up the path to the door, my father said, "Granddad. Simple. Classic. I like it."

I pretended I didn't hear him, then held the door open for him to walk through.

CHAPTER FIVE

Thane

FRESH FROM MEETING with a hospital administrator, my father and I made our way to meet the Pryer family. Ashlee would have the best care as well as the best accommodations the hospital offered. Not every hospital would have treated us as well, but our family had recently funded a substantial equipment upgrade. It didn't hurt that my current public link to the Bellerwoods lent me clout that money alone wouldn't have.

As I'd been raised to, I didn't waste much time analyzing my decision to care for Ashlee. Weakness was born from indecision. Action bred success, even if the action was wrong, because it maintained a person's momentum. A course correction might be necessary later, but based on the information currently available, I was certain we were doing the right thing.

It was that confidence that made it possible to approach the man that from her photos I guessed was Ashlee's father and extend my hand in greeting as if it were perfectly normal for me to be there. "Mr. Pryer? Thane Rehoboth."

His eyes were strained but kind. Dressed in a blue cotton shirt, jeans and running shoes, he appeared to be a man who spent a good amount of time outside. His shake was firm and his hand calloused, but he looked me straight in the eye when he spoke and I liked him instantly. "Joanie said you stayed on the phone to keep her updated about Ashlee." His voice caught and he cleared his throat. "Thank you. Please call me Kit. This is my wife, Diane."

The woman who stepped beneath the protection of his arm and hugged his side had many of Ashlee's facial features. She was slightly shorter and a little rounder, but a beautiful woman with a gentle presence. "I'm so grateful you were there. I always worry when Ashlee goes into the city alone."

"You're welcome," I said, although that felt inadequate. Nodding to my father, I continued, "This is my father, Ethan—" I stopped before adding his last name. These people didn't care who we were—all of their focus was where it belonged, on their daughter.

Kit shook my father's hand. Diane nodded in greeting.

A younger woman stepped forward. The resemblance between her and Ashlee was striking. "You must be Joanie."

"I am." She shook my hand between both of hers. "Thank you so much for being here . . . for making sure Ashlee was okay."

Emotion unexpectedly thickened my voice. "It was the least I could do. My father witnessed the accident. He was the first on the scene."

She turned from me to him and surprised us both by giving him a tight hug he didn't look entirely comfortable with. "Thank you."

He gave her a pat on the back. "It wasn't her fault. The truck sped right through a red light."

Joanie stepped back and sniffed. "Is he okay? The truck driver?"

Her question took me by surprise. "He appeared unhurt. The police have his information. There'll be consequences."

She shook her head sadly. "Truckers push themselves so hard. I pray for his family as well."

"That's a generous viewpoint." And one I didn't share. He deserved to pay the price for what he'd done.

In a soft voice, she said, "No one wishes for something like this to happen." She glanced around. "When we checked in we were told we couldn't see Ashlee yet, but she's in stable condition."

I nodded. "That's what I was told as well." Looking past her to her father, I said, "We've arranged for her to stay in a suite. There's a sitting room attached. Why don't we move up there? There should be refreshments as well. They'll keep you well informed there."

I led the way to an elevator that opened to a private floor. We were escorted from the elevator to Ashlee's empty suite. On the way, Joanie fell into step beside me. In a hushed voice, she said, "My father doesn't know why Ashlee went to see you."

"Understood." I handed her Ashlee's phone.

She accepted it with a slight smile. "I make fun of Ashlee for not locking her phone. She always says she has nothing to hide so why bother. She can be so stubborn." Pausing briefly before following everyone else inside the suite, she put her hand on my arm and said, "I didn't think she should contact you. I was certain you wouldn't want to know. I imagined her chasing you around while you called the police to get her away from you. Thank you for not being that person."

I frowned. I'd almost been exactly that person, falling shy of it only because I hadn't involved the authorities. Before Ashlee's family started to see me in an inaccurately good light, I felt something needed to be said. "I'm not the biological father of her child. I told her that."

A line appeared between her eyebrows. "I understand." She nodded as if a thought had come to her. "And that's okay." God, she sounded like her sister. "That you're here says everything I need to know about you."

I was sure it didn't, but my father had returned to the door, looking for us. It was neither the time nor the place to hash out more than that.

"The doctor is on his way up to speak to us. You may want to come in," my father said.

Before turning away from me, Joanie searched my face. "Sage has your eyes and I hope your heart. I know you said you'd cover the bill for this, but I'll handle the insurance side and make sure we lower it as much as possible. You have no idea how much it means to us that you stayed with Ashlee. I don't care how long it takes you to admit you're Sage's father or if you ever do because—after today—you're family as far as my heart is concerned."

That rocked me back on my heels and it took me a moment to follow her through the door. What the hell was happening? And why was I choosing to get more involved rather than grab my father and sprint out of there?

Outside of my father and brothers, I didn't invest time in other people. Achievement. Dedication. Loyalty. Success. These were the cornerstones of what I valued.

I avoided anything complicated or emotional. Arranging medical care for a woman I knew nothing about and spending time in a room with her family while we waited to hear how she was promised to be both.

But there I was, joining her family and my father waiting for news on Ashlee's condition. The doctor entered the room, introduced himself, then started right in. "Ms. Pryer is in stable condition, but the next few hours will determine how we'll need to proceed. She suffered a brain contusion. Our first concern was a potential bleed. That would have required surgery. The risk now is swelling. You brought her to the right place, though, because we have the best and least invasive equipment to monitor this in the country. We currently have Ms. Pryer on medicines to combat the swelling and in a hyperbaric oxygen chamber. Current research has suggested that damaged tissue is starved of oxygen immediately after an injury. Thanks to your generosity, Mr. Rehoboth, we're able to address this in a way very few facilities can afford to." The doctor had directed his appreciation toward my father and I didn't correct his misconception even though the donation had been under my watch.

Ashlee's mother asked, "Can we see her?"

The doctor shook his head. "Not yet. We have her sedated. The hyperbaric chamber coupled with the medication should minimize swelling, but if it doesn't, we may need to operate."

Diane gasped and clutched her husband's hand. Joanie moved closer to her mother and put her arm around her. "It's going to be okay, Mom. You heard what the doctor said; we're in the best place for her to be treated. She's going to be okay."

Diane nodded without speaking.

The doctor asked if there were any other questions. When there weren't, he said he'd check in again in about an hour, promising that he'd know much more by then. On the way out, the doctor stopped and addressed my father. "You were right to bring her here. Had she gone to the general hospital they wouldn't have been able to address the swelling as well as we can. She may recover with little to no lasting effects from this and that's not something many can say after receiving the kind of head trauma she did."

My father shook his hand. "Thank you. Your hospital can expect to receive an expression of our gratitude soon."

Of course my father would say that. I would have waited to see if the damn space station fiasco bankrupted us first, but what do I know? I'm just the man signing the checks now.

Alone again with the Pryer family, my father and I exchanged a look. Was it time to go? I did a quick assessment of the others in the room. "It looks like it'll be a long night for you. I'll have food sent up."

Her parents thanked me then went to sit on one of the couches.

Joanie crossed the distance to where I was and lowered her voice. "Are you leaving?"

"I don't belong here," I said firmly.

She looked from me to my father and continued to speak in a voice soft enough that her parents couldn't hear. "You are both always welcome."

My father beamed a smile at her.

I groaned inwardly. He needed to take an emotional step back.

Joanie continued, "My husband Mike is watching the kids while we're here, but I'll have to go back in the morning to help him with them. Sage is a little spitfire." She took out her phone and swiped it open. "This is her this afternoon making a cushion and sheet fort with my boys in the living room."

The video began to play before I had a chance to tell her

it wasn't necessary to show us. Three mop-haired boys, all looking under the age of ten, were collecting a massive pile of what appeared to be the cushions from several couches. In an authoritative voice, young Sage directed the boys on the proper placement of each cushion for stability. They protested and one went against her advice only to see his section fail. She picked up two cushions and showed him her idea. It held well enough for her to add a roof to it.

"You were just like that with Jesse," my father said. "He always had to learn the hard way, but you liked to do it right the first time."

I shot him a look designed to silence him.

Joanie swiped to a photo of Sage with her hands on her hips looking as if she was reprimanding the tallest of the three boys. "She's a stickler for following the rules, but I don't see that as a bad thing. She knows what she wants and doesn't settle for less."

"That also sounds like you," my father interjected.

I could have kicked him when I saw how much pleasure that brought to Joanie's face. "Dad, stop. You know she's not mine."

Joanie gave us each a long look then put her phone away. "Listen, Sage is an amazing kid, but I respect your decision. You don't owe her or us anything. Ashlee knew that. Sage couldn't have a family who loves her more than we do, so one day she'll be okay with that as well. When she started asking about her father, Ashlee got it in her head that you might want to write her a letter or share something you'd like us to tell her about you—but tonight will be enough. Even if you never want to see us again, we'll be able to tell her that you saved her mommy's life and made sure she'd be around to take care of Sage." Joanie's eyes filled with tears and I felt like an asshole. "That's the best gift any man could give his daughter."

"She's not my—" I stopped because she clearly didn't believe me anyway. Although I'd pushed my own questions about my birth parents out of my daily thoughts, I was empathetic toward Sage's curiosity. "Tell Sage whatever she needs to hear." I glanced toward my father. "I understand the questions a person asks themselves about where they came from. I'm adopted. I never knew my biological mother. Still, my father and family were—are enough. I'm sure Sage will come to feel the same."

Joanie's eyes rounded. "You're *adopted?*" Her attention turned to my father. "You, sir, have a special place in my heart now as well. If you ever want to try on the grandfather hat—"

"Granddad," my father said without missing a beat. "My other son is expecting a child soon. Hearing about Sage helped me choose what I'd like to be called."

"Granddads can send cards or visit as well," Joanie said with a warm smile.

"I'd like that," my father responded, and I began to question my own sanity. Even if I had a twin and Sage ended up being biologically his, that wouldn't make Sage my father's granddaughter. Oh my God, unless he already considered my possibly imaginary twin another of his sons. Scott had broken my father.

"We should go, Dad," I said in a tight voice.

My father nodded, then turned to address Ashlee's parents. "Kit. Diane. You have my number. Please keep us updated."

"We will," Kit said, looking down at his wife in his arms. "Thank you again."

"We'll be back in the morning," my father added.

I shot him another look. Had he lost his mind as well? "Good night everyone. I hope you receive good news about Ashlee soon." With that, I practically dragged my father into the hallway. As we walked toward the elevator, I said, "Dad, we're not coming back in the morning."

"Of course not," he said with far too much sarcasm for my comfort. "We don't want to get that involved. All we want to do is meet them, arrange for Ashlee's care, fall in love with your niece, then walk away and forget about them. Pick a lane, Thane. It's not like you to sit on the fence about something that matters."

"This isn't a potential client or an investment opportunity. I have no idea if that little girl—"

"Sage."

"If Sage is actually related to me. The sperm donating twin theory is nothing more than that at this point." I took a deep breath. "And, frankly, I'm concerned about how quickly you went from stranger to Granddad. You don't trust anyone, why the hell do you believe anything those people say?"

He pressed the elevator call button. "Because you do."

We stepped into the elevator and turned to stand shoulder to shoulder. "I don't. Not yet."

"Thane, I've known you your whole life. We wouldn't be here if you didn't believe Sage was your niece. Now, you may need to confirm it before feeling comfortable admitting it, but that doesn't change what we both know. You'll either be here at the hospital tomorrow morning or you'll be at your office wishing you'd allowed yourself to be."

"I hate it when you're fucking right."

His laugh was deep and knowing. "Well, I am your father."

We stepped out of the elevator together. "Yes, you are. Dad, I don't have time for this. Bellerwood is breathing down my neck."

My father stood tall and proud, looking suddenly a lot less retired. "I'll handle Bellerwood. Take care of your niece's mother. Find your twin. No space station is more important than that."

I stopped just inside the glass doors. "Since when is the family company not our priority?" It certainly had been for as long as I could remember.

"I never missed one of your martial arts competitions."

"Because you liked to see us kick ass."

"Because I love you and you have always been my priority. Family always should be."

Gratitude for all I'd been given in life flooded in. Ethan Rehoboth wasn't a perfect man, but he was the foundation our family had been built on and if he said something, he meant it. "I love you too, Dad."

We made our way to where his driver was waiting next to his car. "Dad, if I actually have a twin, there was something seriously wrong with the adoption agency you and your wife used. Two sets of twins separated at birth. That doesn't hit right."

He nodded and slid through the car door his driver held open. I joined him. Neither of us spoke until the door shut behind me.

"I've considered that and later, when the dust settles, we'll look into it," he said. "For now, I know you believe keeping Jesse and Scott out of this is what's best for them, but it's not. Rehoboths don't go to battle solo. We're stronger together, and together is how we'll win."

"Win." It's what he'd always pushed us to do. "What does that look like in this situation, Dad?"

"Different than how I used to define it." He took a moment to choose his next words. "I've done a lot of self-reflection this past year."

I met his gaze. "Don't go getting soft on us. You were exactly the father Jesse and I needed."

The smile he shot me didn't reach his eyes. "There were parts I could have done better."

"That could be said of everyone—"

"Let me say this, Thane. It's important."

My father wasn't normally one to talk about his emotions. Jesse and I had always known he'd loved us, but not because he'd necessarily told us. He'd shown us instead. Yes, he'd always pushed us to excel, but you wouldn't have wanted to be the fool who spoke poorly of Ethan Rehoboth's sons. Or, worse, implied we weren't his because of how we'd come to him. He didn't lose his temper often, but that was a button no one pressed twice.

I nodded for him to continue.

"I've always blamed the failure of my marriage on a lack of loyalty on her part, but I put my financial goals before my relationship with her. She thought I resented that she couldn't have a child. I wasn't involved in your adoption process—that was all her. I see now that she was trying to make us into a family. When my focus remained on work, she left."

"Leaving behind the two children she'd promised to care for."

"Yes, and that angered me—and hurt me, but I should never have shared that anger or my bitterness with you. At first I became a better father to prove to myself . . . and possibly her . . . that we didn't need her."

"Clearly you were correct in that assessment."

"For a long time I felt I'd won, but she wasn't a horrible woman, Thane. After she left us, she married someone else and had children with him so even that might have been my fault. I hear they're happy."

"Good for her," I said with a touch of bite to my tone.

He sighed. "I'm not explaining this well. I was bitter for a long time because I couldn't see my life was actually better because she'd come into it. I would never have adopted you and Jesse if not for her. Life throws the unexpected at all of us—but it's our choice to decide if it's a tragedy or a blessing."

"Blessing?" Okay, now I was certain my father was losing it. He'd never been the slightest bit religious. Still, if it brought him comfort, I wouldn't take that from him. Instead I tried to lighten the mood with a joke. "Me, perhaps, but Jesse?"

My father chuckled then sobered. "Yes, Jesse and even Scott. You asked me what winning looks like now, and my answer involves all of you. Winning means Jesse and Crystal stay married and raise a healthy and happy family together. Scott and Monica do the same on that damn farm of his. And you? You've always held yourself and those around you to an impossibly high standard. You get that from me. I know I'm tough. You've always put the family and the business above anything you wanted for yourself. You get that from me as well. But it's time for you to do something for yourself. You need this."

"Dad, we have a lot riding on the Bellerwood contract."

"Exactly—we. That's why we'll have a family meeting."

I looked out the window, tried to imagine that going well but couldn't.

"Bellerwood needs to be there," my father added. "He's family now. It's time he starts acting like it."

I turned back and met my father's gaze. Never had I been prouder to be his son. "I'll call everyone and set that up."

"After you leave the hospital."

"After I leave the hospital."

CHAPTER SIX

Ashlee

As I woke the next morning, it took me a moment to realize I wasn't in my own bed. Snippets of the night before came to me. I remembered part of the ambulance ride and being told not to move my head. I wasn't sure if the flashes of memories were of events that had actually happened or if I'd dreamed them. I remembered floating in a well-lit tunnel that hummed. There'd been voices all around me at times and then an eerie silence during which I'd wondered if I was dead.

I wasn't floating anymore, nor was I in heaven if the throbbing pain I felt on the left side of my head was anything to go by. I touched my face and realized there was an IV in my hand.

Still a little dazed, I looked around the room. My mother was there and, as soon as she realized my eyes were open, she rushed to my side. "Kit, she's awake."

My father joined her at the side of my bed. She took my other hand in one of hers. "How do you feel?"

My mouth was dry and my voice hoarse when I said, "Confused. What happened?"

"You were in a car accident," my father said. "You don't remember it?"

I shook my head and instantly regretted the movement. "No."

"What do you remember?" my mother asked.

Not much I felt ready to share. I remembered deciding to drive to Boston to see if I could meet Thane Rehoboth. I remembered talking to Joanie while I waited for him to come out of his office building then saying good night to Sage. "Sage," I said in a stronger voice. "Where is she?"

My father answered, "Joanie went home to get her boys to school and Sage to preschool. She called and said Sage was asking for you, but not worried when Joanie told her you were with us. She doesn't know you're in the hospital."

I lowered my hand and tested if my other extremities were functioning. My toes wiggled. I could lift a leg. Okay, so those still worked. "I don't remember the accident. Was anyone else hurt?"

"No," my mother said. "Just you. And you're going to make a full recovery. The man you went to see made sure of that. Who is he and why have we never heard his name?"

"I don't understand. Whose name?"

"Thane Rehoboth. He and his father were the ones who called 911 and had you brought here. I never knew hospitals had rooms like this. Your father and I slept on a bed—a real one, better than a hotel bed. And there's staff that keeps coming by to see if we want anything. Get better quick because I bet staying here is costing your friend a small fortune."

"Diane," my father cut in, "she doesn't need to worry about that. Take as long as you need, baby. The money to pay for this will come . . . it always does."

"Thane said he was paying," my mother said.

"We can't let him do that," my father countered.

"Insurance doesn't cover places with butlers, Kit."

My father frowned. "If we have to take out a loan against the truck wash, we take out a loan. It'll be fine, Diane."

Whatever my mother had been about to say was interrupted by a deep male voice. "Good morning. I hope I'm not interrupting."

"Not at all," my father assured.

"She's awake," my mother said in a rush.

A tall man with the most beautiful, strong jaw approached the side of my bed. A flash of embarrassment came and went as I realized who he was. This was the man I'd gone to Boston to meet—the man I'd hoped I could get to write a letter to Sage.

And he was gorgeous. My heartbeat quickened on the monitor as he stepped closer. "How are you feeling?" he asked me in a husky voice I might sell my soul to wake to every morning.

I raised a hand to the bandaged side of my head. "I've

been better." After attempting and failing at a smile, I said weakly, "And surprisingly I've been worse."

"She nearly drowned once," my mother said. "Scared ten years right off my life."

"She'd been swimming in the shallow end of a lake near our house and started feeding the ducks part of her lunch. Something scared them away. One little duckling was separated from its mama. We told her to leave it because the mama would come back, but Ashlee never did listen when she thought she was doing the right thing. She grabbed that duckling and started swimming quicker than any of us could catch her."

"I've always been fast," I added with a shaky smile. God, I felt like shit.

My mother squeezed my hand at the memory. "Thank God your father is a better swimmer than I am, because when you went under and didn't come back up . . ."

I gave her hand a tight squeeze. "But I got the duckling back to its mother."

She smiled down at me. "You sure did. You just forgot you weren't a strong swimmer."

I looked from her to the man I could only remember seeing in photos. His expression was difficult to interpret. He didn't seem happy to be there, but didn't look in a rush to leave.

My father asked, "So, how do you two know each other?"

"We don't," Thane answered before me. "Not really. We met briefly when I was on my way to my car to retrieve something for my father."

My father exchanged a look with my mother. "You never met before yesterday?"

Thane's gaze sought mine. "Never."

As I stared into his eyes, I forgot where I was, that I was in pain and how absolutely unattractive I must have looked. Time slowed, and for a moment, there were just the two of us and the strongest feeling that we'd been in that place together before. "I don't remember meeting you," I admitted.

He frowned then his expression softened. "Your head received quite the hit. Hopefully I'm the only thing you've forgotten."

Attempting again to lighten the mood, I said, "I don't know, but then how would I? Can't miss what I can't remember missing."

My mother interjected. "The doctor said it's common to not remember an accident. The brain has a way of protecting us from the unpleasant."

"Was that what you were?" I asked while still holding Thane's gaze. "Unpleasant?"

A slight smile stretched his lips. "If you don't remember, I have a second chance to make a first impression and I'm taking it."

I chuckled, which moved my head just enough that it

started throbbing again. I groaned. "Sorry. I'm not good company right now."

He leaned closer. "Are you in pain?"

I could have denied it, but I was in a hospital bed with tubes attached to me so there wasn't much point in pretending. "A little."

He pressed a call button. Immediately a nurse was at my bedside asking me to rate the pain and if the throbbing felt like it was internal or not. I touched where the bandage was before answering. "I'm not sure, but I think on the outside."

The nurse turned to my parents and said, "The doctor will want another scan done. I'll wheel her down. It shouldn't take more than thirty minutes unless they find something."

Find something? My eyes rounded.

Thane stepped closer and laid a hand on my arm. "You're going to be fine. The doctor said you have a hard head."

I laughed and groaned. "It's cruel to make me laugh." As the nurse began to arrange my IV for my trip to wherever she was taking me, I blurted out a question that surprised me. "Will you be here when I get back?"

"Yes," he answered without hesitation then moved to stand with my parents as I was rolled away.

I strained to remember meeting him the day before, but couldn't. It must have gone well, though, or he wouldn't have been there looking like he cared if I got better. Had I convinced him to meet Sage? Was that why he wanted me to live?

Or was he mesmerized by how beautiful I looked in a hospital gown?

I smiled a little at that thought.

The nurse saw my smile and said, "We need to get you better quick. That is one fine looking boyfriend you have. I wouldn't want to miss a moment of that if I were you."

I almost told her he wasn't mine, but decided to keep that tidbit to myself.

CHAPTER SEVEN

Thane

WAITING IN A room with Ashlee's parents should have felt less right than it did. I made myself a coffee and joined them in a sitting area. After they thanked me again and inquired about how my father was doing, I felt I should address what I'd heard when I'd walked in earlier.

My gut told me Kit preferred things told to him straight, so I didn't dance around the topic. "My family has a special relationship with this hospital. Although I appreciate that you'd like to assume the cost of Ashlee's stay here, it has already been handled."

Kit's face tightened and Diane took one of his hands in hers. "We can't let you do that."

I took a deep breath and sought a rationale that would have him agreeing while retaining his pride. "When my father witnessed the accident he became personally invested in the outcome—"

"Only your father?" Kit countered in a tone that implied he didn't believe me.

"I felt the same."

Kit rubbed a hand over his stubbled chin. "I have no doubt you care about my daughter. My question is how much? I am grateful for all you've done and have had time to do a little reading about head injuries. With the hit she took, had Ashlee gone to the general hospital and received different care, her quality of life"—he seemed to choke up over what he was envisioning—"might have been dramatically impacted. The doctor tells us that barring any complications, she could have a complete recovery." His eyes teared up. "So, when I ask you about your relationship with my daughter, it's not because I'm not grateful. I just don't believe that you're as invested in her welfare as you are because you met her once in a parking lot. There's more between you, isn't there?"

I'd been called stoic more than once in my life and had embraced the title, but seeing the strong man before me expose how gutted he was by what happened to his daughter had my own eyes clouding with emotion. Holy hell. This was a close family who clearly loved each other very much. Watching Diane quietly support her husband by holding his hand and leaning against him was one of the most beautiful fucking things I'd ever seen.

Still, Ashlee had chosen not to tell them she'd sought me out and I felt I should honor that. "Respectfully, if there were more between your daughter and me and she hadn't told you—it wouldn't be my place to."

RUTH CARDELLO

"I like him," Diane said softly. "And he's right. Ashlee's a grown woman. She'll tell us when she's ready."

Kit visibly composed himself and nodded. "I would warn you to take care of my girl, but from what I've seen, you've been raised right."

"I'd like to think so," I said even as I fought back a wave of guilt about the misconception his family had about me . . . even Ashlee. I'd been honest with her as well as her sister. Short of producing evidence of a twin, there wasn't much more I could or intended to do to correct them.

Diane interrupted my thoughts by asking, "So, you're helping to design a space station. That sounds fun."

I smiled at her innocent take on my role in the project, even though fun wasn't a word I would have chosen to describe the process at all. Challenging. Rewarding. Lately, mostly frustrating. "It's something."

"And you work with your father?" Kit asked.

I nodded. "I did. My father started our company. My brother Jesse and I took it over when he retired. We've put a lot into staying ahead of the tech trends, and that's what helped us land a contract with Bellerwood. We designed the life support system."

"Sounds like a pretty important role," Diane said with a sweet smile. "Your mother must be very proud of you."

I inhaled sharply and sat back, not happy that my reaction had been so obvious. Normally the mention of the women who'd found it easy to walk away from me as a child didn't have the power to affect me, but my emotions were running closer to the surface since meeting Ashlee. "I wouldn't know."

She leaned toward me. "I'm so sorry. Sometimes I say things without thinking."

Her apology shifted my focus from myself to her. The last thing I wanted was to add anything more to this sweet woman's day. "No, I'm sorry." Unless they were close friends, I didn't discuss my parentage with anyone, but for the second time in the past two days I blurted, "I'm adopted. I never knew my biological mother and my father's wife moved on early enough that I have no memories of her."

Clutching a hand to her chest, Diane said, "Well, you seem to have a close relationship with your adoptive father."

"I do."

"And you have a brother?"

"Also adopted," I said. "With a twin we weren't raised with, but who has become a brother to me as well."

Her smile was teary. "That's beautiful." I understood that not all of the emotion welling in her eyes was due to what I was sharing. We were all holding a storm of feelings in.

"Have they met Ashlee?" Kit asked. *Oh, he's good.*

"Not yet." I froze at my own choice of words. "No" would have been the appropriate answer. Clear. Simple. Fitting to where this was going which was no further. "Not yet" implied Ashlee and I were headed somewhere together and there was no way in hell that was happening.

Above everything else, there was a good chance she'd borne the child of my twin. He was the one her daughter was yearning to meet. If any relationship were to develop because of how Sage had come to be, it should be him—not me. To change the subject, I said, "Your daughters look like they get along well."

Diane smiled. "You could say that again. Joanie's five years older than Ashlee. When they were little I worried that the gap would be too much for them to bond as well as they have. I wasn't surprised at all when, after having three children of her own, Joanie offered to carry one for Ashlee. If their places had been reversed, Ashlee would have done the same without hesitation. Seeing siblings take care of each other like that is every parent's dream."

I nodded. The Pryers had more in common with my family than I was comfortable hearing about. It filled me with a yearning I couldn't label.

Just then the door to the family room opened and my eyebrows hit my hairline. I surged to my feet. "Sorry, I need a moment."

Kit rose to stand as Jesse and Scott entered the room. He addressed them first. "Hello. Can we help you?"

Jesse looked at me. "Scott was determined to come as soon as Dad told him where you were. I figured you'd appreciate me running interference if necessary."

Scott rolled his eyes. "I love you too, Jesse," he said with humor.

Not seeing any way around it, I introduced my brothers to the Pryers. Since my father had apparently told them some of what was going on, I hoped he'd also told them enough to keep them from bringing up my possible twin. "Diane. Kit. These are the brothers I told you about. The one in the suit is Jesse. Scott is the one in jeans. I used to be able to tell them apart by the smell, but now they both have barn animals."

My joke seemed to put Diane and Kit at ease. They shook hands with my brothers. Everyone sat before I could stop them.

Scott whistled. "This place is nice. If I'm ever sick I'm calling you, Thane, so you can hook me up. The last time I went to the hospital they left me in the hallway until the doctor had time to stitch me up."

"You mean the vet?" Jesse joked.

Scott laughed, thumbed at Jesse while speaking to the Pryers. "He's an acquired taste—like vinegar. It's best to take him in small doses."

I remained standing, trying to figure out the best way to get my brothers to step outside with me without being obvious about it. "So, this is a surprise," I said.

"Dad said you might need our support . . . so here we are," Scott said, relaxing back into his chair.

How much had my father told them? There was no way to know or ask. All I could do was ride it out and try to mitigate the situation.

"You have a farm?" Diane asked Scott, which was the perfect question to get him talking about safe topics. I'd never appreciated Scott's ability to describe every rescue animal on his farm in detail until then. It was a light conversation that seemed to soothe Diane.

I met Kit's gaze a few times before looking away again. He had questions he was holding back. There wasn't much I could do about that.

Jesse said, "Dad gave me a heads-up about a few things that have been going on at work. We thought we'd drop by to see if you needed anything, then take you out to lunch to discuss how we should move forward."

"I told Dad I'd call you when I left here."

Jesse shrugged. "You know Dad."

I did. Our father was not the type to sit back and wait for things to unfold. I'd be shocked if he didn't show up at lunch with Bellerwood in tow. "I do." I nodded toward the door that led to Ashlee's room. "After Ashlee returns and I hear how her scan went, we can head out."

My brothers sometimes drove me crazy, but the way they accepted my plan without question warmed my heart. They were there for the same reason I made an appearance whenever I felt they were struggling—we were family and that meant we would always be there for each other.

Jesse often came across as brash, but he seemed to respect the strain the Pryers were under. He spoke quietly to Kit about the Pryer's truck-washing business. The two talked about the economy and hiring trends like peers. Crystal had grounded my previously full-of-himself brother. Scott, well he'd always worn his heart on his sleeve. I wouldn't have been surprised had he moved over to curl up on Diane's lap for a cuddle.

Twins. One was a shark. The other a puppy.

If I actually had a twin would he be as different from me as Scott was from Jesse? There was no denying there were traits they shared as well. For example, they were both there, ready to fix whatever was broken together.

Nature vs. nurture. Would they have been more alike had they been raised in the same household? It made me wonder about the life my twin may have lived. If he'd made a donation to a sperm clinic, there was a good chance he'd done it for the money, which meant we likely would have very little in common.

"I hear you're going to be a father," Kit said to Jesse and I marveled at how my brother lit up at the mention of his unborn child.

Time flew as Jesse talked about his wife, their plans for splitting their time between the farm and the city, and how happy he was. Scott shared that he hoped he and Monica would find themselves in the same situation soon.

"And you?" Kit asked. "Do you see yourself settling down and starting a family any time soon?"

I nearly threw up in my mouth, but held back the "Hell,

no" that I would have felt comfortable exclaiming had Ashlee's parents not thought we were somehow involved. Instead I took a breath and forced a smile. "I'm taking things as they come."

At least that wasn't a lie.

Diane reached across and gave my arm a pat. "That's a wise choice. Life isn't a race and it rarely unfolds the way we'd plan for it to anyway."

"That's the truth," Kit said in agreement. "And, yet, somehow it always works out."

She nodded and hugged him.

I could see where Ashlee and Joanie had gotten their optimistic attitude and their ability to accept what others might have fought about. There was so much about the Pryer family I liked.

When the door to Ashlee's room opened, a nurse popped her head out. "Good news, there is no new swelling. Some pain is normal, but we've given her something to help alleviate it. She's fading in and out, but she's asking to speak to Mr. Rehoboth."

Me? I looked around.

Her mother waved for me to go. Her father said, "You might as well, we're not going anywhere."

I gave my brothers each a long look that I hoped they correctly interpreted. They'd done well so far, but Ashlee's father might start grilling them as soon as I left the room. Jesse gave me a nearly imperceptible nod. Scott? Who could tell if he understood? I'd have to trust him to be smart enough to read the situation.

When I stepped into Ashlee's room she was lying flat. I approached her bed and hesitated.

The nurse said, "It's okay. She actually feels better than she did before the scan, just a little loopier. Don't expect her to remember much of what you say, but she was adamant that she wanted to speak to you."

I stepped closer and smiled down reassuringly when Ashlee's eyes opened. "Hey."

Her answering smile was slightly lopsided. "You're still here."

"I told you I would be."

She paused then said, "My parents don't know why I went to see you."

"I know."

"They probably think you and I—"

"They do and it's okay."

She smiled again. "I'm sorry."

My heart melted a little just then. "No need to be. They're wonderful."

A tear fell from the corner of one of her eyes. "Yes, they are. I feel so bad about putting them through this."

"Hey. Hey." I stepped closer and held one of her hands. "You're not the one who went through the red light. None of this is your fault." God, it felt right to have her hand in mine, to be there for her. How right shook me to the core.

"No, but it was my idea to go to your office to see if I could catch you coming out." She searched my face. "I was so afraid I'd say the wrong thing but I mustn't have. You're here."

What could I say to that? "You did fine."

Her eyes closed for a moment before reopening. Once again she gave me a long look before asking, "Did you and I kiss or did I imagine that?"

There was nothing inherently sexual about standing beside a woman in a hospital bed, but you couldn't have convinced my cock of that. It hardened with an enthusiasm I assured it was misplaced. "You imagined that."

"Real or not, it was nice." Her eyes closed again and her lips curled in a smile.

Leaning down to test how it would be in reality was a temptation I nearly gave into. Instead, I released her hand and straightened. "I'm glad. Now get some rest."

Her eyes flew open again. "Will you be here later?"

"I have work I need to get done, but I'll be back."

She made a circle around her face. "Because you don't want to miss a moment of all this loveliness." She chuckled at her own joke.

She was pale with a bandage on her left temple. There was bruising beneath her eyes and her hair was sticking up in every direction, but somehow she was still so beautiful I had trouble looking away. "You look fine."

"Fine," she chuckled again. "That's you. Did anyone ever

tell you that you're gorgeous? My opinion may be affected by the fact that I haven't had sex in years, but I would break my sabbatical from men to be with someone like you."

Well, okay then. "Years?" I really should have ended the conversation. She was stoned on whatever they'd given her, but I had to know.

She shrugged while appearing to focus on the clock on the wall behind me. "It's easier. I don't want to introduce Sage to a lot of men who won't matter in the long run."

She was a good mother. "That sounds sensible."

"I love Sage. I don't want a man who couldn't love her the way I do." She gave me a long look. "Could you love someone else's kid?"

"Any good man could."

"Yes," she said slowly as she closed her eyes again. "That's what I'm waiting for—a good man. If you come across one, send him my way."

"I will."

"But don't tell him what I said about me not having sex. That makes me sound desperate."

"I wouldn't think of mentioning it."

"And my parents," her words slurred, "please don't tell them you're Sage's father."

"I won't." That was an easy promise to make.

"Thank you. I might sleep now," she said with her eyes closed.

Without another word, I slipped out of the room and

returned to where the Pryers were still talking to my brothers. "Whatever they gave her for the pain was strong. She's asleep."

"Good," Diane said. "She was up most of the night. She needs the rest."

My brothers came to stand beside me. "Lunch?" Jesse asked.

I nodded.

As we walked out of the hospital a few minutes later I did my best to put what Ashlee had just said out of my thoughts. All of it. Not one damn part of it had been good for me to hear. I didn't want to think about her with other men. Hearing that she hadn't been with one for years was worse, though, because it made me want to volunteer to help her with that.

She'd imagined kissing me? I'd imagined us doing a hell of a lot more than that.

However, if Sage ended up not being related to me, fucking Ashlee would have been a bad idea. It would mean I opened the door to a seriously troubled woman.

On the other hand, if Sage ended up being the biological daughter of a twin of mine, fucking her was an even worse idea. I hadn't lied to her. I'd just watched my brothers make the mistake of not being honest when they'd met their future wives. That was a chaos I wanted to avoid.

I halted mid-step. Future wife? Where the hell had that thought come from?

Jesse stopped beside me. "You okay, Thane?"

I shook my head. "No. I'm not. Nothing is currently *okay*."

Scott gave me an enthusiastic pat on the back. "That's why we're here."

I was about to tell him not to touch me then met Jesse's gaze. We knew each other well enough to not need words. And he was right. I wasn't upset with Scott and he'd take harsh words to heart. "I appreciate that, Scott."

Jesse said, "Dad texted. Bellerwood is at his house and he'd like us to join them there."

"Walt is at Ethan's?" Scott asked. "What don't I know?"

Probably so much I didn't know where to start. Still, if we were a family and this was about working things out together, it was time to bring him up to speed. I suggested the conversation happen once we were in the car. As Jesse drove, I told Scott about the demands his father-in-law was making on me and how he was stalling the project until one of us figured out how to stabilize his bean paste into a fuel for the station.

Scott was silent for a moment. "That sounds like Walt. You should have said something."

I glanced back at him. "Monica has been through enough with him."

At the mention of Scott's wife, his expression went all goofy and he punched me in the shoulder from the backseat. "You're a good brother, Thane."

He wouldn't have said that had he known how close I'd come to hitting him back. Jesse and I had been raised to kick other people's asses, not each other's. Scott's hands-on approach to affection was something I was still getting used to.

Jesse said, "Easy there, Scott. You know he hates that."

"Sorry," Scott said with a smile.

My irritation instantly fell away. He meant well. "What did the two of you think of the Pryers?"

"They seem like a very nice family," Jesse answered first.

"Will we be planning a third wedding soon?" Scott joked.

My hand fisted on my thigh. "Scott, what did my father tell you about why I was at the hospital?"

"Not a lot. He told me where you were and that you could use more support from your brothers. I know you and I are not as close as you and Jesse are, but I had no idea you were dating anyone."

Jesse met my gaze in the rearview mirror. He'd gotten the whole story from my father. I would have bet my life on it. Scott was family now, but when it came to inner circle sharing—trust took time. His view on things tended to be different than ours.

Should I tell him?

Jesse pulled the car over as if he'd read my thoughts. Although I hated to admit it, he was right again. Scott would never truly be one of us if we didn't let him in.

Without fanfare, I began with how the day before had started, the conversation I'd had with my father, and then what Ashlee had said to me in the parking lot. I went on to describe the scene of her accident, how I'd ended up talking to her sister on the phone, and how the situation had become a bit of a runaway train.

"No, shit," he kept saying. "Really? No way."

I left off the last conversation I'd had with Ashlee, but I did explain that I didn't feel I could say much until I resolved if I did indeed have a twin.

"You sound certain that you have one."

"Well, I've never made a deposit at a clinic."

"The DNA test could be wrong," Scott said.

"I've considered that." I had.

Scott tipped his head to one side. "But?"

"Bellerwood implied a few months ago that I might have a twin. I dismissed it as another one of his mind games, but if the DNA test is valid, it explains a lot."

"Do you want me to talk to Monica's father? See what he knows?"

"We'll do it together. It's part of what we need to discuss with him today." A silence fell over the car.

Scott finally said, "You've gotten yourself into quite a pickle, but Monica and I will help out however we can."

A pickle? I smiled. It was something Scott's adoptive father would have said and it struck me as funny enough that I laughed. "That's what I'm in—*quite a pickle.*"

Jesse pulled the car back into traffic. "Scott, my family used to make a lot more sense before you came along, but I can't say I hate the way it's changed."

"I feel the exact same way." Scott shot a smile at us that had both Jesse and me smiling as well. "Although I'm a little afraid to meet Thane's twin. What if he's even more uptight? Imagine that. Thane as the chill one?"

"Don't make me kick your ass," I joked.

"Don't scuff your designer loafers trying," he tossed back and we shared another laugh.

CHAPTER EIGHT

Ashlee

THE DAY HAD been a long one, full of more tests and treatments, but I was feeling better than I had that morning. Choosing slight discomfort over foggy brain, I'd declined receiving more painkillers. It was a decision I was glad I'd made when Joanie had shown up after lunch with Sage.

At first Sage had looked terrified and I'd questioned my sister's decision to bring her, but as soon as she'd cuddled up to my good side, I'd changed my mind. Mommies get hurt, just like children do, but she needed to see that I was still alive.

I rallied the best I could, pushing myself to sound better than I felt. Snuggled to my side, she told me all about how Alfie had given up his bed for her and was sleeping with his brothers in the other room while she was there. "And he's not even mad at me about it, Mommy."

I smiled at that. I adored my nephews and knew the feeling was mutual. I told Joanie that if she gave me another day to heal, I'd love to see all of them as well. Alfie especially, so I could thank him for being so good.

I usually read to Sage, but this time she read to me and there was no medicine that could have made me feel better than seeing my little baby wanting to care for me. She asked me if my head hurt. I told her it did a little.

"When are you coming home?" she asked.

I told her I wasn't sure, but it wouldn't be too long. To distract her, I asked her about her friends at preschool. She told me a long story about a toilet issue that may or may not have been caused by someone stuffing socks down it. When I asked her who had done it, she told me she suggested the teacher check which kids went home barefoot. Sage assured me she'd had both of her socks on when she left.

I chuckled. "You have excellent detective skills."

"I pay attention," she said with confidence. She sat up and scanned my face. "You look tired, Mommy."

"I am, Sage, but sleep is helping me heal faster so I can come home sooner."

She snuggled down against my side. "I wish I could sleep here with you."

I wished she could as well, but my night was still full of people checking in on me and oxygen treatments. "Maybe when I'm feeling a little better."

I couldn't say how long we lay there, simply holding each other close, before Joanie pried her off me. Joanie and I exchanged a long look. I knew she wanted to ask me how I was really feeling but couldn't in front of little ears. Instead she said, "I convinced Mom and Dad to go home. I can come back later if you'd like. Mike said he's fine watching all the kids if you want me to sleep over."

"Why does Auntie Joanie get to stay?" Sage asked unhappily.

It was a fair question. "She wouldn't be in the same room as me, Sage. She'd be in another room by herself. You wouldn't want that."

Not looking fully satisfied by the answer, Sage still accepted it. "I'd want to be here."

"I'm still working with doctors at night, Sage. They have all this amazing machinery that is healing me up fast."

"Does it hurt?" she asked with wide eyes.

"Not at all," I answered honestly. "One of them is like taking a nap on a cloud."

She nodded then buried her face in Joanie's neck. Over her head, Joanie said, "Well, if you change your mind, call or text. Doesn't matter what time. I have an overnight bag in my car already."

"Thank you, Joanie. For everything." And that included the little girl she was caring for while I couldn't. "They say if things keep healing as fast as they are, I could be home by the weekend. I'll have to be careful for a while and they suggested I take a week or two off work, but I was lucky."

"Yes, you were." She wiggled her eyebrows. "Even with him. He's yummy."

RUTH CARDELLO

"Who's yummy?" Sage asked, lifting her head.

"No one." I shook a finger at my sister. "Auntie is being silly."

"I want something yummy," Sage said. "Can I have a cookie when we get home, Auntie Joanie?"

"If you're good," Joanie answered, giving Sage a kiss on the head. "And only after dinner."

Sage turned to look at me. Her voice was solemn. "I haven't kicked or hit anyone, Mommy. And I won't do it ever again. I miss you."

Tears filled my eyes. "Oh, baby, this wasn't your fault." I wiped at my eyes. "But not hitting anyone is a good choice. I love you, Sage."

"I love you too, Mommy."

Joanie shifted Sage's weight. "Call me if you think of a single thing you need. Mom and Dad will be back in the morning. After I get the kids to school, I can be as well. Or we can do this again. Next time we'll stay longer."

"I get to come back tomorrow?" Sage asked.

"You do," I said then mouthed a thank you to my sister. "Bring a coloring book tomorrow so you can make a picture for me to hang on my wall."

"Horses or fairies?" she demanded.

"Your choice."

Joanie asked Sage if she was ready to go home and help make dinner. After shooting me a quick look, Sage said she was.

After they left, my parents came in briefly to make sure I would be okay if they slept at home that night. I assured them that I was looking forward to getting as much sleep as I could squeeze in.

Alone, I closed my eyes and rested for I have no idea how much time. Sleep wasn't possible with the noise of the monitors, the light throb of discomfort on one side of my head as well as the bright lighting in the room. Still, it felt good to partially shut down and empty my mind.

I didn't move at the sound of someone entering the room. If it was a nurse checking on me, they'd leave without bothering me. If it was time for another treatment or scan, they'd rouse me.

The sound of a chair being moved closer to my bed did get my attention. I turned my head in that direction and opened my eyes. There, beside my bed, was the suit-clad, muscular man I was beginning to wonder if I was imagining. *Do all brain injuries come with gorgeous guardian angels?*

He smiled. "I'm no angel."

I groaned and closed my eyes. How had I said that last part aloud? "People with head injuries cannot be held responsible for what they say." Embarrassment flooded in. There was no surfacing from this with any pride, was there?

"How are you feeling?" he asked as if I hadn't just made a fool of myself.

I opened my eyes slowly and forced myself to meet his gaze. "A little better."

"That's good."

I raised the back of my bed so I was sitting up and arranged my blankets over me.

"No more hospital gown?" he asked.

I glanced down at the long sleep T-shirt I'd changed into earlier. "My sister brought it." When I realized my nipples were visible nubs since his arrival, I pulled the blanket higher to cover them. Sports bra. *I'm definitely going to ask Joanie to bring one tomorrow.*

My hand went to my hair. Not wanting to mess with my head, I hadn't brushed it since the accident. *I'm being ridiculous. Thane isn't here because he's attracted to me. He cares only because he saw me all bloody. And, maybe, just maybe he's curious about his daughter.*

"Sage was here earlier."

His expression gave nothing away. "How did she handle seeing you?"

"Better than if she'd come yesterday. Or even this morning. I don't like how I am on pain meds."

"I can understand that. I broke a bone in my foot once and didn't take anything for it after I left the hospital. I don't like feeling out of control."

He did get it. "Yes. In my teens I had to undergo several surgeries, they're the reason I couldn't have a child the usual way. Anyway, the last one involved the removal of a tumor. Withdrawing from the meds they sent me home with was scary, and I wasn't even on them that long. Since then I've decided to manage on over-the-counter meds or nothing. I don't even drink much. One or two at the most."

"I'll have a social drink now and then, but that's it. My brother Scott jokes that I need to relax, but I figure there'll be time enough for that when I'm dead."

I smiled at that. "My parents told me they met your family. Both of your brothers as well as your father?"

"Yes."

Hearing about his daughter had obviously affected him enough that he'd told his family about Sage. His brothers' desire to meet my family had to be a good sign. "My parents said they thought your family was very nice."

"My family said the same about yours."

"My mother got a kick out of the fact that your brothers are twins. She said they were identical in appearance but very different in personality."

"That sums them up."

Never having been in a situation remotely like the one we were in, I struggled with what to say. My memory of earlier that day was cloudy, but I remembered that he'd visited me. At least, I thought he had. "Thane . . ."

"Yes?"

"Were you here this morning?"

"I was."

I strained to remember what we'd talked about. "I was medicated."

A slight smile stretched his lips. "Yes, you were."

"If I said anything inappropriate—"

"You didn't." He leaned closer and I was sure I'd never seen more beautiful eyes. They were the same as my daughter's and not at the same time. My body warmed and tingled in a way I would have thought impossible considering my injury.

"Good," I said breathlessly, unable to look away from his face. We were strangers but somehow he was also the father of my child. That had to mean something. It seemed to matter to him. Lacking a better topic, I asked, "How was your day?"

The smile he directed my way warmed me from head to toe. "More productive than expected. How was yours?"

I could happily spend a lifetime basking in his gaze. "Surprisingly busy. The best part was the long snuggle I had with Sage. Being away from her is hard."

"I imagine it would be. If you're too tired for company, I can go." His eyes darkened. "Or I can stay. I brought my laptop and could get some work done while you sleep if you feel better with company."

Could a person fall in love with someone before they knew much about them? I was beginning to think I could. Thane was caring for me the way Mike would care for Joanie—the way I'd always yearned for a man of my own to do.

How was that possible? What the heck had I said to Thane in the parking lot that had earned this kind of response from him? Still, sleeping with him watching over me felt like too much too soon. "I'm not tired," I lied.

"Don't be shy about telling me to go if that changes," he said in that deep voice that I wished I could listen to a hundred books narrated by.

"If you hear me snoring that'll be the first clue," I joked.

His laugh was as sexy as the rest of him. I had to remind myself that there was a good chance his presence at my bedside had less to do with wanting to be with me and likely more to do with wanting to hear about his daughter. "Sage will be back tomorrow afternoon if you'd like to meet her."

His expression closed and he sat back. "That's not a good idea."

There was a pain in his eyes that moved me to say, "She doesn't need to know who you are. You could be an out of town friend visiting because you heard I was hurt."

He shook his head. "Your parents already think there's something between us. I don't want to confuse the situation more."

I searched his face. "But you'd like to meet Sage."

He ran his hands down his thighs and emitted a sound somewhere between a groan and a growl. "Maybe."

His hesitation was understandable. Hell, he'd just gone from being blissfully unaware of where his sperm had gone to hearing he had a daughter who wanted a father. That had to take a moment to come to terms with.

When I'd first decided to try to find Sage's biological

father, I'd prepared myself for the possibility that he might not be someone I'd be comfortable introducing her to. The world was full of all types of people and I wasn't naïve to the danger some of them could bring to our otherwise safe and happy life.

But Thane? He was everything I'd prayed Sage's bio-dad might be. He was kind, intelligent, caring, and from a family who seemed willing to accept her. The way he'd stepped in to care for me told me he would protect and care for Sage as well.

Although I hadn't met his siblings or father, I loved that they'd been at the hospital. My mother had described the relationship he seemed to have with them as solid and supportive—the way our family was. I didn't want to get too hopeful, but I was beginning to think he might be someone who would want to be in Sage's life . . . even if it was only on her birthday or holidays.

Some might have felt threatened by the appearance of a potential second parent, but I'd learned a lot about love through Sage's birth. Joanie had carried her, birthed her, would also love her as if she were one of her own . . . but that in no way lessened what Sage and I were to each other. More people caring about a child was never a bad thing. Love, when it was healthy, made everything that didn't make sense in life seem insignificant.

Like the fact that Thane had donated sperm to a clinic with no desire to know about what they used it for. I had no idea what his mindset had been back then or if he'd put any thought into what he'd done since. None of that mattered because he was here now and, from what I could tell, with only the best of intentions.

I really need to stop imagining him naked. He needs time to meet his daughter and sort all of that out without the complication of me throwing myself at his feet and offering myself to him.

"Normally I would tell my parents why I went to see you, but I'm not sure if that would complicate things more."

He nodded once. "I'd appreciate a little time before you do."

"Of course." There was likely also some embarrassment involved in how he'd come to be Sage's father. "I'll tell them . . ."

"I told them we met for the first time in the parking lot, spoke briefly before the accident, and that seeing you hurt was why I felt invested in your care."

Our gaze met and held again. "But they didn't believe you."

"Not for a second."

"I could tell them you're an old friend, no different than I was going to tell Sage."

"Would they believe you?"

I wrinkled my nose. "I'm not a good liar so probably not."

"Then for now say nothing."

My eyebrows rose. "And let them think we're a couple?"

His eyes darkened again and there was a flare to his nostrils that was sexy as hell, but when he spoke his tone was cool. "Your father asked me about us."

"And?" My breath caught in my throat.

"I told him that if you hadn't mentioned me, it wasn't my place to. Your mother suggested that you be allowed to tell them about me when you're ready. There's no need to say anything."

"If they ask, I'll just say we're not ready to talk about us yet."

"Yes."

"And that's true." It made sense. I smiled and curiosity overtook my restraint. "What did I say that convinced you to meet your daughter?"

His expression darkened and the look he gave me had unexpected steel in it. "Sage. Is. Not. My. Daughter."

I blinked quickly. Was he not ready for the title of father? Actions spoke louder than words. If he actually didn't care about her, he wouldn't be here. His family wouldn't have met mine. He'd asked for time and it seemed like a fair request considering everything. "Okay."

He leaned closer again, holding my gaze the whole time. "I'm serious. I never went to a fertility clinic. Sage is not mine. I know that doesn't make sense to you. It doesn't yet make sense to me. But as soon as I unravel this situation, you'll be one of the first people I explain it to."

Not everyone could face reality head-on. My parents had

helped me understand that when my fathers's brother lost his wife but continued to speak about her as if she were still alive for a year afterward. Some had labeled him delusional, but my father had asked us to give him the grace of patience as he worked through his grief. I watched him go through stages of denial, anger, sorrow so deep we thought he might not pull himself from the depth of it, and finally acceptance. But none of it had happened overnight. It had taken time.

Maybe coming to terms with something you wished you hadn't done but could no longer deny that you had was similar. Thane wanted things to have happened differently, so for now he was holding to a reality he could handle.

Did that make him someone who couldn't be around Sage? I didn't think so. I hadn't seen anything bad enough to concern me. Coming to a decision to let him have the time and the reality he'd asked for, I repeated my earlier response. "Okay."

We spent a moment in a silence that was broken by a nurse checking in to see how I was. It was the same nurse who'd assumed Thane and I were a couple. She looked pleased to see him there with me. "I see you're in good hands," she said with a wink, then retreated quickly.

It was difficult to meet Thane's eyes after that.

"It appears she's also under the impression that we're a couple," he said.

I swallowed hard. "An understandable mistake. You're paying for my stay. Your family was here. You're here . . ." I raised my eyes to his. "It's a lot to do for a stranger. Anyone might read more into it than is there."

His lips pressed together in a tight line before he spoke. "And they'd be wrong too. I'm here because it's important to me that you fully recover. Your daughter needs her mother."

That gutted me on so many levels.

Sage did need me and this man was ensuring I could be there for her. Did I need to push him for more?

But there was more. "Did you lose your mother?"

He stood and for a moment I thought he wouldn't answer my question. When he did, his voice was full of so much pain I wished I could cross over to hug him. "I never had one to lose. Not one anything like you."

"I'm sorry."

"Not your fault." His hands fisted at his sides, then relaxed. "And not something that I care about anymore."

Clearly that was not true. He'd experienced a loss that went a long way to explaining why he was at my bedside.

"Did she die in a car accident?"

He shook his head, looking once again like he might not speak further on the subject, then he said, "My family is less conventional than yours. My biological mother gave me up. I have no idea why. The woman who adopted me left soon after she also adopted my brother Jesse. Thank God, my father is a solid human being who stepped up and raised us well enough that none of that mattered."

But it had. "Your biological father?"

"No," he growled. "I have no idea who he was. The man who adopted me is the only parent I have ever or will ever need. Knowing where Sage's DNA came from will not make or break your daughter's happiness. The family you surround her with, the love you give her, that's all she'll need."

In the softest voice I could muster, I asked, "Will that family include you?"

He ran a hand through his hair. "I don't know yet."

At least he was honest. I respected that. I brought a hand to the injured side of my head when it started to pound.

He stepped closer and looked over my monitors before demanding, "Is something wrong?"

"No. Sorry. My head still throbs now and then."

All tension left him and his expression softened. "You need your rest. I should go."

I searched his face, thought about all he'd said, and decided that as strange as all of this was, I was okay with him watching over me. "If you meant what you said about being able to get some work done while I sleep, I'd feel better if someone were here with me."

He sat back down. "There's nowhere I need to be."

I lowered the bed again and closed my eyes briefly, but was too tense to sleep.

When my eyes fluttered back open he touched my arm briefly. "What's wrong?"

"The lights are so bright."

He found a switch and dimmed them, then asked, "Better?"

I nodded and tried again, but my thoughts were still racing. The pounding in my head was equally distracting. I met his gaze again.

His smile was gentle. "What else?"

There was something incredibly comforting about his voice. I hesitated, then decided I had nothing to lose and asked, "Could you tell me something about your childhood? All the beeping is hard to tune out. I don't care what you tell me, but your voice is so deep . . . I think I could fall asleep to it."

The oddest expression came and went on his face. "Now there's something a woman has never said to me before, but sure . . . I'll give it a try. Jesse's a pain in the ass, but consistent about it, so that might be repetitive enough to put you out."

I smiled. "What's your earliest memory of him?"

Thane began describing the day he and his brother had hidden from their nanny in the pantry of their house. He remembered being very young, under the age of five. Their choice of hideout had come with the most incredible revelation—their father had a sweet tooth. There were shelves of cookies, chocolate, small cakes. By the time their nanny had found them, he and Jesse had eaten enough to make them both sick. No reprimand necessary. That's the day his father introduced them to one of his favorite terms "natural consequence."

When Thane paused, I closed my eyes and asked him to tell me another story. This one started with he and Jesse hiding in their father's home office to discover if he was actually the government spy they'd suspected he was after watching a movie with parents who had been. I don't know if their father ever realized they were there because Thane's voice lulled me into the first peaceful sleep I'd had in days.

CHAPTER NINE

Thane

I WOKE TO the sound of a female voice saying, "Oh, Kit, look who's here. Keep your voice down, he's sleeping."

I sat forward and stretched.

Ashlee's father said, "Not anymore. Good morning, Thane."

"Morning." I rose to my feet.

Diane went to her daughter's side and smiled down then waved for us to step together into the other room so we wouldn't wake her. "She has more color today. How was she last night?"

"Good," I answered. "They're still running tests on her every few hours, but everything is coming back positive. In a few days she should be able to go home."

Kit came over and clapped a hand on my shoulder. "We hated leaving her, but I should have known you'd be here."

There wasn't much I could say to that, so I didn't touch it. Instead, I checked the time on my watch and said, "I need a shower and change of clothes before I start my day so I'm going to run."

Diane held up a hand to stop my retreat. "One thing first."

I stopped. "Sure."

She wrapped her arms around me and gave me a hug so tight it knocked some of the air out of my lungs. I wasn't quite sure what to do with my arms at first so they hovered above her for a moment. When I met Kit's gaze and saw the emotions shining in them I hugged Diane to me and said, "There's no reason to believe she won't make a full recovery."

Diane nodded against my chest then stepped back. "Thank you. I needed that. If I didn't think it'd hurt her more than help her, I'd crawl right into that bed with her and hug her as well. There is nothing worse than watching your child suffer."

I'd never experienced that, but her pain was palpable. "She must be feeling somewhat better," I assured her, "because she's no longer on pain medication."

Kit smiled. "She never liked them. Thank you for being here." He shook my hand and looked as if he was close to hugging me as well. I stepped back and nodded.

"Will we see you later?" Diane asked.

Ashlee had said Sage would be there during the day. I wasn't ready for that. "I might return tonight. Unless you'll be here."

"No, no," Diane said. "Poor Ashlee is probably sick of us

by the time we leave. She needs you with her as well."

I wasn't certain about that, but I was finding it difficult to imagine not wanting to be at her side that night. Why? I wasn't allowing myself to question it too deeply. Once she was out of the hospital and back to her life with Sage I would step away.

This was about making sure a daughter didn't lose her mother. That's all it was. I excused myself from the room and headed to my apartment to change. I was fresh from a shower and stepping into a clean pair of trousers when my phone buzzed with a call from Jesse.

"You need me at the office or with you today?" he asked as soon as I answered.

"I'm fine either way. Besides, although I hate to admit it, you handled Bellerwood better than I have been. Do you think he's actually going to move forward with the station now?"

"Your problem with him was you were too nice. He was holding how much you care about Scott and Monica over you. He had to believe we were willing to take them down as well as him to get him to back up."

Jesse could sell that well. When it came to being an asshole, no one could play the role better, although there'd been times I'd wondered if it had been a struggle for him at all. Either way, Bellerwood had removed the expectation that we could force Scott to produce a fuel source from our agreement.

And the only price? The ten minutes or so it took to reassure Scott that Jesse hadn't meant anything he'd said. I couldn't blame Scott for questioning Jesse. I'd thought getting married and fatherhood had softened my brother, but Jesse had gone for Bellerwood's jugular—threatening to ruin not only him, his project, but also his name and anyone associated with him. How? Jesse left the details out, but spoke with enough conviction that I was half convinced he had something on Bellerwood.

Not for the first time in my life, I was glad Jesse and I were on the same side. With Bellerwood in a position where he was less resistant to working with us, I took the opportunity to demand he tell me what he knew about the twin he'd told me not to look for.

"A twin?" he'd said absently as if a person could forget something like that. "Oh, yes."

"How do you know I have one?"

He'd withdrawn inside his head for a moment, then said, "I don't. Not with one hundred percent certainty."

I'd growled out, "What the hell does that mean?"

My father told me to hold my temper. Me? I wasn't the one who'd threatened to ruin Bellerwood, but after taking a deep breath I understood the difference. Jesse's aggression had been strategic and therefore productive. Mine had been an expression of frustration and a show of weakness. He'd taught us early to recognize the difference and act accordingly. In a much calmer tone, I asked Bellerwood to explain what had led him to believe I had a twin at all.

Bellerwood waved a hand at Jesse's twin. "Scott. I couldn't have a daughter of mine cavorting with a man I knew nothing about. So I had my people do some digging. The adoption agency you, Jesse, and Thane were placed through was funded by Charles Simmons."

The name meant nothing to me. A quick look around the room confirmed that no one else seemed to recognize the name either. "Should I know who that is?"

Bellerwood shrugged, not putting much emotion into our exchange. "He was a well-known psychiatrist in Austria fifty or so years ago. He lost his license and fled to the US after he was accused of performing unethical experiments on minors."

You could have heard a pin drop in the room. "What kind of experiments?"

Bellerwood shrugged again. "That's irrelevant to what you're asking, outside of what he was researching."

"And that was?" my father pressed.

"The degree to which a person's environment affects their behavior and character."

"Nature vs. nurture?" I asked.

"Yes," Bellerwood confirmed. "What one is born with opposed to how their environment molds them is difficult to determine. I've read his papers on it. Fascinating stuff."

"And he studied us?" Scott asked.

"I suspect he did more than that," Bellerwood said. "In

his early work he wrote about the limited number of twins he could study. There were also too many variables he considered out of his control, especially if the twins had already reconnected before he met them, which was most often the case."

A dark thought gripped me. "So he deliberately separated Jesse and Scott?"

"Why stop there?" Bellerwood said. "Simmons was wealthy, angry that his work was not being recognized by his peers, and I suspect more than a little obsessed to prove his work was worth his methods. It's my understanding that he placed children in families with the condition that the family let the child be interviewed annually by a 'social worker' aka a researcher under his employment."

My father said, "There was someone who claimed to have the right to speak to both Thane and Jesse, but I put a quick stop to that as soon as I found out about it."

Scott added, "My parents said there was someone who used to come around and ask me questions but they eventually stopped."

"Likely because Simmons had lost access to your twin. The research he was doing required collecting data on both children."

"Where is this Simmons?" I demanded.

"Long dead," Bellerwood said with no affect in his tone at all. "And his research, if he didn't have it destroyed before he died, is somewhere my people couldn't find."

"I have a twin," I said slowly as the reality of it sunk it.

"Or had one. There's no way of knowing if he's still alive." Bellerwood seemed to wander away into his own thoughts again.

"You don't have any information about him?" I asked, stepping closer to him.

Bellerwood shook his head. "Why would I? You weren't the one marrying my daughter."

I ran both of my hands over my face. This was really too much.

"We'll find him," Jesse had said firmly.

"Yes we will," Scott had added with conviction.

My father had walked over to Bellerwood then and laid a hand on his shoulder. "Walt, we're family and this is a family matter. Whatever you know about the adoption agency and this Simmons man, you need to share with us."

Bellerwood looked around the room then nodded. "I'll have my people forward you what they found." He didn't offer to do more than that, but I wasn't surprised. Hopefully his people already had the answers I was looking for.

"Earth to Thane," Jesse said, bringing me back to the present as I drove. "I asked you if want help squeezing information out of the researcher Bellerwood's people found or if you want me to do it."

"I can handle it." I'd played nice with Bellerwood because I cared about Scott and Monica. There was no one associated with separating and studying twins that I had the tiniest bit of sympathy for.

That was still true an hour later when I stood in the driveway of a timid-looking man with round spectacles and watery eyes. I'd met him under the guise of wanting to buy a car from him, but I quickly set him straight that I'd come to talk to him about Simmons.

At the mention of the name the man had turned to flee, but I'd grabbed him by the arm and stopped him. "We can have this conversation here or somewhere it'll be harder for anyone to hear you call for help."

Wide-eyed, the man looked around. "Follow me. No one should see you talking to me."

He led me into his first-floor apartment and closed the door behind us before saying, "You're Thane Rehoboth."

"I am."

He gulped visibly. "You've done well for yourself."

"I'm not here to talk about me. You worked as a researcher for Simmons."

"A long time ago and for a very short time."

"Were you the person sent to interview me?"

"Not exactly. You were too young to answer questions, but I was your caseworker. At the time I was taking notes on the milestones you met."

"Were you also assigned to my twin?"

He took off his glasses and wiped a hand across his eyes. "I was."

"Where is he now?"

"I don't know. I haven't seen him since I quit working for Simmons, which was when you were both just over a year old." He replaced his glasses. "I didn't know Simmons was doing anything nefarious. I thought all the families knew about the study and had agreed to it, but none of the parents were aware that their child had a twin. At first, I thought, what was the harm? Right? Families were receiving the babies they yearned for and the children all seemed healthy and happy. But it felt less and less ethical every time I visited. I didn't like lying to the families. I started feeling so guilty about it I said I couldn't do it anymore."

"And you quit? Did you consider telling the families the truth?"

"Someone broke into my house and took my notes and photos. All they left was a note that told me if I didn't keep my mouth shut they would kill anyone and everyone I cared about. I had a new wife. We were planning to have a family. I was too scared to talk."

"Thirty years is a long time to be too afraid to say something," I said coldly.

He swallowed visibly. "I'm not a brave man. That might be why my wife left me. Listen, I'm no hero, but I quit as soon as I knew what I was doing was wrong."

I ran a hand through my hair. No, he wasn't a hero and I could have told him that doing nothing was as bad as continuing his involvement, but I didn't care about him. I cared about the twin he might be able to help me locate.

"Name. I need the name of my twin."

"Zachary Danford."

"Where was he placed?"

"On a small farm in Connecticut."

"Farm?" Oh, of course, Simmons must have wanted to keep as many of the variables in the experiment the same. "Which farm?"

"It was a long time ago. I don't remember."

I stepped closer and took him by the neck, slamming him against the wall. "Try."

Sputtering, he said, "It was Serenity's Loss. Or Cross. Serenity's Crossing. That's it. Down in rural Connecticut. That's all I know."

It was a solid lead. "Don't go anywhere. If I have to ask you another question and have to track you down I won't be as understanding about your role in this."

The man's head wobbled in a semblance of a nod before I let him go.

It was late or I would have headed to Connecticut straight from there. Instead, I decided what I needed before then was another restless night in a hospital chair.

I do have a twin.

Sage is almost definitely my niece.

I really need to stop imagining Ashlee naked.

CHAPTER TEN

Ashlee

THE BANDAGE ON the side of my head was fresh and significantly smaller. I hadn't been allowed to wash my hair, but my hair was brushed. Under the protective eye of my mother, I'd even taken a shower.

The doctors said I was healing faster than expected and if all continued as it was, I was out of the danger zone. I wasn't experiencing dizziness, vision issues, or any of the more severe side effects of a head injury. They credited my recovery to how quickly I'd received treatment as well as the availability of the hyperbaric chamber.

Whatever the reason was, I was grateful to finally be free of the IV and back on my feet. It was nice to have my ladies supported again with a loose-fitting sports bra beneath the T-shirt my parents had brought. Oh, yes, changing out of my long T-shirt and into shorts and a shirt had me feeling much more like myself.

Being able to sit in a chair rather than staying reclined in my bed made a huge difference in how worried Sage was when she visited. This time we read stories on the couch together, then snuggled and watched a movie on her iPad. I was careful to not move my head too much and the nurse warned me to remain as calm as possible. Some movement was good, since there was a concern that I might develop a blood clot. Too much was bad since having a brain bleed was still possible.

So move, but don't. Got it.

I called the tutoring center I worked for to update them on my progress. My father had already told them I wouldn't be back for a week and why, but my doctor said he wanted me out of work for two weeks with no driving before he cleared me to return.

Good thing I have savings.

Recovery from anything was no fun, but I'd been in that place in my teens when the doctors had found a tumor protruding out of my uterine wall. Healing from that had been painful and emotional, but I'd survived and beaten it. This would be no different.

My parents stayed long enough to have dinner with me, a delicious steak dinner provided by the hospital and served by staff at a table like we were in a restaurant. Afterward, my father said, "Unless you'd like us to stay, Mom and I are going to head home. Thane said he'd stay with you tonight."

"He did?" He hadn't said anything to me about that, but I had been asleep when he'd left.

My mother gave me a kiss on the cheek. "You chose well.

He's such a nice man."

I nodded and didn't correct her. Thane and I weren't a couple. He'd explained why he felt involved in my recovery. Still, I couldn't help but wonder if he felt something more for me.

Yes, it was too soon.

Sure, his only impressions of me had been as a parking lot stalker and an overly adoring hospital patient, but would a man who wasn't interested spend another night by my bed, watching over me? Yes, he cared about my welfare, but I'd slept with men who couldn't have been bothered to bring me soup when I was sick. Thane didn't need to be at my side to make sure I was well cared for. For heck's sake, the amount of staff devoted to making sure my every need was met was beginning to make my stay feel more like a vacation . . . if vacations included being tested and prodded every few hours.

When my father stepped away to gather a few things, I could no longer look my mother in the eye without admitting, "Thane and I are not dating. There's nothing romantic between us. I'm not even sure we're friends yet. What he said about meeting me for the first time the other night was true—"

"Then I like him even more," she said softly, cutting me off before I had a chance to tell her who he really was. "I know a thing or two about men. The way he looks at you and how he's already brought his family into the mix—well, I wouldn't be surprised if he hadn't already decided you're the one for him. It's like that for some men. I drove your father a little crazy in the beginning, so it took him longer to figure out that we were meant to be together but my friend Gracie married her husband two weeks after they met and they've been together thirty-two years now."

"That's not what's happening here, Mom—"

My father returned before I had a chance to add more and I wasn't ready to have this conversation with him yet. My mother would listen then help me sort out how I felt. My father would instantly become more protective of me and question everything Thane was doing. I wouldn't lie to him, but the whole truth of what was going on could wait another day—especially if Thane had said he'd return.

Things were already weird enough.

After my parents left, I debated what I should wear like a schoolgirl choosing her prom dress. I could change into a fresh set of shorts and a new T-shirt, but I'd look exactly the same. There was no way I was putting on a granny night-gown unless I had to. A quick look in the mirror confirmed that regardless of what attire I chose, I still looked like someone who'd lost a boxing match. My eyes had large dark circles beneath them. The best I could say about my hair was that it was brushed. My lips were dry and chapped. I groaned and turned away from my reflection.

How I looked should not have been on my radar. I told myself all I should be thinking about was how grateful I was to have survived an accident some wouldn't have, and with possibly no long-term effects from it. To be upset that I hadn't surfaced from that instantly, looking fresh-faced and stunning, was ridiculous.

I hugged my arms around my waist. *But do I have to look so bad?*

All that the peek I'd taken of myself had done was confirm that Thane was hanging around because I was raising his child. Anything more than that was just a byproduct of the imagination of my slightly battered brain.

"Hey, you're up," Thane said in that deep voice that felt like a caress of its own.

I spun toward the door and instantly regretted it as I became less steady on my feet. He was at my side in a heartbeat, supporting me by gripping one of my arms. He tossed a small gift bag on the chair to take hold of my other arm as well.

"Are you supposed to be up?" he demanded like I was some errant child he'd caught sneaking out.

I would have pulled my arms free from his grasp, but his touch felt too good. He filled my vision as well as my senses and my body hummed for more of his attention. I licked my dry lower lip and tried to focus on answering him rather than melting into his deliciously wide chest. "Yes."

His hands tightened on my arms and I allowed myself the fantasy that he was as affected by our proximity as I was. Our eyes met and the anger I saw in his was as good as foreplay. What was it about this man that made him impossible to resist? "Get back in bed," he growled.

I coughed on a laugh of surprise because I'd nearly blurted out, "Only if you join me." I was comfortable with my sexuality, but I'd never been bold. Sex was good. Sometimes it was even wonderful. My attraction to a man had never been something I couldn't resist, something so powerful it left me feeling... wanton. Did people even use that word anymore? They would if they ever found themselves that close to Thane. He bent his head closer, his breath tickling my lips, and if he hadn't been holding my arms I likely would have wrapped them around his neck.

I'm not sure how long we stood there, breathing each other in, the air pulsing with what had to be a mutual attraction. *It had to be.* It was too glorious of a torture to endure for long. Fearing that I was about to do something to completely embarrass myself like beg him to kiss me, I made a joke instead. "I would, but you're kind of holding me in place."

He released my arms as if he hadn't realized he was and took a step back. I was both relieved and deeply disappointed. "Sorry."

"Don't be." I forced a smile, shooting for as casual as I could. "Thank you for not allowing me to faceplant. My face already needs all the help it can get."

He frowned, raised a hand to trace the unbruised side of my face, and said, "You're beautiful."

It was so easy to fall under his spell. I fought to keep my

hands to myself as I said, "Now I know you're a liar. This room has mirrors."

His thumb traced over my dry bottom lip and if I'd known any national secrets, I would have spilled them to him for a promise that he not stop. "Beauty isn't just what's on the outside."

I laughed nervously at that. "What a kind way of saying I look—"

He claimed my mouth with a hungry kiss that seemed to take him by surprise as much as it did me. There was no uncertainty in his touch as he pulled me closer. This was a man who knew what he wanted and knew how to get a woman to give it to him. His lips were skilled and had mine opening to an even more skilled tongue. Oh, the way he hungrily explored my mouth was a hot promise of a need to explore more of me and I was all in.

It wasn't until his hands moved to frame my face that he encountered my bandage and broke the kiss off with a swear. He withdrew to a few feet away, and ran a hand through his hair. "Sorry, I meant to say that you still look good, despite the bruising."

Breathing as heavily as he was, I tried to look like I hadn't experienced the best kiss of my life. Seriously, I had a new standard. If a man didn't bring *this*, I wouldn't bother asking if he drank or gambled. I wouldn't settle for less than how Thane made me feel. "Thank you," I croaked, then cleared my throat and tried again. "I like the way you give a compliment."

His eyes met mine and what I'd said sounded worse to me each time it echoed in my head. The night before, I'd referred to him as my gorgeous guardian angel. The things that came out of my mouth when I was around him didn't make sense to even me.

Just as I was starting to worry that I'd finally run him off, a smile started in his eyes then spread to his lips and he said, "I like the way you take one."

"This is a little crazy, isn't it?"

"It most definitely is."

Smiling back, I said, "I have a brain injury. What's your excuse?"

"You're too damn beautiful," he said without missing a beat and my breath caught in my throat. His expression turned more serious. "But I shouldn't have kissed you."

My hand went to my bandage. I could see that a man might feel badly about coming on to a woman in a hospital room. "It's okay. I'm already feeling a lot better."

He looked about to say something but then decided against it. Instead he retrieved the bag he'd walked in with and handed it to me. "My sisters-in-law thought I should bring you something. They picked this out."

It was an odd intro to a gift. He could have said that he wanted to bring me a gift, but there was also something touching about imagining him talking to the women in his family about me. I thanked him and accepted the bag. When

I looked inside, I exclaimed, "Lip balm. Your sisters-in-law are geniuses. Seriously. I didn't realize how dry my lips were until . . ." I stopped there and decided it was safer to check out what else they'd sent. "Hyper-allergenic concealer? I love these women already." There were fuzzy socks and a body lotion for sensitive skin. After replacing everything but the lip balm in the bag, I said, "Tell them I really appreciate this."

I applied an ample amount of lip balm and smoothed it in with a ring finger. "Oh, my God, that's better." Then I made the mistake of meeting his gaze. Was it too much to hope he would compliment me again? With his lips, or his hands, or any part of him really. I swallowed hard.

"I'm glad," he said in a tight voice. "I'll tell them you liked it."

"I do," I answered breathlessly. "And thank you. This was all very considerate." I stopped myself from saying more. *I need to gain control of myself before I scare him off. Tone it down, Ashlee. You know how to flirt with men. Easy on the heavy breathing and ogling.* "I'll put this with my things."

He followed me. After placing the items he'd given me with the piece of luggage my parents had brought my things in, I glanced at my hospital bed then away. When I'd been in more pain with tubes attached to me, having him sit in a chair at my bedside hadn't felt . . . so . . . intimate. I cleared my throat. "My parents said you might stay the night."

My hand flew to cover my mouth as I realized how that

sounded and groaned. Clearly, I'd hit my head too hard. If I wasn't capable of saying anything to him that didn't sound painfully adolescent, I needed to stop talking.

He gave me a long look. If I'd been able to script the moment, this was where he would have told me not to feel awkward around him because he was so damn attracted to me he couldn't say anything that made sense either. He'd kissed me . . . said I was beautiful. So, why did he go back and forth between looking at me with desire in his eyes and seeming annoyed? I wanted to ask, but wasn't sure I wanted the answer.

My phone rang. A quick check confirmed it was from someone I couldn't ignore. "Joanie? Everything okay?"

"Yes and no," she said in a flustered tone that had me instantly tensing.

"Did something happen?"

Thane stepped closer, seeming to go on high alert right along with me.

"I feel bad calling you about this at all. Sage has been doing so well, but at dinner when I told her we would call you to say good night, she started crying for you and she hasn't stopped. Usually I can console her, but she said she wants to see you again. I don't want to bother Mom and Dad. The boys have been trying to cheer her up, but she has them near tears now as well. Do you mind if I bring her by for a little while? I think all she has to do is see you and she'll feel better."

"Of course," I said without hesitation. "I'm still up."

"If I come now we can visit, Mike can put our kids to bed, and Sage will probably fall asleep on the drive back. But if you're too tired tell me—"

"No, I'm fine. Bring her. I could use a cuddle too. Call her over. Let me talk to her."

I met Thane's gaze, but this time without awkwardness. Motherhood trumped ego—at least for me. If he had any issue with me taking time away from him to comfort my child . . . his child as well . . . then Sage and I would both be better off without him.

He didn't look annoyed though. All I saw in his eyes was concern.

Sage was still sobbing when she came on the phone. "Mommy, come home."

"I can't, baby, not yet," I said. "Soon, though. Hey, you saw me today, honey. I'm getting better."

"I don't want you to die, Mommy."

My hand tightened on the phone. The hand Thane placed on my lower back was welcome support. A quick glance at his expression confirmed he'd heard her. I turned my attention back to her. "I'm not going anywhere, Sage. I'm still right where you saw me earlier . . . feeling better all the time."

"I miss you, Mommy. I'm scared."

"I miss you too. And why are you scared?"

"I don't have a daddy. If you die I won't have a mommy

either." She started crying again and it nearly shattered me.

"Oh, baby, all I did was hit my head. I'm not going anywhere." Thane's hand tensed on my back. I looked up at him again. His expression was tight and his eyes dark with emotion. "Auntie Joanie said she could bring you here to see me if you want. Why don't you bring your froggie book? I'll read it to you, we'll snuggle, you'll see that I'm feeling even better than I was earlier today, and then you won't think about losing me anymore."

"Auntie Joanie, can you take me to see Mommy?" Sage asked in a voice so young and hopeful that I doubted even the most coldhearted person could have denied her.

"Of course, Sage. Go wash your face, get your book, and I'll drive you over."

"Mommy," Sage declared with excitement. "We're coming. We're going to snuggle."

I smiled even as I wiped tears from my eyes. "Yes, we are. Now, go wash your face like Auntie Joanie asked."

"I'm sorry," Joanie said. "I tried to—"

"You're doing amazing," I said in a grateful rush. "Joanie, I'm the one who feels bad that I've turned your house upside down this week. They said I should stay for a few more days, but I already feel so much better. I can ask—"

"Don't," she said. "The most important thing is that you get the treatments and follow your doctor's instructions. I hated to call you about this, but she was crying so hard she was starting to make herself sick and that isn't Sage. It was breaking my heart to see her like that."

"You were right to call me," I said. "And thank you. Tell Mike I'll make it up to you guys somehow."

Joanie chuckled. "You don't owe us anything, but I do have to tell you Mike will be glad when you're home. When I couldn't get Sage to stop crying, he tried to talk to her. Don't tell him I told you this, but when she asked him if she could stay with us if you died, he almost started bawling with her."

I sniffed. "Mike is such a good man."

"He is," Joanie agreed. "He told her there was no chance that you were going to die. You're too tough for that. But if anything ever did happen to you, our home was ready and would always be Sage's. I nearly lost it then. So if I crawl in bed with you while we're there and steal a snuggle—I need one too."

"I'll request a larger bed," I joked with a chuckle.

"Sage is ready to go, so we'll head out now. Thirty minutes?"

"Perfect."

The call ended and it took me a moment to realize Thane was still at my side, hand on my back, comforting me with his presence. I was half afraid if I turned toward him he'd step away . . . or kiss me again. I wasn't ready for either. "Joanie and Sage are on their way back."

"I heard."

"Please stay." There, I'd said it. In that moment it didn't

feel important that I'd only met him a few days earlier or that my sister knew what his relationship with Sage was. I didn't want him to leave and I wanted him to meet Sage, even if it was only this one time.

"Ashlee, I'm not—"

"Ready? Her father?" This time I did turn toward him. "It's okay. We don't have to make this into a big deal. Simply be here while she is." I searched his face. "Look me in the eye and tell me you don't want to meet her, and I'll believe you."

Both of his hands settled onto my hips as if it were the most natural thing, as if we were already a couple. "I do want to meet her, but there are things you should know."

"Are you a dangerous person?" I asked, holding his gaze. "Would you ever hurt her?"

"No and never."

"Is anything you've told me about yourself a lie?"

"No."

"Are you married?"

"God, no."

I smiled at that. "My daughter needs me, and I'd love for you to meet her. The rest will sort itself out."

His hands tightened on my hips. "I'm not the 'ride it out and let things sort themselves out' kind of person."

"What kind of person are you?"

"I choose goals, determine my priorities, and put all of my energy toward achieving them."

"Is that what you're doing here?"

"No." He paused. "Yes." He shook his head. "I have no idea what I'm doing here."

A memory came back to me that made me smile. "That's how I felt when I was chasing you around the parking lot."

His head tipped to the side. "I thought you couldn't remember that."

"It's coming back."

He made a face. "In my defense, that morning I'd won a paternity case against a woman who'd also claimed her child was mine."

My eyebrows rose, which seemed to make him aware of how that might sound bad.

He quickly added, "I had never done more than unwillingly share my food with her." When I cocked my head to the side questioningly at that one, he added, "I took her to dinner once and she'd used that opportunity to claim I was the father of her child." He stopped, ran his hand through his hair, and growled, "Anyway, that's why I was an ass when you walked up to me."

He seemed genuinely embarrassed, and I believed him. "Does that happen to you often?"

"Lately yes. A recent project has made it seem that my family is much better off than we are and that has some people . . ."

Well, no wonder he's reluctant to admit he's Sage's father. "That must be difficult to know how to navigate."

He held my gaze. "It is. I came close to calling security on you and I'm not proud of that."

In the scheme of things, his initial reaction to me felt inconsequential. "I can forget it again if that helps." I shot him a smile that he returned.

"You'd do that for me?" he asked in jest.

"This once, yes."

Time slowed again as the look in his eyes began to reflect the heat spreading through me. There was suddenly nothing comforting about his touch—it was all promise and need. My hands came up between us, sliding beneath his jacket to explore the wide expanse of his chest. It was a bold move, but one that felt more right than anything I'd ever done with a man.

Whatever this was . . . it was real and raw and impossible to resist. My lips parted in anticipation. His head bent and those delicious lips of his gently grazed over mine.

"Excuse me," a female voice said. "Ms. Pryer, I was asked to take you down for an oxygen treatment."

Feeling bereft after Thane's immediate withdrawal, I forced a smile to my face. "Of course." Then I remembered who was on their way, and in a mild panic said, *"Sage and Joanie."*

"I'll meet them," Thane answered in a tone that instantly calmed me. "And explain where you are."

"I'll be as quick as I can be."

Thane touched the side of my face gently. "You'll take as

much time as you need to. Sage will be fine."

I nodded, then went up on my tiptoes and gave his cheek a quick kiss. "Thank you."

His face flushed as if we hadn't already kissed more than once. "Go."

I followed the nurse to the door, stopping briefly to look back at him. It was still difficult to believe he was there, that we'd gone from me waiting in my car outside his office to this. Was it unlikely? Yes. Impossible? I didn't believe in the word.

I had no idea where this was going, but I trusted him to be there to meet Joanie and Sage. One step at a time. I shot him a grateful smile before following the nurse out of the room.

CHAPTER ELEVEN

Thane

A MAN DIDN'T reach his late twenties without having one or two brushes with women who camped out in his thoughts, despite his attempts to oust them. Ashlee was the mother of my brother's child. That mattered more than how drawn I was to her.

Until I clarified the situation with her, she was under the misguided impression that my denial of being Sage's father was a case of me wanting to take things slowly. Rather than explaining my poor behavior the first time we met, I should have told her I wasn't the one she was looking for. I should have told her what I'd discovered and promised to introduce her to Zachary Danford when I located him.

Why hadn't I?

I wasn't looking for a relationship.

I certainly didn't need to start one with the mother of a child from my twin.

So, what was holding me back?

As hard as it was to admit to myself, I'd already begun to

feel protective of Ashlee. I did want to meet her daughter . . . my niece . . . and I wasn't ready to step aside and hand both of them over to a man I knew nothing about beyond that we had the same DNA.

I really need to stop kissing Ashlee.

"Mommy." A little girl burst into the room, sprinting past me as if I weren't there. Ashlee's sister was right behind her.

"Sage, I asked you to walk," Joanie said in a reprimand that had no bite to it. She stopped when she saw me. "You're still here." She smiled. "I approve."

Sage was in front of Joanie in a heartbeat demanding, "Where's Mommy?"

I answered. "She's getting a quick treatment, but she'll be right back."

"She said she would be here." Sage's face bunched up.

Joanie bent so she was eye to eye with her niece. "We talked about this being possible. Your mommy is here to get better. The treatments don't take long and they don't hurt her. Remember what she said about feeling like she was lying on a cloud? That's all they're doing to her. They give her extra oxygen so she heals up faster. You want that, don't you?"

Sage nodded solemnly.

Joanie took Sage's hand in hers. "Then we'll sit and wait. And you'll see, she'll be back before we know it."

"Okay."

Joanie's phone beeped. She read a message then grimaced and looked at me. "It's Mike. The boys are all riled up about something. If I take this call, could you—?"

"Absolutely," I said even though I knew nothing about kids and Sage hadn't yet acknowledged my existence.

"I'll be as quick as I can be," she said and I smiled. She and Ashlee might not be identical twins, but they were two peas in a pod.

"We'll be fine."

To Sage, Joanie said, "I need to call Uncle Mike real quick, Sage. I'm not going anywhere, but I'll be right over there. Okay? Stay here with Thane."

Without giving Sage time to agree or not, Joanie moved to the other side of the room and held her phone up to her ear. "Mike? What's wrong?" A moment later, she said, "No, those are not his pajamas. They don't even fit him. He should give them back to Alfie. He has his own pair. What? He peed in his?" She lowered her voice as if realizing we could hear her.

Eyes on her aunt, Sage said, "Josh pees his pants when he gets nervous."

I nodded and said nothing since it was not an area I had experience in.

Sage looked up at me. "Are you a doctor?"

"No."

She took a moment to size me up. "Who are you?"

"One of your mother's friends." I hoped that much was

true.

"I don't know you."

"You're right. We've never met."

"Are you dating my mommy?"

"No." I loosened my tie, suddenly feeling like I was being grilled by a pro.

Her eyes lit with excitement. "Are you my daddy?"

It could have been the hope in her eyes, but I found myself incapable of instantly denying that I was. She had my eyes. And damned if she didn't also have my ears. But she wasn't mine and why that made me a little sad confused me. Eventually, I forced the truth out. "No. I'm not your daddy."

She sighed and hugged the book she was holding to her. "I don't have a daddy, but I have cousins. And Auntie Joanie and Uncle Mike. And Grammie and Grampie. Annabelle said I don't need a daddy. She doesn't have one."

"Who is Annabelle?"

"My friend at preschool. Her cat just had kittens."

I nodded.

"I don't have kittens either," Sage said as if that were interchangeable with having a father. She gave me another long look. "Do you have kids?"

"I don't."

"A daddy?"

"I do have one of those."

"And a mommy?"

How honest was a person supposed to be with a young child? I had no idea. "No. I don't have one."

Mouth rounding, Sage asked, "Did she die?"

"Not that I know. I've never met her."

"Like me and my daddy." Sage seemed wise beyond her years. "Do you have cousins?"

"No, but I have brothers and we're close."

She smiled. "I want a brother, but Auntie Joanie had her bits and pieces removed. I don't know how bits and pieces make a brother, but Mommy doesn't have them and now Auntie Joanie doesn't either."

I nodded again.

Sage glanced at the empty hospital bed and her bottom lip began to tremble. "I want my mommy."

"I know," I said gently. "Hey, what book did you bring for her to read to you?"

Sage sniffed. "It's my froggy book. I can read it."

"You can?" I asked as if she'd announced she had the solution to Scott's bean paste fuel volatility.

She nodded. "It's a big girl book, but I remember all the words." Her face began to crumple again. "Mommy loves when I read it."

Oh, boy, she looked closer to tears this time so I hastily asked, "Would you read it to me?"

"You like frogs?"

Not at all, but I lied, "Love them."

She didn't look convinced. "Sometimes I forget a word."

"I could help you with that."

She sniffed. "Okay."

She went to sit on one side of Ashlee's bed. I took the chair beside it. She looked from the book to me. "My mommy taught me to read. Who taught you?"

I couldn't remember. A nanny? Tutors? But that wasn't the answer that would have made her feel better. "My father and my teachers."

She liked that. "Teachers are nice."

I loved that she'd had good experiences with them. "They sure are."

"Can you see the book?"

"I can."

She opened it and started to read. Until then I would have said there wasn't much about children that I liked, but watching her filled me with a sense of hope . . . and wonder? She was so young, but somehow also confident and clear about what she wanted. It wasn't difficult to believe we were related. "I forgot that word."

"Which one?"

Impatiently, she hopped off the bed and walked over to me. "This one."

"Imagined," I supplied.

"Oh, yeah. Imagined." She frowned. "Mommy said it's okay for me to make up a word if I forget, but I want to be right."

Oh, yes, that's my gene pool. "I'm like that too."

She almost returned to her place on the bed, then climbed up on my lap instead. I raised my hands and said, "Oh. You shouldn't. You need to—"

As if it weren't the most awkward experience for me, she settled against my chest. My arm stayed raised in the air above her. "You smell nice," she said.

"Thank you?"

"Uncle Mike smells like gasoline sometimes because he works on trucks. But he doesn't always smell bad. Auntie Joanie tells him to go shower when he stinks."

"That's good."

"I'm gonna start the story over."

"Sure. I guess."

Joanie returned and sat on the bed where Sage had been. "You okay?" she asked with humor.

I shrugged and motioned toward Sage in an attempt to explain that I had invited none of what was going on. Joanie laid a hand over her heart with an expression of approval I didn't deserve. She clearly thought I was warming up to the idea of being Sage's father. There was no way to explain that I wasn't.

Uncle Thane was the most I could be. Before I figured out how to get Sage off my lap, she began to read again and it was so damn cute I forgot to ask her to get down. She asked me if she could read it to me again. I said, "I'd love to hear it a second time."

"Would you read it to me this time?" she asked when she

finished.

I couldn't say no, so I took the book from her and did my best to read it with as much expression as she had. "Read it again," she said, settling more under one of my arms.

I met Joanie's gaze. She nodded for me to, so I did.

Sage was asleep before I finished the book, but I continued reading it anyway. I put the book to the side when I was done then motioned for Joanie to take her. She shook her head and whispered, "Let her sleep. Today was hard on her. And if she wakes now, she'll be upset that Ashlee isn't back yet."

I nodded because although she and Ashlee were wrong about why I was there, Joanie was right to believe I cared about Sage's happiness. Sage was no longer just my twin brother's child or even biologically someone who was my niece.

She was family.

And I'd die before I ever let anyone hurt her.

CHAPTER TWELVE

Ashlee

I FROZE AT the door of my hospital room and instinctively motioned for the nurse beside me to not make a sound. The sight of Sage asleep on Thane's lap under the watchful eye of my sister had my heart thudding wildly in my chest.

My sister's body language was relaxed. Thane's tie was loosened and his hair was slightly mussed. He looked exactly like a father who'd come home from a long day at work then read a story to his daughter until she fell asleep.

In a hushed voice, the nurse said, "I'd snap a photo and frame that moment. If you have any hard days, focus on all you have to go home to."

"I will," I promised. Sage and the family I already had were more than enough blessing for me to be grateful for. Kisses aside, all of this had to be even more confusing for Thane than it was for me. He was holding his daughter, one he'd likely made himself okay with never knowing a thing about.

Although it had been exciting to imagine myself with

Thane, in that moment I knew his relationship with Sage was more important than any attraction he and I might have for each other. I didn't want to do anything to rob her of the opportunity to know him.

I need to stop kissing him.

As if sensing my presence Thane looked up and met my gaze. Wham, what I felt for him rocked through me. I was reminded of something my mother had once told me when I'd wanted to give Joanie one of my dolls and was trying to decide which one I cared about the least. My mother had said the best kind of gift, the ones that truly mattered, were the ones that were the hardest to give—not the easiest.

I'd given Joanie one of my favorite dolls and had yet to regret it. My mother had been right . . . when the decision was made out of love it was never wrong.

For Sage, I'd put aside what I wanted. Both she and Thane needed this time to get to know each other. And us? If we were meant to be, Thane and I would survive the wait.

I smiled, walked into the room, and sat down beside my sister. "Thank you both for this."

At the sound of my voice, Sage roused and scrambled over to me. She threw her arms around my neck and clung to me so tightly I nearly burst into tears.

Thane rose to his feet and said he needed to make a few calls but he'd be back. I thanked him again and let him go.

"He was so good with her," Joanie said once he was out of the room.

I scooted back onto the bed so I could hold Sage. "Sorry it took so long."

Sage was the one who answered. "It's okay, Mommy."

I smiled and kissed the top of her head.

Joanie asked, "How do you feel?"

"Surprisingly good," I said. "It's amazing what a difference the therapy makes."

"Can you come home tonight, Mommy?" Sage asked.

"Not tonight, but soon," I said, cuddling her close.

"Guess what?" Sage said. "Josh peed in his pajamas again."

Joanie wagged a finger. "We're not going to talk about that. Especially not when we get home. Right? It's not something anyone needs to mention."

Sage raised and lowered a shoulder. "As long as he doesn't pee in my pajamas."

I rolled my eyes and met Joanie's gaze. "That sounds fair." We both gave in to a smile.

Joanie nodded. "If Josh pees in Sage's pajamas I'll come trade places with you because my own brain will have exploded." She made an explosion move with both of her hands.

Sage and I laughed. I said, "Hopefully, it won't get to that point."

After a short silence, Sage said, "Mommy, your friend is nice and he can read."

"Wow, is that right?" Joanie and I exchanged another

smile.

Joanie said, "I was wrong about this one and you know I hate to be wrong, but there's no denying I should have trusted your instincts."

Over Sage's head, I said, "I hope so. Things are a little weird, but I think they'll all work out."

With the audience we had, we were limited as to what we could say.

"Mommy, can I read my froggy book to you?" Sage asked.

"I'd love that." I settled us both down and Joanie handed Sage the book.

When she came across a word she usually stumbled over, Sage paused, and pointed at it. "Your friend taught me that word. *Imagined.*"

"His name is Thane," I said.

"Thane." Sage tried out his name. "I like it."

"I'll tell him you approve," I joked.

"He has beautiful eyes," she said.

I looked into hers, loving how much they were the same. "So do you, baby."

"He never met his mommy," she said. "His daddy taught him to read."

"I've met his daddy. He's a very nice man."

Her eyes rounded. "Was he very old?"

"Not very."

"Was his name Grampie?"

Joanie was the one who answered this time. "He said he prefers Granddad."

"He sounds nice," Sage said just before losing interest in that topic and returning to reading a book we'd read a hundred times before. I found comfort in the routine of it and I sensed that she did as well.

Our time together passed quickly, and when Sage started to look drowsy, I suggested Joanie take her home. Joanie agreed and scooped her up. "We'll be back tomorrow," she promised. "Hopefully only once."

I stood and gave them both one big hug. "I'll be home before you know it, Sage. Be good."

"I will be," Sage mumbled against Joanie's shoulder.

Thane appeared at the door as they were leaving. He said good night to Joanie. She said she hoped to see him again soon.

Alone again, my body began to yearn for me to close the distance between us, but I had come to a decision I needed to state. "Thane, do you mind if we talk?"

"Certainly." His expression was cautious. He took a seat on one of the couches as I sat on the other. Had he also decided we needed to put some space between us?

"I loved seeing Sage snuggled up to you."

"But?" His tone gave none of his feelings away.

"There isn't a but—not really. I just think we should focus on one thing at a time. You should get to know your daughter before you and I . . . before we even think about . . ."

"Sage is not my daughter," he ground out.

I'm doing this badly. Still, I couldn't hold back a question. "What are you so afraid of?"

He took a deep breath. "I understand your confusion. My DNA did match with Sage's. I'm not, however, her father. Although, I do believe I'm her uncle."

What? "Her *uncle*?"

"If all the information I have is correct, the donor at the fertility clinic was my twin."

"You have a twin?" It seemed late in the game to mention it, and not entirely believable. *"A twin?"* I lost a little respect for Thane in the face of what sounded like a desperate fabrication.

"Yes."

"Does this twin have a name?"

"Zachary Danford."

Okay, for someone who was lying he was quick with details. "I don't believe you. My family met yours. If you actually had a twin, that seems like something one of them would have mentioned."

He ran a hand through his hair. "None of us were certain he existed."

"Oh, I see." I didn't. Not at all. And I was getting frustrated. "Listen, if you want Sage to think you're an uncle instead of her father, I have a problem with that. I'm okay with not telling her anything, but I also won't lie to her."

"It's not a lie. I have a twin."

"Then where is he?"

"I don't know."

"But you do know that he was the one who went to the fertility clinic?"

With a slight smile, he said, "Unless I also have a triplet, I feel it's safe to assume it was him."

Shaking, I rose to my feet. "I don't get you. Do you think you're being funny?"

He stood as well. "I don't find any part of this amusing. I was simply stating an ironic fact. Until recently I thought the idea of a twin was ludicrous, so my confidence that I don't also have a triplet has been shaken."

"Stop," I said as my head began to throb. "None of this makes sense."

"We're in agreement on that." He stepped closer. "I know where Zachary was as a child. I'll find him."

Bringing a hand to my bandaged temple, I asked, "You'll find the twin you discovered you had as soon as I showed you proof that you were a DNA match to Sage?"

"Yes—"

"Just say you don't want to be a father," I snapped and stepped back. "It's okay. I'm good with whatever you decide, but don't lie to me."

He closed the distance between us. "I've never been anything but honest with you."

"Sure," I said as disappointment settled in. I'd wanted

Sage's father to be as wonderful as he'd seemed, but my fantasy of what was possible had apparently clouded my ability to see him as he was. I walked away from him toward the other room. "I'm sorry. I'm tired."

"Do you want me to go?"

"Yes." Perhaps because it was late, but I was having difficulty reconciling the man I'd started to think Thane was with a man who would make up a twin.

"This will all make more sense when I produce Zachary."

"Please go."

He lingered a moment longer. "Nothing I said was a lie." An emotion burned in his eyes I couldn't decipher. "I'd stay and try to convince you, but you look exhausted."

"Wow, a lie and an insult. You're batting a thousand."

"Ashlee—"

"Good night, Thane." For Sage's sake, I added, "If you wake up tomorrow and feel up to telling me the truth, you're welcome to come back. If not, please don't bother."

He turned and left without saying another word.

CHAPTER THIRTEEN

Thane

I STARTED THE next day by driving to Scott's house and telling him we were going on a road trip. "A long one? A short one? Do I need to pack anything?" was all he'd asked.

"Short. We'll be back tonight."

He'd explained to Monica that he was heading out for the day with me, gave her a kiss, and hopped into the passenger seat of my car like a dog excited to go for a ride. We were about a mile from his house when I said impatiently, "You have no idea where we're going. How are you okay with that?" Jesse wouldn't have been. Not for a second. He would have come with me, but not until he knew all the facts and had given his opinion on how we should proceed.

"I trust you. Plus, you wanted me with you and that means a lot to me." He shrugged, changed my radio station from classical music to country and started drumming along with his fingers on his knees. "And whatever we're doing, I bet it's spontaneous and wouldn't hold up to Jesse's scrutiny."

My hands tightened on the steering wheel. "Correct."

"That's my kind of mission. Are you getting a puppy?" he joked.

He really was an idiot at times. That alone should have had me rethinking my plan. I didn't have to be the one chasing down clues. I could have hired a detective. I glanced at Scott. Was I doing this all wrong?

"Don't give me that look, Thane," Scott said, sounding more amused than bothered. "I know you're glad I agreed to come. Just say it."

Rehoboths were strong, faithful, tenacious, but none of us were particularly good about expressing our emotions. We won by doing, not by asking ourselves how we felt about our goals.

"I do appreciate that you're here."

"See, that wasn't hard. I'm curious, though. What is it you need me for? Moral support? My charm? What are you up to, Thane, that requires my specific set of skills?"

"You're a farmer."

"That's a little vague—but I'm still in."

I reminded myself that his joking manner wasn't indicative of a lack of intelligence. In no way would I ever condone whatever sick experiment Simmons had made us a part of, but the differences between Jesse and Scott were often striking—just as how they were strangely similar in other ways. They liked a lot of the same foods. They both had a strong sense of self as well as family. So many of their facial expressions were the same. Their humor, though, was entirely different. Jesse's was more subtle and cutting. They handled conflict differently. Jesse and I had been raised to avoid unnecessary confrontation, but if it came to us . . . we struck first, struck hard, and took down our opposition so forcefully they would never think to come at us again. Scott was a nurturer. He sought to understand the cause of his opponent's aggression and tried to diffuse it.

"You're good with people," I said. "You pay attention to things I might not. We're headed to Serenity's Crossing, a dairy farm. Zachary Danford was placed there by the adoption agency. I haven't been able to track down Zachary's current location through traditional methods. So, we'll start with where I know he was."

"Your twin. Of course."

"The farm owners will probably be more comfortable talking to you than to me."

"Because I speak farmer?" He looked far too amused.

"If you're unable to take this seriously—"

"No. I get it. This is important." He raised his hands in mock surrender. After a moment, he said, "Are you grumpy because you've been sleeping in a hospital chair instead of your bed? How is Ashlee today?"

"I don't get *grumpy*, and I have no idea."

"Oh. Jesse told me you were going to see her last night. What happened?"

"Nothing. She's getting better quickly. There's no longer

a need for me to be there."

"I thought brothers didn't lie to each other."

I said nothing for a moment. "They also don't push for information that is none of their business."

"So touchy. You messed it up, didn't you?"

"There was no 'it' to mess up."

"What did you do?"

I sighed. Scott could be relentless when he was curious about something. He said it was because he cared. I wasn't sure it wasn't a case of not being taught boundaries as a child. Still, once again, he wasn't wrong. I'd definitely mishandled my last conversation with Ashlee. "My goal today is to find out something that will lead us to Zachary. Feel free to talk to these people like they're your next best friend. Find out everything. I want to know why Zachary is hiding before we meet him."

"What makes you think he's hiding?"

"No driver's license in his name. No medical records. It's as if he disappeared after he was placed. Unlike us, his adoption wasn't recorded with the courts."

"I hope he's still alive," Scott said with a grimace. "Sorry, I'm sure you do too."

"I have zero feelings about him one way or another. All I want out of this are answers."

"For Ashlee."

And Sage, but I didn't share that. "Yes."

"I really liked her family."

"You would. They're similar to your own."

"Say that again but in a tone that makes it sound less like a slam."

I inhaled audibly. Is that how it had come across? I hadn't meant for it to. "What I mean is that they're . . ." None of the words that came to mind fit what I was trying to say. "Normal."

"I thought you were about to say 'simple' and I'd have to kick your ass."

That earned an eye roll from me. Scott was the type to catch and release insects that made it inside his house. He wasn't kicking anything. "I've never implied I felt your parents were not wonderful people."

He wagged a finger at me. "See, that right there is where you miss the mark. You had an opportunity to tell me you think they're amazing."

"Do you require my validation to assess the attributes of your parents?"

"And that's you being an ass because you're feeling defensive."

I groaned. "Are you trying to rile me?"

"No, I'm teaching you the ways of farmers. We don't accept bullshit."

My temper began to rise. "I can't believe I thought bringing you along might be helpful."

"That was a joke, Thane. People make them. The correct response is to laugh. You do have a sense of humor, right?"

Rather than answering, I began to calculate how much of the day would be wasted if I turned the car around and drove him home before heading to Serenity's Crossing. Short-term annoyance might be outweighed by how much easier the rest of the day would go without him.

"How many friends do you have, Thane?" Scott asked. Before I had a chance to answer, he added, "Real friends. Not people you're connected with through your work. I'm talking about people who want nothing from you except the joy of being with you."

I slowed, preparing to take an exit that would allow me to swing around onto the highway heading back to his house.

Scott pointed to the exit. "Do you always run away from things that make you uncomfortable?"

"No. I remove myself from situations I consider a waste of time."

"So, yes."

I drove past the exit but snapped, "If you wonder why you hear things last in our family—this is why." It was a dick thing to say, and I regretted it as soon as it was out of my mouth, but I was too agitated to apologize.

"Because you, Jesse, and your father have a certain way of seeing things and any challenge to that view is considered a threat?"

"I didn't say that."

"You didn't have to. Hey, you came to me today. All I

did was ask a few questions and suddenly I'm a 'waste of time.' So, you can spin this as my fault, but it might be time for you to dig deeper and try a little honesty."

What wasn't I being honest about? I'd told him where we were going and what our objective was.

He continued, "You obviously felt something for Ashlee. Whatever happened between the two of you is bothering you. So, maybe stop using me as your verbal punching bag and tell me what happened the last time you saw her."

Verbal punching bag? That pulled me back. I might be what some would consider uptight and blunt, but I didn't see myself as unkind. If I was taking my frustration out on Scott, it needed to stop. He'd accused me of not being honest. To me, being factual covered that. To him, it required vomiting every detail surrounding a situation. "I met Sage," I admitted.

"Her daughter. Your niece."

"Yes. She's smart, and curious, and not at all afraid to make known what she wants."

Scott smiled. "Like you."

I nodded. "She even has my eyes."

"That must be confusing."

Confused. It was as good of a description to how I felt as any. "She's family, Scott. My family."

"Then she's mine as well," he said in a quiet tone that brought us right back to being brothers on the same team. "That's good, right?"

"I was never meant to meet Ashlee or Sage. Not the way we did, anyway. They were looking for Zachary."

"Because you're not Sage's biological father?"

"Correct. It's him they need to connect with."

"Okay, let me wrap my head around what's going on in yours." He lowered the music. "Why is it a problem that they met you first?"

I shot him a dark look that likely revealed too much.

He said, "Oh. Okay, I'm beginning to understand. But you do know that fatherhood is about more than matching DNA?"

"That's not what this is about."

"Of course not. Although Sage is technically from Ashlee and Zachary, they were never together."

"I'm perfectly capable of comprehending how in vitro fertilization works."

"Zachary is not Sage's father. His sperm helped to create her. It's not the same thing. He made a DNA donation with the understanding that he wouldn't be expected to play a role in the child's life. For all you know he'll be relieved to learn that you're looking after his offspring."

"I don't care how he may or may not feel about anything."

"Are you worried about Sage? She sounds like a sweet kid who wants a father figure." When I didn't say anything, Scott added, "But this isn't just about her. What did Ashlee say that has your nuts in a twist?"

146

I gave him a warning side look that only made him smile. "I told her about Zachary."

Scott slapped a hand on his thigh. "You got that out of the way. Good for you."

"Not as good as you'd think. She didn't believe me."

After making a sound deep in his throat, Scott said, "It would seem far-fetched. Would it help if Jesse and I went to see her and explained our own story?"

"No," I said without hesitation. "I intend to find Zachary, introduce Ashlee to him, and let her decide on her own how she'd like to proceed."

"Sounds . . . so methodical. Not sure I'd go with that plan."

"I didn't come to you for advice."

His smile was bright and unwavering. "Actually, I believe you did. And, since I love you, I'll help you through this. What was the last thing Ashlee said to you?"

I considered not telling him, but there was value to hearing an opposing viewpoint on an issue. "She said if I woke today and felt up to telling her the truth I was welcome to go back to see her. If not, I shouldn't bother."

"Ouch. She's not happy with you."

"She made that point quite clear."

"Did you call her this morning?"

"No."

"Send her flowers? A note?"

"No. We're not in a relationship."

"That's a debatable point."

"Furthermore, I'm doing something of much more consequence for her."

He made a doubtful face. "Does she know that?"

"She doesn't believe I have a twin. Telling her where I'm heading today wouldn't have been a productive conversation."

He stewed on that for a moment. "You can't let her believe the worst of you until you can produce a twin."

"Now that I've prioritized finding him, it shouldn't take long to locate Zachary."

"You need to take her feelings into consideration."

I arched an eyebrow in his direction. Scott had been pretending to be Jesse when he met Monica. They'd had to sort through that lie before they could move on. "The way you did when you first met Monica? I've been nothing but honest with Ashlee."

"Aha, see what you did right there? You compared you and Ashlee to me and Monica. It's okay to say you have feelings for Ashlee."

"I care about what happens to her as well as her daughter."

Scott brought a hand to his chest. "Look at you, all grown up and falling in love."

"Shut the fuck up."

He laughed then took out his phone and I would have worried who he was texting if his sudden silence hadn't felt so much like a gift. A few minutes later, he put his phone away and said, "Don't be upset."

I inhaled sharply. "What did you do?"

"I sent Ashlee a bouquet of flowers from you with a note that said you were sorry about the misunderstanding and that you'd drop by to see her later today to explain everything to her. I chose the one with a teddy bear so she'll have something to give Sage."

A wave of anger came and went in a heartbeat. Ashlee was still recovering. My pride didn't matter as much as her stress level. "Was there one with a stuffed frog?"

"No, but I could definitely make that happen."

"Sage likes frogs." I told him briefly about the book she'd read to me.

Scott took his phone back out and made a call to the florist he'd used. He made sure it would get to Ashlee early and they would have a stuffed frog suitable for a young child. If the one they sent looked like the character of the book he gave them the title to, he promised to follow the delivery with a large tip.

When he ended the call, I found it difficult to speak for a moment. I thought about what I'd said to him earlier about him being the reason we didn't share everything with him. He wasn't the problem, we were. "Scott—"

"I know and you're welcome." The smile he shot me was warm and supportive.

Still, I felt something needed to be said. "I'm glad you're

here."

"We're family."

Family. What that looked like was in a constant state of evolution lately. Change was unsettling and not without mishaps, but I didn't want to go back to life before Jesse had found out about Scott. I loved that both of my brothers had found wives and settled into happy lives with them.

Could I imagine myself doing the same? I wasn't sure.

There was something between Ashlee and me, there was no denying that. If we'd met under normal circumstances, I would have asked her out and slowly explored our attraction to each other.

There was nothing normal about any of this, though. Would she be equally attracted to my twin?

What did a man do in that case? Should I beat my fists against my chest and proclaim her mine because I met her first?

Hell, I was still trying to figure out what I felt for her. Was I gambling that sexual attraction would be worth robbing her of her chance to be with the actual father of her child?

I didn't regret kissing her, but she deserved the chance to meet Zachary before we took things any further. She might decide to be with *him*.

My hands clenched the steering wheel at that idea.

And I'd be okay with that—because I'd have to be.

CHAPTER FOURTEEN

Ashlee

THAT EVENING, FEELING restless, I'd moved from the couch in the sitting room to my bed then back to the couch. I'd attempted to read a book I'd started before getting injured, but I couldn't concentrate on the story even though it had been one I'd been looking forward to finishing. Nothing on the television was able to hold my attention. When the nurse caught me flipping through the channels, she told me it was natural to not be able to focus after a contusion. My brain was healing. She suggested I try to remain as calm as possible. Avoid anything stressful.

So I definitely shouldn't have spent the day rehashing every conversation I'd had with Thane. I shouldn't have jumped to my feet in anticipation every time someone walked through the door then been stupidly disappointed when it wasn't Thane.

Flowers had arrived from him during Sage's visit or I might have refused them. The stuffed frog that looked so much like the one in her favorite book? Well, that was either an incredibly considerate touch, or a sign that he was a master at manipulation.

I'd wanted to spill everything to Joanie, but her morning had been hectic and she'd once again put everything else aside to make sure Sage had a good long visit with me. She was so happy to see flowers arrive from Thane, believing it meant his feelings were deepening for me, that I didn't show her the accompanying card. Had Sage not been there she would have asked me to read it to her, but we were on the same page when it came to keeping kids as out of adult business as possible.

I would have asked my mother to be a sounding board for Thane's bombshell of a twin story, but she'd woken up with a head cold. She and my father were going to take it easy for a day. For my mother that meant she'd probably head over to my house to clean it. During the day I worked for my parents. My father was likely using that time to organize and go through my work so I'd have less pressure when I returned.

Or my mother was really sick and my father was worried enough to stay home with her. Both possibilities made my head ache. I'd texted Joanie, asking her how Mom was doing. She'd told me not to worry about anything beyond getting better. It wasn't an easy answer to accept. Everyone was already doing so much for me. The better I felt, the more impatient I was becoming to go home and get back to normal.

From the couch, I looked across the room at the bouquet Thane had sent. It was a bright assortment. Clearly meant to cheer someone. On the card had been a typed apology for what he'd called a misunderstanding. As someone in the unenviable position of having just suffered a head trauma, I was willing to concede that my attention span was suffering . . . but I wasn't otherwise impaired or confused. Thane had clearly said *his twin* was Sage's biological father. I didn't misunderstand that.

Was it true or a lie? That was what I wanted to know, even though I wasn't sure which to hope for. If he'd panicked and made the twin up so he could continue to deny that Sage was his . . . well, that wouldn't say much about his character. I couldn't imagine Mike or my father doing anything remotely like that and they were the standard I held men to.

On the other hand, if he actually had a twin he hadn't been sure existed . . . how did that happen? And that I had no idea, was an uncomfortable reminder of how very little I knew about him.

If there were actually two Thanes wouldn't the other one have shown up as a DNA match? I absently rubbed at one of my temples as my head began to pound.

I remembered the nurse saying I shouldn't allow myself to stress over anything while I was healing. How was I supposed to do that when the gorgeous, attentive, family-approved man I'd foolishly begun to fantasize about making a permanent fixture in my life threw me a twin curve ball?

I couldn't imagine Thane admitting he'd lied. Very few people had the balls to do that. It was more likely that he'd say, "I've never been anything but honest with you" or try to gaslight me into questioning if I'd heard him correctly.

I wanted answers, but the idea of actually having that conversation was exhausting. I was an optimistic, things-will-work-out-if-you-plow-forward type of person. But I wasn't an idiot. The world was as full of liars and cheats as it was good, honest people. The trick was being able to distinguish between the two and choosing to fill your life with only the latter.

A memory from college returned. I'd had a circle of friends while I was there, no different than I had back home, but my best friend had always been Joanie. If given the choice between spending an evening meeting new people or heading home to play board games with my family, it had always been an easy choice for me—family every time. Some had called me introverted. Antisocial. Snobby. The labels didn't bother me. I found no joy in drinking and trying to impress strangers. People came and went. My sister? My family? They were forever.

Where did someone like Thane fit in? Had I given his biological match too much importance? As DNA matching became something people gave each other as gifts for the holidays, it was likely that I'd find more people who were somehow related to my family. Would they matter? I wasn't sure if they should.

My childhood hadn't been full of cousins and distant relatives, but it had been a happy one. My father's parents had retired to a warmer state. We rarely saw them, but they were nice enough people. We didn't often see my father's siblings, even though he spoke to them frequently. My mother had never been close to her parents. She'd distanced herself from them long before I was born.

Life wasn't perfect, but together we rose above the challenges of it. Sage would be okay without a father. I shouldn't have rushed to find him. I'd pull back and tell Sage about him when she was eighteen and better able to understand that not every father is a daddy.

A quick look at the time on my phone confirmed it was getting late. I leaned back into the couch, closed my eyes and thought, *Thane's not coming. I wasted all that energy worrying about a man who doesn't even keep promises.* Massaging my scalp through my hair in frustration, I thought, *I'm done. When he shows up, if he ever does, that's what I'll tell him.*

"Are you up for company?" Thane asked.

I groaned, dropped my hands to my sides and opened my eyes. Of course he couldn't have come earlier when I might have still looked human. Sitting up, I reminded myself that what he thought of my appearance was no longer important. "No, but come in."

He sat in the chair across from me. "Bandage free today. You look better every time I see you."

I hated how my body warmed beneath his gaze. Narrowing my eyes, I tried to focus on being angry with him. His compliment was likely meant to soften me to his lies. I kept my tone civil. "Thank you for the flowers. Sage loved the frog."

"I'm glad and you're welcome." He placed his hands on his knees for a moment, then sat back. "I'm not good at this."

"Lying?"

His eyebrows rose. "Is that what you think I'm here to do?"

"I have no idea why you're here." I folded my arms across my chest, doing my best to ignore how my breath caught in my throat when he loosened his tie absently. *No, no, no,* I told my body. *We are no longer lusting after him. Stop it.*

He rubbed his knuckles along his jaw. "That's understandable, I suppose."

My gut was twisting and churning. I wanted to shake him and demand he say whatever he'd come to. The anticipation was unbearable. Regardless of what he said, though, I was no longer sympathetic when it came to him needing more time. If he was man enough to donate his sperm to a clinic, he should be man enough to face the natural outcome of that act.

No more flirtations.

No more embarrassment.

I held his gaze and waited for him to choose a lane.

He sat forward. "If you came to me with what I'm about to tell you, I wouldn't have believed you. Not without proof. I'm still trying to wrap my own head around it."

I shook my head slowly. *He's going to double down on his lie.* My stress level lowered, replaced by a flood of sadness. *At least I have my answer.* I let my anger go right along with my feelings for him. "You don't have to say more, Thane. It's okay. You didn't seek me out. I cornered you at your business." Breathing in calm, exhaling negativity, I said, "You went above and beyond when you took on my care. You don't owe me anything."

His hands flexed on his muscular, unfairly tempting thighs. "Things are not okay. You shouldn't say they are when it's not how you feel."

I sat up straighter. "Don't tell me what I can or can't say. You're no one to me."

That snapped his head back. "I can see how this would be confusing."

"I'm not *confused*," I bit out. "I'm disappointed."

"Stop and listen to me."

I was trying to but I was so angry. "You say you're all about goals, Thane. What's your goal here? What do you want?"

We sat there, eyes locked on each other, neither giving an inch. He blinked first. "Zachary Danford exists. Well, Zachary does. Anyway, Scott and I spoke to the parents of the woman who'd taken Zachary in. Nothing we heard was what we'd hoped."

"Zachary, the man you claim is your twin."

"Yes, only his last name was legally changed every time his mother remarried which happened at least three times. If he hasn't changed it again, we're looking for a Zachary Brown now."

Could that be true? If it wasn't, his ability to lie convincingly was terrifying. I considered myself a good reader of most people. My gut told me he was telling the truth. "Why wasn't he raised with you?"

"My father didn't know about him. I'm adopted. We were never told about Zachary."

I ran my hands over my eyes. "Aren't your brothers, Jesse and Scott, also twins? I remember my parents saying something about that."

"They are. Until about a year ago, we didn't know Scott existed either."

"Because they'd also been separated before adoption?" That sounded too sinister to be true.

"Yes. Jesse came from the same agency. My father was told nothing about Scott."

"Why would anyone do that?"

"Their goal is still a matter of speculation at this point, but what they did is not. It appears that they deliberately placed twins in different socio-economic situations then collected data on the effects each placement had on the children."

"Like a scientific experiment?"

"Exactly like that."

"How do you know it wasn't a bizarre coincidence?"

"I met one of the researchers tasked with collecting data on me as a child. He quit when it became obvious to him that there was something unethical going on."

"A researcher? And he just admitted all that?" It sounded too detailed to be a lie and something that would be easy to disprove.

"By his own admission, he's not a particularly brave man."

I raised a hand in question. "So if I asked you to call your father, he'd back everything you just said?"

"He would."

"And your brothers? They'd tell me the same story?"

"Yes. Would you like me to get any or all of them on the phone right now?"

I rubbed at my temple as it began to pound. It wouldn't make sense for Thane to lie about something that would be so easy to disprove. Unless his whole family was in on the lie, but what would be the purpose of that? They certainly weren't after money. I hadn't been awake when Thane's family had visited, but my parents and sister had nothing but good to say about them. "If I believe that you have a twin and he's the one who is actually Sage's father . . ."

"That would make me—biologically, at least—Sage's

uncle."

I closed my eyes briefly. If that were true, did that make everything else he'd said to me true as well? I struggled to sort through our conversations and make sense of them in that light. When I couldn't, I stood. "I'm sorry. I need a minute."

After making my way into the bathroom, I splashed water on my face and steadied myself by gripping the edge of the vanity. Thane isn't Sage's father. What do I do with that?

Normally, I was good about riding out the unexpected, so why did I want to sink to the floor and cry? I met my eyes in the mirror and saw anger in them. Who was I upset with? Thane? Me? And why?

In the quiet of the bathroom, I admitted that I'd allowed myself to imagine a future where Thane and I meant something to each other. I'd let the comfort of his presence spawn an impossible fantasy where he and I plus Sage equaled a family as happy as what Joanie had with Mike. I tried to make myself feel better by acknowledging that my car accident had left me feeling vulnerable. It was true, but there was no denying part of me yearned for a loving partner. My parents had modeled what a healthy relationship looked like. I'd watched Mike transform from smitten to devoted and it had inspired me to hope that one day I might find the same.

I couldn't let yearning skew my ability to make sensible decisions. What was the saying . . . play stupid games, win stupid prizes? Deciding to plow ahead with finding Sage's father, regardless of his desire to be found or the legality of it, had not only put me in a painfully awkward position with Thane, but it had also nearly gotten me killed.

No different than when I'd almost drowned trying to return that duckling to its mother. When will I learn? This is no longer just about me. I have to do better for Sage.

And that meant healing so I could care for her rather than putting all of my energy into sorting a situation out that wouldn't be a problem if I hadn't made it into one. With resolve I pushed myself off the vanity, inhaled deeply, and returned to where Thane was waiting for me.

His expression was guarded. "Are you okay? Would you like me to call a nurse?"

Excellent, I look as bad as I feel. "No, I'm fine, but we do need to talk." He held my gaze while I chose my next words. I continued, "I believe you, but I am not currently in a place where I can handle this. Maybe my brain is still scrambled. Maybe I'm exhausted. All I know is that I wish I could go back in time and not have found you."

His eyes darkened and his jaw tightened.

"I'm not saying that to hurt you, it's just all so over-whelming . . ."

He raised a hand. "I understand."

My hand instinctively went to my temple. "I need time to process all of this."

"Of course."

"You should go."

He nodded.

His easy acceptance of my dismissal filled me with a confusing amount of anger. I wanted to take his bouquet of flowers and toss them at him. "And stop coming to see me."

"If that's what you want." I hated that he looked perfectly calm and composed while I felt like I was falling apart.

I waved a hand wildly through the air and stormed, "None of this is what I want." Not the hospital. Not my pounding headache. Not the fact that the best kiss I'd received in my lifetime had been delivered by a man who was likely relieved that he'd never have to see me again. "Just go."

He walked over to where there was a pad of paper and pen and bent to write something. When he straightened, he said, "This is my number. Text me and I'll come. Tomorrow. Next week. A year from now."

I didn't make a move toward it. We stood there for a few minutes locked in an awkward silence. I refused to say anything out of fear that speaking at all would lead me to asking him not to leave. I had no idea what held him there, but he seemed reluctant to go.

He stepped closer, touched my cheek gently and said, "It was thoughtless of me to lay all of this on you while you're still recovering. When you're feeling better, if you have questions or simply want to see me again, I'm only a text away."

I swayed when he withdrew his hand. As I gathered the

courage to admit I didn't want this to be the last time I saw him, he bent and gave me a tender kiss that knocked my ability to speak clear out of me. It took every bit of the strength in me to not throw my arms around his neck and melt against him.

My senses were in overload even after he raised his head. In a low tone, he growled, "No matter how this turns out, I don't want to turn back time and never have met you." Without saying more, he turned on his heel and left.

I stood there, his last words echoing my thoughts, wondering what I was supposed to do next.

CHAPTER FIFTEEN

Thane

HALFWAY TO MY house, I changed direction and drove to my father's. I didn't tell him I was coming. It was late enough that he should be home, but if he wasn't, the added drive would at least give me time to clear my head.

I hadn't meant to kiss Ashlee again, but when it came to her I wasn't in full control of my stupid self. Looking back at our interactions, there were so many of them I could have handled better.

Had I not dismissed her so completely that first night, there was a chance she might not have gotten into the accident she did. Yes, I'd made sure she was physically taken care of, but I should have waited until she was out of the hospital before I dropped the "I have a twin" bomb on her. It wasn't as if I hadn't heard her doctor say she might have difficulty concentrating while she healed. But no, instead of keeping that in mind, I'd let my emotions get the best of me. I'd allowed myself to feel cornered and become reactive.

I wasn't proud of that.

When things became uncomfortable or chaotic, I tended to distance myself from my emotions and act. It was what I'd been raised to do. Action was power. Facts mattered more than feelings. All of that might have been a recipe for success in business, but it wasn't working with Ashlee.

The truth had been too much for her to process.

Rather than take advantage of her while she was at her most vulnerable, I should have held myself in check and given her time. She was right to ask me to leave.

Ashlee was likely worried about her health, her daughter, the job she wasn't able to work . . . you know, little things like that.

My focus had been clarifying that I wasn't Sage's father while sorting through how attractive I found Ashlee.

I'm such an ass.

I announced my arrival at the security gate at the end of my father's driveway and was let in. Growing up, we'd been financially comfortable, but hadn't required the level of security our newfound visibility necessitated. The space station contract had added zeros to our net worth and changed our lives, but not all for the good.

I was met by my father's butler who said my father would meet me in his study shortly. Important conversations were best conducted in places conducive to civil discussion. I'd made many major decisions in my father's home office. It was where we met when I wanted to share a win or talk through a loss. There was a comfort to knowing that despite how much had changed, some things hadn't.

Dressed in a cotton robe over his pajamas, my father looked ready for a photo shoot for successful retirees. "Coffee?" he asked.

"No, but thank you."

"Bourbon?"

I weighed that one before refusing it as well. My goal was to clarify my thoughts, not cloud them. "Dad, have you ever been in love?"

He turned on the gas flames in the fireplace and motioned for me to choose one of the seats near it. "Sadly, I have not."

"But you were married," I said after I sat.

"I suppose, Thane, that explains why she didn't stay. I cared about her, and she cared about me, but that's not enough." He gave me a long look, then asked, "Are you falling for the Pryer woman?"

I shook my head. "I don't believe so. I was better off before I met her and she essentially told me she wished she hadn't found me."

"Ouch."

"I was completely focused on work and getting Bellerwood to move forward with the station. Jesse had stepped away, but I was picking up the slack."

"You were."

"I haven't had a relationship last more than a few months, but that's how I've always preferred it."

"I'm the same."

"When things end with a woman, I'm not bothered by who they're with next."

"That's sensible."

"And they don't affect how I feel about myself. When things are good, they're good. When they stop being good, we end it. No regrets."

"You do have a reputation for being good to people."

"So why do I feel worse about myself every time I'm with Ashlee?"

My father sat forward and his eyes narrowed. "You tell me."

I rehashed the epiphanies I'd had when I'd left her earlier. "She told me to stop going to visit her. And what did I do? Respect that? No, I kissed her again, because my brain stops working when I'm around her."

My father looked away then back. "Was she upset when you kissed her?"

"No," I said with a frown. "I don't think so. That's not the point. She's in a hospital room telling me to leave and not return. No woman has ever told me that before."

I didn't like the way my father looked like he was holding back a smile. "She dented your pride a little. Sounds like it was needed."

Was that what had me all jumbled up on the inside? "If this was about my pride, would it feel this confusing?"

With a grimace, my father said, "I'm not good at wading

through the minds of others."

His honesty was something I'd always respected about him. "We have that in common."

"I've never cared much about what others thought of me."

"Exactly."

"Except you and Jesse. Your happiness has always been important."

"Same."

"It was difficult at first for me to expand that circle of caring to Scott and his family."

All I could do was nod along. It had been the same for me.

My father continued, "Then Jesse added Crystal and Scott married Monica. My concept of what family was and what my role was had to evolve."

"Yes. Mine as well."

"At first I wasted time asking myself if it was all for the best, but life doesn't stop changing because a person isn't ready for it to. Not mine. Not yours."

"I don't hate that I'll soon be an uncle." I flexed a hand on my thigh. "Or that I'm already one."

"Good. I'm warming up to the idea of having children running around the house again. From what I hear Sage is adorable."

"Sage?" I took a deep breath. "Dad, you did hear the part where Ashlee asked me to stay away from her, right?"

"I did," he said with a twinkle in his eye. "Right before you kissed her."

"It didn't change her mind and it wasn't meant to."

"I see. So when you left her you told her to not bother to contact you again."

I held his gaze instead of responding.

He cackled. "If I know my son, and I do, you gave her your information and told her to call when she wants to see you."

That was exactly what I'd done. "Her daughter is my niece. I needed to leave the door open between us."

"Um-hmm."

"We were there the night Ashlee was hurt. It makes sense that I'd feel invested in her rehabilitation. I'd feel the same about anyone I'd met under those circumstances."

He glanced down at his bathrobe. "I'm inappropriately dressed to be wading through this much bullshit."

That brought a slight smile to my face. "If I was looking for someone to agree with me, I see I chose poorly."

"That you did." He paused for a moment, then added, "I've never cared about a woman enough to talk to my father about her."

I surmised that from his earlier confirmation that he'd never been in love. I wasn't certain why he'd felt the need to circle back to that. "And?"

"But," he corrected, "you're here. Think on that for a moment before you tell me you're not interested in having more with Ashlee."

"I've already put my interests ahead of hers on too many occasions."

"You and I have spoken about the danger of judging past events through the lens of hindsight. You had no reason to trust her when she showed up at your workplace. No one could have predicted that someone would run a light and collide with her car. So, wipe both of those off your list of what you could have done better. Now, as far as waiting until she felt better before locking lips with her or divulging who Zachary is . . . you probably should have waited, but you didn't. So, the question isn't what you should have done differently. That's already sealed and done. I want to know what you intend to do from this moment forward, because that's what matters."

I trusted my father's advice because it always came from a place of wanting me to succeed. "I believe I've located my twin. A few years ago Zachary Brown bought fifty-four acres in Maine."

"Oh, Lord, another Scott?"

"Not as far as I can tell. The details around how he ended up on a farm in Connecticut are murky. I spoke with the parents of the woman who raised him. There was something not right about their daughter. She moved around a lot, married and divorced several men. Her parents called her paranoid, unstable, and borderline something that was never officially diagnosed."

My father's expression darkened with concern. "Why wasn't he removed from her care?"

"Scott did a phenomenal job of getting them to open up about that. Their daughter had violent tendencies and the ability to spin the truth. Bottom line, they were afraid of her and more grateful that she moved away than concerned for a child they had no blood relation to."

Hands fisting, my father growled. "What disgusting excuses for human beings those parents are."

"An apt description of them. They're older now, alone, and unable to afford to hold on to their land much longer. I feel no sympathy for them."

"Nor do I. Your twin certainly did not have the idyllic childhood Scott did."

"Not at all. Zachary's last name was changed each time the woman who called herself his mother remarried. From what I've been able to uncover, he changed schools ten times. Never graduated from high school. Had more than one run-in with the police, mostly disorderly conduct and fighting. His 'mother' went missing a few years ago. He was investigated for playing a role in her disappearance, but no body was found and there wasn't enough evidence to convict him. Somewhere around that time he sold his sperm to the clinic. I don't know how he parlayed that into a large land purchase, but there's nothing anywhere about him online after he moved to Maine."

"Did his mother ever resurface?"

"No."

"Doesn't sound like someone you should introduce Ashlee and Sage to."

"Exactly." I let out a breath. "This would have all gone easier had I simply allowed her to continue to believe I was Sage's father."

"You did the right thing. The truth matters, Thane."

"That's what I keep telling myself, but Ashlee is not in a space where hearing any of this would do more than hurt her. She needs to heal and put some distance between all of this and her child."

"And you as well?"

"If it's for the best for them—yes."

"And I was starting to imagine myself as a granddad of two this holiday season."

I sighed in frustration. "She's not mine, Dad. Neither of them are."

He smiled. "Yet."

It was the way he'd always challenged Jesse and me when we encountered something that felt impossible. He'd never allowed us to say that we couldn't do something. We were, however, instructed to rephrase it as, "I'm not capable of that *yet*."

"I'm good, Dad, but I can't change a person's biology."

My father shrugged. "First, you and I both know that family isn't determined by blood."

We were proof of that.

He continued, "Second, you and this twin of yours came from one cell. It's my understanding that your DNA and his are identical."

"I believe so."

"Because for a short period of time, you and Zachary were one person."

It was a stretch. "I suppose so."

"So, when you look at the child and see yourself in her . . . that's not your imagination . . . biological father . . . biological uncle . . . these are just labels you shouldn't allow to define your relationship with her."

"You're right."

"Often, but it never hurts to hear one of my sons tell me so." After a moment, he asked, "What does your heart tell you to do about Ashlee?"

"My heart?"

"You know, that thing below your brain but above your dick."

I barked out a laugh at that. "Oh, that thing."

"Yes, that thing." He was smiling along with me.

I gave his question a moment to sink in before answering, "Ashlee needs time to heal. Everything else can wait until she's ready for it."

"I'm proud of you, Thane. You've grown into a good man."

"I had the best role model." Unlike my twin. My stomach churned at the stark difference in how we'd been raised.

"I'll make arrangements for Jesse to cover for me, then I'll take a few days off. I need to meet this twin of mine."

"And help him if he's in trouble."

It wasn't a question. I'd already made up my mind to and my father knew it. "Yes."

"He may resent you and all you have."

"He may."

"That won't be easy on you."

"I'll be fine."

"Or him."

"I'll try to make this as painless for both of us as I can."

"You can handle this, but my door is always open if you need to talk when you get back."

I rose to my feet. "I know and thanks, Dad."

CHAPTER SIXTEEN

Ashlee

THE NEXT MORNING, I was cleared to go home. Joanie picked me up at the hospital while Sage was in school because no one thought it was a good idea to tell Sage I was going home until the doctors actually let me leave. Last minute changes in release plans were not unheard of.

As we made our way through the busy morning traffic of Boston, I did my best to focus on how good it would feel to make Sage dinner that night and read her a story in her own bed, before falling asleep in mine. I didn't realize I was clutching the seat belt strap until Joanie asked, "Are you having flashbacks?"

"What?" I released the seat belt. "No. Not really. I still don't remember the accident but my body must because it's pumping adrenaline through me."

"That'll pass," she said with a sympathetic glance my way. "At least you don't have to work for a couple weeks."

"I refuse to sit around and do nothing."

"Talk to Dad; he spoke with your doctor and you're

supposed to take it easy." As she merged onto the highway, she asked, "Would you like the good news or bad news first?"

"Always start with the bad news."

"Right. Dad told me they had to fill your tutoring position at the after-school center. They said they should have room for you again in the summer."

"Great. Well, there goes my vacation money." A car sped by my window and I had to close my eyes briefly to re-summon calm. "And the good news?"

"You'll have more time to get to know Thane?" Her smile was so bright and I ached from the memory of when I'd felt more was possible between Thane and me. "We haven't had a chance to talk without an audience. Mike wanted me to tell you that, although we keep joking about you watching the boys, if it helps you land a rich husband, we'll watch Sage a few nights."

I smiled at that. "Tell Mike that's a kind offer, but it won't be necessary."

"What happened?"

I massaged my temples even though I didn't currently have a headache. "It's a long story."

"No better time to tell me. At home, I can't even go to the bathroom without being interrupted. I love Mike and the kids, but I swear they couldn't find their socks if they were on their own feet."

"That bad?"

She chuckled. "People say these are the years I'll miss. Will I? I remember being able to read whole books in one sitting and ending the day with a glass of wine. I'm thinking I'll also enjoy when the kids are old enough for that to be possible again."

"I understand, but I also have to say it got a little lonely without Sage around asking me to color with her or snuggle and watch her favorite show for the hundredth time."

Joanie nodded. "So, back to Thane."

I looked out the passenger window for a moment before answering. "You were right. I never should have tried to find Sage's father. I get these ideas in my head about how things should be and then no amount of good advice can sway me. I stupidly believe I know better than everyone around me. I'm sorry about how much my latest bad idea affected everyone else's lives as well."

"I'm not sure I like you this humble," Joanie said and I turned back to face her. "Before you continue on this apology tour, I want you to ask yourself something. Would I have offered to carry a child for someone I didn't think would be the most amazing mother?"

"No, you wouldn't," I answered in a thick voice.

"You inspire me, Ashlee. Even when we were little, you couldn't sit back and not help if I had a problem. If we were at war, you'd be fighting in the front line. In a fire, you're the crazy person who runs back in to save others. I've never seen you be anything but kind to people and you tend to put their welfare before your own. So, before you tell me what happened between you and Thane, know that I'm already prepared to kick his ass for it. I'm team Ashlee, and I always will be."

Tears welled in my eyes. "You know I feel the same about you. I love Mike, but I'd help you bury him if he ever hurt you."

That got a laugh from Joanie. "I need to tell him you said that. It'll break his little heart, and have him sleeping with one eye open, but it's too good not to share."

I chuckled and wiped at my eyes. "Mike knows and he loves me anyway. I may have said exactly those words to him at your wedding."

Her smile fading somewhat, Joanie said, "What happened with Thane, Ashlee?"

"In my head or in reality?"

"I have a pretty good idea what was going on in your head and we were probably all on the same page. I expected him to be the one driving you home today."

"I expected the same." And that's what hurt.

"So, where is he? Did you tell him you were going home this morning?"

"I haven't spoken to him since last night."

"Well, hon, if you didn't tell him, how was he supposed to know to be here?"

I rested my head against the car seat. "Things got weird between us. He started telling me all these things ... I believe him, I think. I don't know."

"What did he say?"

"You met his father. Did he seem . . . normal?"

"Yes, but now you're starting to freak me out." Joanie's eyes widened. "What did Thane say?"

"At first he was adamant that he's not Sage's biological father. I thought he was saying that because he needed time to get used to the idea."

"But?"

"Then he told me he was adopted and his brother was adopted from the same agency. They both have twins they didn't know they had. So, Sage's father is actually some man named Zachary who Thane is tracking down. Something about an experiment with researchers. My head still hurts every time I try to make sense of it."

After a moment, Joanie said, "Mom and Dad met Thane's twin brothers. They said they were different, but both very nice. Mom did mention something about them being raised apart, but she didn't have a ton of details on it and I didn't ask."

"When Thane first told me he had a twin, I didn't believe him. I thought he was a liar. Last night, he came by and tried to explain it to me better and I told him to leave. I said it was too much for me to handle and that he should stop coming to see me."

Joanie sighed. "In your defense—*what the fuck?* You're in the hospital with a brain injury. Did he miss that part?"

I raised a hand to my bandage-free temple. "My brain was jostled, not put through a blender. I get headaches, but I'm not impaired."

"Your doctor told us that your concentration would be temporarily affected. It's normal. If you'd hit your knee, it would be sore for a while and you'd want to let it rest while it heals. Your brain is the same."

"How does someone rest their brain?"

"By not working and not trying to unravel what sounds like the plot of a psycho thriller. I'm glad you told him to back off. Telling you all that right after your accident? When your brain still isn't right? What was he thinking?"

"Are you trying to make me feel better or worse? They wouldn't have released me if my brain wasn't right."

"You know what I mean. It's stress you didn't need."

I nodded. That much was true. "Sorry. I didn't realize I could be 'brain-defensive.'"

"No, I'm sorry. I wasn't thinking about how what I said might come across. All I meant was that—of course that was too much for you. Want to start over and tell me everything you can remember him saying and I'll help you sort it through?"

"I'd like that."

I spent the next several minutes trying to remember the precise wording he'd used as I walked Joanie through both conversations. Because Joanie was not only my sister, but also my best friend, I also told her about the kiss and how he'd said he wasn't sorry we'd met.

When I finished, she said, "Either that man is completely psychotic or you walked into his life and turned the whole thing upside down."

"He's not psychotic." I sighed. "At least, I don't think so. Jesse and Scott are real and twins. The news is full of crazy, evil people doing crazy, evil things. Separating twins as some part of an experiment? It's not beyond my ability to believe, but it changes things."

Joanie nodded in agreement. "Because of Sage."

"Yes. I can't expose her to something this confusing, not while she's so young."

"Or endanger her by involving her." Joanie shrugged. "We don't know how dangerous the people are who orchestrated all those placements."

Joanie's words sent a chill down my back. "I hadn't thought of that, but you're right."

"So, what are you going to do?"

"I don't know," I said slowly. "I told him I needed time to process this. I suppose I should do that."

"That sounds like the safest plan."

"I'm a mother. Safety needs to be my priority."

"Yes," she said without as much conviction as I expected. "But tell me more about that parting kiss . . ."

I blushed. "It was . . . incredible."

"Then give yourself the time you need." She glanced my way, smiled, then returned her attention to the road. "Just, you know, not so much time that he meets another woman loony enough to chase him around a parking lot."

I laughed into my hand. "And here I am trying to determine if *he's* normal."

"Normal or not, you caught his attention. What happens now? Who knows? You'll either figure this out"—my sister reached out and took one of my hands in hers, giving it a supportive squeeze—"or you won't."

We exchanged a smile and I said, "Wow, that's deep."

She nodded. "It sounded more inspirational in my head. Hey, I haven't had a good night's sleep in a week. Pretend I came up with something amazing and wise."

I gave her hand a squeeze in return before releasing it. "I will. Hey, thank you for coming to get me today."

"Always," she said easily.

And just like that, the panic inside me lessened. I might have messed things up with Thane, lost my part-time job, and wrecked my car . . . but I still had everything that mattered.

We were almost back at my house before I asked, "Do you think I should text Thane to tell him I don't hate him?"

"I think you should do whatever your heart tells you to."

"Even though there might be a dangerous element to getting involved?"

"Ashlee, I say this as someone who couldn't love you more, but you have never let that stop you and somehow it always works out."

I looked at the passing cars. "Even this time?"

"Have you forgotten that I broke my arm a few years ago trying to put a blanket on the top shelf in my closet? You can stay home, play things safe, and still get hurt. No one will let anything happen to you or Sage. Besides, if that adoption agency is still around, I want to be part of taking it down."

"You do?" It was a bold statement from a sister who normally played it safe.

We stopped for a red light and she turned to meet my gaze. "Someone exploited innocent children. Hell, yes, I want to make sure they're never able to do it again."

It could have been that my brain really wasn't quite right yet, but I agreed without hesitation. "Me too." Sage's safety was a concern, but the only way she'd grow up to be a strong, loving woman was if we modeled what that looked like for her. "So, I should text Thane?"

Joanie laughed softly. "Yes, but tell him you need a week or so to rest your head."

"I'm fine." When she didn't agree, I said, "You're a jerk."

"Hey, if a sister can't tell you when you're not yourself, who can? You still look a little shell-shocked. When you meet me at the door looking ready for a fight—that's when you can see him again."

I didn't understand what she was seeing in me that was different until I sat on the arm of my couch and felt tired from the ride home. I was relieved when she told me to take a nap and that she'd drop Sage off when she got out of preschool. I would have told her that neither was necessary, but humbling as it was—I did need the help. "Hey, Joanie."

"Yes?" she asked as she prepared to leave.

"I know those are my jeans you're wearing. My brain isn't that scrambled."

She was laughing as she closed the door behind her and I smiled because a pair of jeans was a small price to pay to have a saint for a sister.

CHAPTER SEVENTEEN

Thane

A WEEK LATER I was swimming laps in the private pool I'd had installed in my apartment building. It was one of the few luxuries I allowed myself.

Okay, I also had a private chef.

A butler.

Someone who maintained my cars for me.

Cleaning staff.

And someone who did my shopping.

All of that was common for a man who worked as much as I did. In theory, I had no issue with doing any of that myself, but it wasn't where my time was best spent. Cleaning my own kitchen didn't move my family's company forward or secure our place in the market.

Success required one hundred and fifty percent dedication. I couldn't remember the last time I'd taken a vacation, indulged in a hobby, or slept in. Anyone who believed that luck had played a role in Bellerwood choosing my family's company to design the life support system for his space station, didn't understand how much time, sweat, and sacrifice "luck" required.

Scott had asked if I had friends who weren't work associates. I didn't, nor did I see them as necessary. When I wanted companionship, I found a woman willing to spend some no-strings-attached time with me. When I needed to talk out a problem, I had my father, my brothers, and if it was work related, a team of loyal, long-time employees.

I pushed off the pool wall with the precision taught to me by the Olympic gold medalist my father had paid to teach Jesse and me to swim. Although my father had seen no real benefit to being on a swim team, he laid a foundation for us to excel at whatever interests we had.

We were Rehoboths and to my father that meant nothing we did could be mediocre. Some might have called his unwavering high standards unfair, but I'd always considered them a gift he'd given us. He believed in us and wanted us to have that same faith in ourselves. Confidence was a difficult skill to hone from the comfort of one's couch, so my father put us out there in the thick of battles and made sure we understood that everything worthwhile required some amount of struggle.

Live purposefully, my father often instructed, and that was what I strove to do daily—in business as well as my personal life.

Lifting weights added bulk and strength to my frame. Years of Krav Maga training gave me physical power, speed, and focus. Swimming quieted the noise of my thoughts and allowed me to problem solve with greater clarity.

As I swam, I replayed the conversations I'd had with Jesse over the past week. I'd gone to his home, had dinner with him and Crystal, and updated them on what Scott and I had uncovered about Zachary. As expected, he'd had questions. So, so, many questions.

The hardest to answer had been why I'd gone with Scott and not him. There's often a fine line between being honest and being cruel. I was blunt by nature, but that didn't mean I didn't care about Jesse's feelings. So, instead of sharing the whole truth, I said, "Owning one cow and donkey doesn't make you a farmer. I needed someone who knew how to talk in a way that put these people at ease."

Jesse had nodded. "Scott is definitely skilled at talking."

Crystal had playfully smacked Jesse's arm. "And getting people to like him. Scott's all heart."

Arching an eyebrow, Jesse challenged his wife. "And what am I?"

She beamed a smile at him. "A good, but slightly arrogant man I am happily going to spend the rest of my life with."

He bent and kissed her smiling lips. "I accept that."

I didn't ask for an appraisal of myself from either of them because I already knew how they saw me. Crystal had diagnosed me early on as having the classic oldest-child syndrome and she wasn't wrong. I did tend to follow the rules, prefer things to be done correctly, and shoulder the responsibility of fixing whatever mess Jesse made. Jesse saw me as less daring than he was. One of us had to be or our company wouldn't have weathered the times his ideas hadn't panned out. He chased new talent and contracts; I made sure we fulfilled our obligations and maintained a reputation for high quality, innovative services. Neither of us would be where we were had we not honored our differences.

In an odd role reversal, it was Jesse who called for caution when I asked him to cover for me at the office so I could go to Maine. "And do what?" Jesse had asked. "Walk right up to him, introduce yourself, and tell him that you're falling for the woman who used his sperm to make a baby?"

My temper had flared. "Keep Ashlee out of this."

Crystal had excused herself, claiming she needed to check on something in the kitchen. They had staff and their own chef, but I let her remove herself from a conversation I wished I could have removed myself from.

"I would if she wasn't affecting your judgement," Jesse said in a harsh tone, then sighed. "I'm sorry, but you need a reality slap. I appreciate how welcoming you've been to Scott. Hell, half the time you're still nicer to him than I am, but your twin situation is very different than mine was."

"Because mine wasn't fortunate enough to be raised by perfect parents?"

"Listen to yourself, Thane. Feeling protective of someone you know very little about is how you invite trouble."

"And how do you suggest I get to know him without contacting him? He's living off grid in Maine." I took a deep breath. "He's my twin, Jesse. You of all people should understand why I need to meet him."

"And you should, but not right now. Thane, I'm about to become a father. Our contract with Bellerwood is held together by a thread and a threat. A few months from now, when the dust from both settles, you can take all the time you want. Right now . . ." Jesse looked away then back. "I need you."

That had me standing straighter. "What are you not telling me?"

Jesse ran a hand through his hair. "Crystal is having a tough final trimester. She was told to stay calm and take things easy. Preeclampsia can go bad quickly. We may be checking in to a medical center as a precaution."

"I had no idea."

"She was on bedrest because they thought this was where things might be headed. We had a scare the other night and it really shook me up. With everything we have and all we've done, you'd think we'd have more influence over the things that matter the most—but we don't. When Crystal started seeing spots in her vision and we thought we might lose the baby, there was nothing I could do but hold her and wait."

I stepped closer and laid a hand of support on his shoulder. "What do you need?"

My normally bold and brash brother blinked a few times

before answering. "Right now, I don't care about anything beyond Crystal and our baby, but I know I have to. I realize I'm being selfish, but you didn't know about your twin until recently. He's not in any danger. I'm asking you to not move forward with contacting him until I'm holding my son in my arms and this damn contract is behind us. Three months? Six, tops, you'll be free to do whatever you want. By then it won't matter if that situation blows up and makes the news. But right now . . ."

"Of course," I said without hesitation. "Whatever you need, Jesse. You know that."

"Thank you." He slapped his hand over mine then stepped back. "If your twin didn't sound so—if he was more like Scott—"

"I agree." Zachary had been a person of interest in more than one criminal investigation—one for a missing person and one for wrongful death. Both times he hadn't been convicted, but that didn't mean he was innocent. Scott, on the other hand, ran a rescue for unwanted farm animals. The difference between them was glaringly obvious.

Jesse was correct, also, that as far as I knew, Zachary wasn't in any danger. I wouldn't have circled back to finding him had Ashlee not sought me out. We'd gone our whole lives without knowing each other, we could wait a few more months.

Jesse called me out of the blue the next day and surprised me again by saying, "Crystal and I talked after you left. I've always steered clear of your personal life, but she wanted me to tell you something and I am not about to refuse her anything right now."

"Oh-kay."

Jesse cleared his throat. "She wants you to know that Ashlee didn't find the wrong twin. She thinks you should call Ashlee and explain everything to her again. If it's still too much for Ashlee, Crystal offered to call her . . . Monica as well. They seem to think you should fight harder for this one because she sounds like she was meant for you."

"Wow."

"I know. It's a lot, but now I can at least tell her I passed the message along to you."

"I can call Crystal myself if you don't think that would add stress."

"She'd love that. So far she's not proving to be very good at taking things easily and resting. She asks about updates on you and Ashlee like someone addicted to a soap opera. Anything new I should tell her?"

"No. Ashlee asked me for time and I'm giving that to her."

After a moment, Jesse said, "Before Crystal got pregnant, I probably would have told you to man up and go after her, but you're putting what she needs above what you want—and that tells me Crystal is right. You don't owe anything to this twin of yours nor does Ashlee. Take your time with her, Thane. Do this right."

"I'm trying to." The emotion tightening my throat made it difficult to get the words out. "Tell Crystal her message hit me hard. I originally thought Ashlee should meet Zachary before she and I could move forward, but I'm beginning to rethink that. He sounds troubled. What if instead of introducing Ashlee and Sage to Zachary, I'm meant to protect them from him?"

That question was still circling in my thoughts when I pulled myself out of the pool and toweled dry. It had been a long week, one made even longer by the fact that Ashlee was on my mind each night as I went to sleep and impossible to drive out of my thoughts each morning as I woke.

All week, Ashlee had had me obsessively checking my phone messages. I couldn't remember the last time I'd wanted anything as much as I wanted to hear her voice again.

Waiting was a sweet torture.

Distracting.

Consuming.

Exciting as hell.

But I did it, because she was worth it.

CHAPTER EIGHTEEN

Ashlee

TWO WEEKS HAD passed since I'd left the hospital. Fourteen days and fifteen hours since I'd spoken to Thane, but who was counting? Just me.

After putting Sage to bed, I texted Joanie. **Kids asleep?**

She called me almost immediately. "Thank the Lord, yes. What's up?"

"I'm going to do it. Right now."

Her voice rose an octave. "Call Thane?"

"I thought I should start with a text . . . you know, test the waters with a toe."

"Okay, that makes sense."

"But what should I write? Hey, the doctors cleared me for work so . . ."

"You could just say hello. See what he responds."

"Just hello?"

"It's probably better than leading with a brain update."

I laughed. "You're right. Okay. I'm going to do it. Do you want to stay on the line?"

"Sure."

I'm a grown woman—a mother—how can I be so nervous to send a simple text? I took a deep breath and typed: **High** and nervously hit send when I meant to correct what my phone had auto added. "No!"

"What?"

"I just spelled hi wrong."

"How do you do that? It's two letters."

"I don't know. I was going to write hello, then decided to write hi instead but my fingers must have skimmed over the extra letters. After two weeks of not hearing from me, he's going to wonder why I've decided to announce I'm on drugs."

"You can always play the brain damage card."

I rolled my eyes and groaned. "How would that be better? I know people joke that men like dumb women, but somehow I doubt Thane is one of those men."

I checked my phone. He had answered me.

Low

When I read his message to Joanie, she laughed and said, "Quick, write 'Up.'"

I did.

He answered, **Down**

I impulsively wrote: **Too late**

Just in time

"He's either flirting with me or I've accidentally opened the thesaurus feature on my phone."

Joanie said, "Be blunt. Be bold. Tell him you've been thinking about him."

"Just like that. Just throw it out there."

"Yes."

"Should I apologize? He paid my medical bills and the last time we spoke I told him to stay away from me."

"He's had two weeks to get over what you said. You can apologize over a glass of wine."

"I don't drink."

"You know what I mean. Just act cool. This is not a big deal. Grow some girl balls."

How could I not laugh at that? I flexed my fingers and typed: **For dinner?**

When he didn't answer immediately, I added: **You and me**

I read my texts to Joanie then said, "He's going to think I have lingering damage."

"Wait. Give the man a moment to answer. For all you know he's running around the room high-fiving the air. Don't assume the worst."

"Okay. He's typing. He's still typing. Oh, my God, what could he be saying that requires this long to write? He's explaining that he's with someone else. Or just no longer interested—"

"Did he actually write any of that?"

"No, so far, it's just three dots. Three horribly vague, taunting my soul, dots." Seconds stretched to what felt like an eternity.

Free tomorrow?

I read his text aloud.

Joanie said, "I'll talk to Mike, but we can watch Sage. If he has something going on, Mom and Dad could as well. Say yes."

Yes "Done."

Let's get together early.

Okay. I would have agreed to any time. I couldn't believe he'd said yes.

Casual? Expensive? Or a surprise?

My breath caught in my throat. "Joanie, he wants to know if I want casual, expensive or a surprise."

"I like his style," she said. "What do you want?"

"A surprise, I guess. I don't know. The men I've dated always asked me to come up with something to do."

"I love it when Mike plans a date for us. Sometimes it's so corny. I can't wait to see what Thane surprises you with."

A surprise, I wrote after hesitating. When it came to doing things for others, I had no problem charging ahead without a thought about myself. I wasn't sure where my nervousness was coming from. I added, **I'm not supposed to drink alcohol, have caffeine, ride a bike, or play a sport yet.**

As soon as I'd sent it, I groaned.

Okay.

"What's wrong?" Joanie asked. "What did he say?"

"Is this a mistake, Joanie? This isn't someone I met at a party and don't care if I ever see again. He's related to Sage.

Should that make him off-limits?"

After a pause, Joanie said, "If you're not sure, give yourself more time. You're still healing."

"This isn't about my head."

"What are you afraid of, Ashlee? Talk to me."

I opened myself to her question and the answer wasn't easy to admit. "I'm scared. When I'm with Thane I feel like we have such a strong connection—different and more intense than I've ever had with a man. What if he doesn't feel the same?"

"It'll suck. You and I will ditch the kids and go to the movies or shopping. Maybe take a yoga class together. And you'll go on. You're an amazing person. Thane may see that or he may not, but you'll never know if you don't give him a chance."

She was right.

Are you working yet? he asked.

No, I start Monday.

Sage?

She goes to daycare at 9.

I'll pick you up at 10.

I swallowed hard. **What should I wear?**

Something comfortable to walk in. See you at 10.

Thank you.

Thank you? Why had I said that? Wow, was I out of practice? I read our conversation to Joanie and she chuckled and asked in a singsong voice, "Guess who has a date with a hot guy tomorrow?"

I smiled. "I do."

"I'll get Sage from daycare. Don't feel that you have to rush back. I texted Dad and he said they'd love to have her at their place for dinner if your date goes long. Do you know what that means?"

"Dad likes him?"

"Bingo. So, don't overthink this, Ashlee. You haven't been on a date for ages. Let yourself enjoy it."

A memory of him returned. For just a moment I was back at his office building, looking into his eyes for the first time. A giddy excitement rose in me. "Joanie, I'm going out with Thane tomorrow."

She laughed. "Yes, you are. I just wish you were happier about it."

Feeling lighter than air, I joked, "What should I wear? I had the perfect pair of jeans, but I can't seem to find them. They would have gone so well with the blue sweater I also can't locate."

"You really should be more careful with your things." I could imagine the twinkle in her eyes as she added, "Or start buying clothing that don't look good on me."

"Seriously, what should I wear?"

"I was hoping you'd ask. After I drop off the kids at school, I can come over and we can do your hair, makeup, outfit selection. It'll be just like old times. What do you think?"

"No hairspray. You know I hate it."

"I know."

"Then yes. Let's do it."

"I'll bring some outfits with me. This is going to be so exciting."

Exciting. Yes. My life was full of warm, wonderful moments, but since having Sage I wouldn't have called it exciting. I took pride in my appearance, but I couldn't remember the last time I'd dressed to impress a man. Somewhere along the way I'd shelved my sexuality and thrown myself into the role of mother.

I'd forgotten what it was like to have my heart race at the thought of seeing someone. Joanie was right—there was no way to know if Thane felt the same—but even if he didn't, meeting him was awakening a side of me I was relieved was still there.

I should warn you, Mr. Rehoboth, it's been a long, long, oh, so long time since I've had sex. When we get to that stage, if we get there, I'm either going to pass out from excitement or tear your clothes off with my teeth.

Have I mentioned it's been a while?

CHAPTER NINETEEN

Ashlee

M Y APPEARANCE THE next morning could best be described as simple and casual, while in fact it had taken a great deal of effort and negotiation. Joanie was a genius at applying makeup so it enhanced while still looking natural. It was my clothing that we'd gone back and forth with.

All Thane had said was that I should wear something I was comfortable walking in. Walking where? Up a mountain? Down city streets?

I didn't want to wear jeans on our first date, but considering he'd made it sound like we'd be outdoors it wouldn't be shocking if he showed up in them. In the end I chose a short-sleeved blue A-line dress. It had a playful slit up the waist that would have been revealing but instead was lined with a lighter blue plaid material. Since I didn't know where this date would take us, I slid a pair of biker shorts on, low socks and blue tennis shoes.

Okay, so it wasn't high fashion, but when matched with

my hair in a loose braid and the irrepressible smile on my face I was pleased with the end result.

"Perfect," Joanie said when I spun before her. "You look confident and effortlessly sexy."

I looked down at my dress then met her gaze and smiled. "I'm feeling more like myself every day. Thanks for coming over to help me get ready. You wouldn't think a little head injury would shake my confidence, but it did."

She glanced at the clock on the wall then around the room. "Do you want me to leave before he arrives?"

"No," I said as I considered both scenarios. "You're a big part of my life and if he ends up being part of it too, he should get used to that."

She smiled then hugged me. "That's essentially what I told Mike on our first date. You had walked me to the door and grilled him about where we were going. Do you remember?"

"I do. Dad told me I made him proud that day."

"Oh, Dad cross-examined him before our second date and I believe Mom took him aside before our third. Looking back, I'm surprised we made it to a fourth."

"I'm not," I said with all the love I felt for her in my eyes. "He jokes that you're the best thing that ever happened to him, but I don't believe he's joking. I love when I catch him looking across the room at you and smiling. Dad looks at Mom the same way when she's telling a story to someone. Just so you know, you and Mom are why I'm still single. You both went out and found such good men. I won't settle for less."

She adjusted the material on the shoulder of my dress. "Just remember that good doesn't mean perfect. Mike and I disagree, we just keep our squabbles behind closed doors. And we both always apologize. We learned that during the first year of our marriage. When you love someone there shouldn't be a scoreboard. It doesn't matter who was more right or more wrong. What matters is that you're both keeping your vows faithfully and your actions loving. Does that mean he won't sometimes come home from work and leave a trail from the doorway to the shower? No. But it does mean that when I tell him how frustrating that is, he cares and tries to not do it the next time. When I use one of his tools and accidentally leave it out I respect how irritating that can be for him and let him rant a little. Because at the end of the day, he was exhausted when he shed his clothing across the living room and I was distracted and probably tired as well when I left his stuff out. Neither is perfect, but we talk it out, apologize and move on."

"I can't imagine Mike lecturing you about anything."

"That's because he respects me enough to do it when we're alone. I do the same. If you're in a marriage, you need to be a team—otherwise what are you doing together?"

"How did we go from you helping me to choose the right dress to marriage etiquette?"

Joanie stepped back, rested her hands on her hips and

said, "You brought up your standards and I wanted to make sure you had realistic ones. You and Thane seem to have a real connection. It's good to see you honoring your needs for once and not just Sage's. I love how you put her first, but motherhood shouldn't be all sacrifice. You deserve a little something for yourself."

To lighten the mood, I joked, "I wonder how Thane would feel about being called *a little something*?"

Joanie wrinkled her nose. "You might want to save that for the second date."

I was still laughing when my doorbell rang. "He's here."

"You've got this, sis."

Squaring my shoulders I walked past her, opened the door, and inhaled sharply when Thane filled the doorway. Several times over the last two weeks I'd wondered if I'd imagined how good simply standing near him felt.

I hadn't.

He had a quiet, but strong presence that set my heart racing. I felt vulnerable in a delicious way. And those eyes of his pulled at my heart. Was it because they looked so much like my daughter's? It felt like more than that. I said the first thing that came to mind. "A *suit*?"

He held my gaze. "Always."

My mind filled with X-rated visions of when that claim wouldn't be true. In the shower. In bed. With me in both of those places. "That's nice." *What is it about this man that has me sounding like a young girl speaking to her first crush?*

Joanie stepped forward. "Hi, Thane."

The smile he shot her was friendly. "Good to see you, Joanie."

"Same," she replied.

I used that exchange to recover my ability to speak coherently. "Joanie lives a block away. My parents are a two-minute walk as well. I love having them all so close."

"What a great way for Sage to grow up," he said without missing a beat, and my heart started thudding wildly in my chest again.

He gets it and doesn't look bothered by it.

"Well, I'm outta here. Have fun today," Joanie said.

Without looking away from Thane, I answered, "Thanks, Joanie."

"Nice to see you again," Thane murmured, his gaze locked with mine.

The silence that followed was broken by the sound of the side door of my house opening then closing. It was only then I realized I hadn't invited Thane in. He was still standing in the doorway. I opened my mouth to say something but the words were lost when one of his hands slid along my jaw then back to cup my head, holding me in place for a kiss that rocked through me.

It was no tentative kiss. There was no question in it. It was a declaration of intent, a claiming of territory. His lips moved across mine like they'd done so hundreds of times before and would hundreds of times more.

The world around us fell away. My hands came up to rest flat against his strong chest, sliding beneath his jacket as I savored the warmth of him. I had so many things I wanted to ask him, but none of that mattered more than the desire burning through me.

His tongue teased my bottom lip. I opened for him with an eagerness I couldn't suppress. Slowly he explored my mouth, dancing intimately with my tongue with a skill that had my lower region firing up.

When he finally raised his head, I would have been embarrassed had I not been too turned on to feel anything else. "I've thought of nothing but seeing you again for weeks," he growled.

In a fine display of my wit, I simply looked at him.

His grip on the back of my head gentled and he frowned. "Sorry, when I planned this date, I imagined giving you a gentle kiss at the end."

Breathlessly, I answered, "Planned kisses are overrated."

We exchanged a smile. "Good, because I lose my head when I'm around you."

"Had to lead with a head joke?" I teased and loved how his eyes lit with humor.

His other hand went gently to the side of my head that had been injured. "How are you feeling?"

"One hundred percent better. The doctors still want me to be careful for a while, but I don't have any pain or symptoms anymore." I felt something needed to be said out of the gate. "My concentration is back to normal. It wasn't at the hospital. I'm sorry I shut you down each time you tried to explain. I couldn't—"

"No, I'm sorry I didn't wait for you to feel better before laying all of that at your feet. Of course it was too much."

I told myself to not read into the fact that we'd just apologized to each other in the same manner that Joanie had described she and Mike would. There was still so much Thane and I didn't know about each other. First dates were supposed to be fun and carefree. "Where are we going today?"

His smile returned. "What kind of surprise would it be if I told you?"

I glanced down at my feet. "I wore tennis shoes because you said we'd be walking but am I underdressed?"

A heat flashed in his eyes and his grin was pure male amusement. "Never."

I shook my head. "That's not what I meant."

"Me neither. Where did your mind just go?" He bent and murmured into my ear, "Don't be afraid to tell me."

I would have, but my focus returned to how every inch of my body was coming alive for him. I clung to his shoulders to steady myself. Over the years friends had shared stories with me on how chance meetings with a man could lead to casual sex. One had even told me she'd "accidentally" slept with a man on a first date because he'd been so much fun she hadn't wanted their date to end. Later, she'd been devastated when he'd ghosted her.

I didn't believe in judging people for living a lifestyle I wasn't interested in, but at the same time I hadn't been able to imagine myself being so overcome by the moment that I'd be so impulsive.

When Thane raised his head and our eyes locked again, I understood exactly what my friend had given herself over to that night. I wasn't a virgin. Desire was something I'd experienced, but this was a whole different level.

You make me laugh and I enjoy when you touch me is entirely different than *Oh, God, don't stop touching me because I may die if you do.* How would sex with someone like Thane be? Something told me rather than feeling relaxed afterward, sex with Thane would leave me shattered but in the most incredible way.

If Thane had stepped inside my house and closed the door behind him, I had no doubt that our clothing would have started flying off. I tried to come up with a reason why that wouldn't be a good thing and couldn't.

"You ready?" he asked.

I nodded, afraid if I spoke it would only be to whisper yes over and over again.

He offered me his hand. "Do you need anything? A purse? Your phone?"

I blinked a few times and stepped back, needing to put physical distance between us. "Yes. Both. I'll be right back."

As I hunted down my phone, I took several deep breaths.

Holy shit. I need to get myself under control before he thinks I am actually impaired.

When I returned with my things, Thane was standing in my living room looking at the photos on my fireplace mantel. All of the photos were candid shots: Sage fishing with my father. Me teaching Sage to fly a kite. Sage in a pile of leaves with her three cousins. Mike showing Sage how to lose at chess. Joanie and me at the hospital holding Sage the day she was born. All of us, our parents included, in matching ugly sweaters in front of a Christmas tree—laughing because we thought we were hilarious. "Sage is one lucky little girl," he said in a thick voice.

I stood there awkwardly hugging my purse. "I like to think so."

"It's obvious how much you love her." He looked around the room before meeting my gaze again. "That's one of the many things I find beautiful about you."

I swallowed hard. "Some men find it a turn off. One even told me he could never care about someone else's child."

"Thankfully, my father never felt that way."

I winced and kicked myself for my lack of sensitivity. "I'm sorry. Sometimes I speak before I think."

His expression remained warm. "I find it refreshing and there's no need to be sorry. Some people are sensitive about being adopted. I'm not. My father is an amazing man who never made Jesse and me feel like anything but his. Blood ties matter, but to me loyalty and dedication matter more."

"I understand. Joanie's husband isn't blood, but Mike's a brother to me now. He won my heart by being so good to my sister."

Thane didn't instantly respond to that, and I made the mistake of meeting his gaze again. The air sizzled with an attraction that appeared to be, thankfully, mutual. My breathing slowed, time stalled, and I was certain he would kiss me again.

"I have a car waiting," he said.

"Oh," I said in a rush. "Of course. Do they charge for the time while they wait?"

He tipped his head to one side. "Who?"

"The rideshare you use."

A smile curled his lips and he shook his head. "No."

"That's a relief." We stepped out of my home; I closed and locked the door behind me. "This is really fun, thank you, Thane."

He bent closer. "Shouldn't you hold off on the gratitude until you see where I take you?"

I shot him a huge smile that reflected the giddiness bubbling up in me. "I know I'll love it. I've never had anyone plan a surprise date for me. The details of it don't matter as much as the time you put into planning it. Where you go is never as important as who you go there with."

He gave me a long look. "You mean that."

I shrugged. "Who have you been with that you sound so

surprised that I might?"

"All the wrong women, apparently." Placing his hand on my back, he began to usher me down my driveway.

"Apparently," I repeated cheekily.

He let out that sexy laugh of his that sent a shiver of delight down my spine. I loved the feel of his hand on my back, the way he took control without being overbearing. He carried himself with a confidence few men had and it looked effortless on him.

It wasn't until we were near the end of my driveway that I saw a stretch . . . van? "Is that—did you—are we riding in that?"

He chuckled then introduced me to the driver who was standing beside the vehicle. I'd ridden in a limo twice before—both times when I'd been a bridesmaid in a wedding. I'd never been in one like this.

When the door slid open my jaw dropped. The interior was white with black accents and a huge sunroof. Each window was covered with white curtains. There were two captain's chairs facing forward on the back wall across from a huge television. It looked like something out of a private plane ad—so impressive I had to lean back and take in the simplicity of the black exterior again. It was a vehicle that had been designed to not attract attention.

With his hand still placed on my lower back, Thane bent near my ear and said, "In order to see what I have planned for you, we need to leave your driveway."

"Of course," I said and climbed into the van as gracefully as I could. I sat immediately, stuffed my purse in a pocket on the side of my chair, and smoothed my skirt down over my legs.

Thane was in the chair beside me, seat-belting himself in. I did the same, then looked around as the door closed. Although it was designed to blend in, I was certain there was more technology in the van than in my entire house. Everywhere I looked there was a knob, button, or remote. "What does this do?" I held up a remote. There were chair and table icons on it.

"Try it."

I pressed the chair button. The television folded up into the ceiling and out of the wall behind it came a leather captain's chair like the ones we were seated on. "No fucking way, how cool is that?" I blushed when I realized I'd sworn.

He smiled. "Press the table button."

I did and a table came out of the wall in front of the chair. Excited, I picked up the other remote and guessed that it went to my seat. "Hold on, this is a recliner?" Laughing, I tested it, then decided I'd rather be seated straight up. "If you told me this thing also flies, I'd believe you."

He chuckled. "Sadly, that's an option that wasn't available, but press the drink button."

When I did, a panel opened and a small robotic table rolled toward us with two champagne glasses and a bucket of ice with a bottle of ginger ale in it. My hand flew to my mouth and tears filled my eyes. I'd felt ridiculous about not being able to drink and even worse about having blurt/texted that to him. He'd not only remembered what I'd said, but he'd shown me he cared in such a sweet way that I didn't know if I could express how moved I was without scaring him off. "Ginger ale. Thank you." I sniffed and wiped at my nose.

"Hey, hey, this is supposed to make you smile, not cry."

"I'm not crying."

After a moment, he asked, "Would you like a tissue?"

I sniffed again. "If you have one."

He pulled one out of a compartment next to him and handed it to me then made a sound deep in his throat. "If this is too much, just say so. I know it's been a long time for you and I wanted to make sure I made things special."

I blew my nose then froze. "A long time?"

He froze as well, as if he was just then realizing he had slipped up. "What?"

I stuffed the tissue in a trash receptacle beside my seat then pinned him with a look. "You just said you knew it had been a long time for me."

He loosened his tie a little. "I did say that."

I looked around the van again and a horrific thought occurred to me. "Did I say something to you when I was drugged up? What did I tell you?"

He grimaced. "You may have mentioned that it's been years for you."

I covered my face with my hand. "Oh, my God, of course I did. Which explains why you rented this sex mobile. Yes, it's been a while, but I'm not the kind of woman who—"

"Ashlee." He took my hand in his. "This is a mobile office. I've been using it to meet with clients all over the East Coast. Now, if you want to have sex in here sometime, I certainly wouldn't say no, but I'm not expecting that to happen today."

I could not have felt more embarrassed had someone stripped me naked, slapped a clown nose on me, and paraded me through the streets. How had I gone from someone who used to know how to flirt and go on casual dates to this? To torture myself more, I asked, "Did I say anything else?"

"You may have asked if all brain injuries come with gorgeous guardian angels."

This time I glared at him. "I remember saying that, but I was hoping you didn't."

Looking amused, he shrugged. "It's not something a man forgets."

"What is it you see in me?" I asked, the question echoing in my head.

He frowned and took a moment to answer. "Who have you been with that you don't know?"

I met his gaze, glanced down at our intertwined hands, then locked eyes with him again. "All the wrong men, apparently."

He raised my hand to his mouth and kissed my knuckles

lightly. "Apparently."

My breath caught in my throat. Could this actually be happening? Being with him felt so—right. "I have an idea. How about we forget that I chased you around a parking lot and then confessed God knows what to you while looped out on pain meds . . ."

"Only if you forget I chased you around a hospital room and dropped my family's drama on you while your head was still bandaged."

"This doesn't have to be awkward. We could be two people who met under normal circumstances. You asked me out—"

"And picked you up in my sex mobile."

I gave his hand a shake, but laughed. "That can go into the file of what we pretend never happened."

Looking like he was holding back a laugh of his own, he said, "It's a substantial sized file. I'm not sure something like that can remain closed."

I tipped my head to the side and shot him a playful glare. "Said like a man who doesn't want a second date."

His grin was shameless. "Said like a woman who has no idea how awesome of a first date I have planned for her."

"Oh really?"

"Really," he growled just before claiming my mouth with a kiss so hot that I gladly let him have the last word.

CHAPTER TWENTY

Thane

ASHLEE PRYER WAS an addiction I had no fight left in me to deny. The way she looked at me smashed down barriers I hadn't known I'd erected around my heart. Being with her felt like sunshine on my face on the first nice day after a long, cold winter.

The taste of her was nearly my undoing. As images of what I'd like to do to her on that retractable table flooded my thoughts, I laughed against her lips. Until her, this van had been nothing more than a mobile office . . . but suddenly I could see how it had potential for much more.

Smiling, she laid a hand on my cheek. "What are you laughing at? Before you say *me*, I should warn you that I can deliver a powerful pinch when provoked."

"I find that difficult to imagine. Support that claim with names and dates."

Her eyes rounded, but I could tell she enjoyed being challenged. "Timmy Stevens. Second grade."

I chuckled. That sounded about right. "I see. And what

had he done to deserve your wrath?"

"He'd made fun of a boy who'd just moved to town. Phil. Timmy started calling him Silly Philly and pushing him around. I warned him to stop, then I took things into my own hands."

"Literally."

She blushed. "He wasn't a nice kid. Words hurt more than a push."

"Yes, they do."

"Phil had it tough because he was small and timid. We were friends until middle school and he was always so worried about what people thought of him. If someone said something unkind to him it would devastate him. At least until I told him my furniture theory. That seemed to help him."

"Furniture theory?"

I loved the way she was a blend of shy and bold. When it was about her she was more like Phil than she was probably comfortable admitting. But when it came to protecting others, she put her own welfare aside and did what she felt was needed.

I thought about the story her parents had shared about her nearly drowning, trying to return a duckling to its mother. She was a quiet hero. My father had explained what those were to Jesse and me when we were little and encouraged us to find that type of person in our employees and our community. Those were the people who valued the welfare of others. They stepped up when others looked away. He said we should fill our lives with heroes. Lesser people would disappoint. When times got tough, the weak would choose themselves every time. Not the heroes. They would stay and if you'd earned their loyalty with your own, they'd fight at your side. My father said the quiet heroes would always win because, although they were often underestimated when they rose up together—they were undefeatable.

Scott was a quiet hero. I'd recognized that as soon as I'd discovered his reason for his bean research was to be able to support his parents when they retired. Some people performed acts of heroism for the glory, and although the outcome might be impressive, it was the quiet hero . . . the one who did the right thing with no expectation of receiving gratitude from anyone . . . that I'd learned to admire. "Tell me about this furniture theory of yours," I prompted Ashlee again.

She looked away then back. "It may sound silly, but it has always worked for me. The world is full of people I call creaky furniture. They say horrible things for no reason other than they're not happy with themselves."

"That's very true."

"Sometimes what they say really hurts and we give their words more importance than we should. For example, if a parent of one of the children I tutor said I was the worst tutor they'd ever had, I'd be devastated. I'd go home and tell Joanie what they'd said. I'd probably tell my parents as well.

The temptation would be to call some of my friends and vent to them too. Because words hurt."

"Yes."

"But I've found that if I imagine that the person who is speaking unkindly to me is nothing more than a piece of furniture, I don't get as upset. If you sat on a chair that squeaked beneath you, even if it did so loudly, it would bother you at the time but chances are you wouldn't carry the memory of that chair with you into the next day. You wouldn't call all of your friends and tell them what that horrible chair did to you and how it made you feel. You wouldn't waste any emotion on it because it's just a chair and some of them squeak."

"That actually makes a lot of sense."

"Now, the caveat is that some criticism should be a cause for reflection. If I really am the worst tutor someone has ever hired, I should want to know why and improve if I can. So the theory doesn't work in all situations. It's really just for the Timmy Stevenses of the world who say things to hurt you for no other reason than because they can."

"Those people are nothing more than squeaky furniture."

"Exactly."

"And you came up with that as a child?"

Her shoulders rose and fell. "Phil needed some way of dealing with bullies. He said it helped."

"Have you stayed in touch? I'm curious how he ended up."

"Last I heard he was working for a building demolition company." She bit her bottom lip, wrinkled her nose at me, and with twinkling eyes, she said, "So I guess you could say he's blowing up furniture for a living."

I barked out a laugh. "Do you think he names every building Timmy?"

Laughing, she swatted at me. "Stop. We shouldn't laugh. Phil was always so nice to me."

"And Timmy?"

She gasped for air then said, "He's an architect."

I pressed my lips together to stop from laughing again. "That's probably a coincidence."

After a moment, Ashlee sobered. "All joking aside, the world is a weird place, isn't it? I mean, if this were a game and I were writing the rules, Timmy wouldn't have ended up more successful than Phil."

I took a moment to consider that. "Success is subjective, isn't it? To me, it's more about quality of life than possessions. And if that's the case, Phil is the clear winner."

She searched my face as if trying to determine my level of sincerity.

I continued, "Phil had years of friendship with you, while Timmy has to live the rest of his life with someone who clearly isn't happy—himself."

She gave me another long look. "You sound like someone who isn't into material things, but what is this?" She referenced the interior of my van.

"A necessity in the business world. Potential clients expect to be wowed when they meet with me."

She glanced around again. "I can imagine this would impress many people." When she met my gaze again, she asked, "Although I think that designing the life support system for a space station would be all someone would need to know."

"I can't take full credit for that project. We have a whole team. And although it's an incredible opportunity, it's not too different than what we've always done, just on a bigger scale."

"And in space."

"Technically in the exosphere, but yes."

"It's still impressive."

I dipped my head. "Well, thank you." For some reason her praise meant more than any award or public recognition could have.

She bit her bottom lip again. "I wouldn't expect you to be as humble as you are."

I laughed at that. "Oh, humble is not how most would describe me."

Her eyebrows rose. "No?"

"Not when it comes to business. I know what needs to get done and I make sure it does."

"And what about other people? Your friends. How would they describe you?"

Scott had asked me the same question. I felt prepared for

it this time. "Outside of my family, I don't have much time to socialize unless it's work related."

"So, your brothers are your best friends?"

"Yes." That about summed it up. Would she, like Scott, see that as an issue?

"Joanie's my best friend. I've worked for my parents during the day and part-time hours at an after-school tutoring program ever since I chose to have Sage. It's the only way I could afford for us to have our own home. Outside of my family, I don't have many friends either. Some people think it's because I'm a snob, but it's really because I prefer to spend my time with the people who matter to me the most. I love my family. We always have a great time when we're together. Not everyone gets that and it's okay."

"What's your idea of fun?"

She smiled. "It doesn't really matter. I love to try new things and see new places, but then I also really enjoy a tea party with Sage or a movie marathon with Joanie and Mike. My parents love to hike and camp so I'm equally happy out in nature, but Joanie and I have splurged and stayed at nice hotels and there's nothing wrong with those either."

"Because for you it's all about who you're with."

"Exactly. I went to college. I could have found a better job than working at my dad's truck wash, but it keeps us close. I manage the office with my mom. We have truckers from all over the country who have been clients for decades.

I was in high school when my parents added a kitchen, tables, and a washroom with a shower to the facility. It's not a restaurant. My mom and some volunteers prepare something each day and anyone who uses our services is welcome to a fresh meal and a shower if they'd like. The volunteers take some of what is prepared each day to our town's food kitchen. There's always more than enough. Sage grew up with big, burly men making goofy smiles at her and getting all teary eyed because she made them miss their own families."

"And Joanie?"

"Mike met Joanie at the truck wash. He moved here, and together they started their own trucking business so he wouldn't have to travel as much. Joanie loves it because it gives her the flexibility to work from home."

The emotions welling within me as I listened to her confused me. The more I got to know her, the more what she'd said to me when we'd first met made sense. She hadn't sought me out for financial support. Ashlee didn't require rescuing nor did Sage. They had a stable, loving family who believed in caring for others. Quiet heroes—all of them.

"And what about you?" she asked. "What's your idea of fun?"

"That's a good question," I answered honestly. "Most of the time I'm working. When I'm not, I'm with my family or working out. I swim a lot. It clears my head, but I wouldn't say I do it for fun."

"So, you'd go on a hike?"

"I don't see why not."

"Movie marathon with a huge bowl of popcorn?"

My kneejerk response was almost to say that I preferred to be productive, but then I imagined her snuggled to my side, her head on my shoulder, with no distraction other than a mindless movie. The idea held a surprising amount of appeal. "With you on my lap?"

Her face flushed delightfully. "Is that the determining factor?"

"Absolutely."

She smiled, looked away, then met my gaze again. "You'd let me hold the remote?"

Loving the sizzle between us, I lowered my voice and growled, "If you're on my lap, you can hold whatever you want to."

Her eyes lit with amusement and desire. "Well then it sounds like we should schedule a movie marathon." Her suddenly husky voice had my cock surging to attention.

"In my sex mobile."

She laughed and wagged a finger at me. "You, sir, need to remember that first dates are when you're supposed to be on your best behavior. A gentleman would kindly forget that I said that."

"Is that what you're looking for? A gentleman?" I released her hand and laid mine possessively on her knee, moving it upward to her midthigh. "Do you want someone you can control?" I inched my hand higher, encountered her biker shorts and slid a finger just below the edge of them. "Or someone who would tell you to take these off because I want less between us?"

Her eyes dilated and her lips parted. "What happened to the gentle kiss you planned to *end* our date with?"

It was impossible to be this close to her and not want more. "I've changed my mind on where that kiss should start and just how gentle it should or shouldn't be."

She swallowed visibly, but her tongue danced across her bottom lip.

I slid another finger beneath the hem of her shorts. My caress still a good distance from her sex, but that wasn't how it felt. It felt wildly intimate and from the fire in her eyes I could tell it was the same for her.

I was a male in my prime with a healthy sex drive. I'd found pleasure with a variety of women, but had never experienced this level of heightened awareness of one. Her scent tickled my senses. I'd carefully planned a date I'd hoped would not only put her at ease, but give us time to get to know each other.

Unrushed.

That was in direct conflict with the desire I was fighting to release my seat belt, free her from her underthings, and claim the sweetness of her sex with my mouth. Inside the van. On top of the van. It wouldn't have mattered. Especially in the age of technology and surveillance, I wasn't the type to indulge in public displays of affection. Whatever this was between Ashlee and me was as potent as a drug. I didn't care who saw what. My hunger for her was a growling beast held back only by an equally strong primal need to protect her.

A man could make a real fool of himself over a woman who tangled him up the way she had me. Jesse was the impulsive one. Me? I was the one who methodically fixed whatever he broke. I made detailed plans, stuck to them, and didn't allow myself the indulgence of impulsiveness.

Planning was a waste of time with Ashlee. All it took was one look from her for my resolve to crumble. Her lack of immediate response, however, to my last comment had me mentally tapping the brakes on my libido. The last two times we'd been together had ended with her asking me to leave. Had I just earned that honor again? It was difficult to say.

When she cleared her throat I prepared for the worst. I began to withdraw my hand from her leg.

"My doctor gave me a long list of what I shouldn't do for a while. Sex wasn't on that list. Although I've done some online googling and brain injuries can result in decreased hormone release which makes it more difficult to . . . you know."

That was not where I thought the conversation was going. "So . . . you'd like to wait until you heal more." That made sense and once again I was inwardly kicking myself for allowing my attraction to her to cloud my judgment. Of course she needs more time. She's not yet back at work.

What the fuck is wrong with me?

"Or we could see if it's even an issue." She'd spoken that last part so softly I nearly asked her to repeat herself. I was certain I'd heard her right, though, when she rushed to add, "It's not like my brain would explode or anything from an orgasm. I'm out of that danger zone."

She was so sincere I had to bite the inside of my lip to stop from laughing. Ashlee was unlike any woman I'd ever known. She was earnest and honest, playful and loving. With her, there were no games. She said it like it was and I found myself loving that. I couldn't hold back the grin that spread across my face. "I'm relieved to hear that. I do want to blow your mind, but—"

She covered her face with one hand and groaned. "I may be out of practice with flirting. How am I doing?"

I chuckled and gently pulled her hand away from her face. "You have now successfully made the idea of going down on you both exciting as hell and slightly terrifying."

Shaking her head, she rolled her eyes skyward.

I took her chin in my hand and brought her face around so our eyes met again, then said, "But you know what I'm not? Bored. I can't remember the last time I laughed on a date. We're starting from a place of not having much in common, but that doesn't feel like it'll matter because I like you . . . and I like me when I'm with you."

She let out a relieved chuckle. "I like you too." Her expression turned serious. "I thought I should be up-front, though. I can't have children and I know that matters to some men. Imagine if I also became incapable of orgasming . . ."

My heart cracked wide open for her right then and there. She wasn't speaking from a place of anger or shame. She accepted who she was while accepting that others might find fault with her. I hadn't known until that very moment that it was possible to fall in love with someone on a first date.

Had anyone told me it'd happened to them, I would have dismissed their claim. Lust was one thing, but love? No, that took time, cultivation, and commitment. A deep attachment like that couldn't happen in a heartbeat.

But it had.

"You're perfect just the way you are, Ashlee. Anyone who can't see that, doesn't deserve to be with you." I caressed the line of her jaw as I spoke. "Sex is important to me, but what that'll look like and how we'll bring each other pleasure . . . we have plenty of time to figure that out."

A man could get lost in those beautiful eyes of hers. "I may be fine. I can't have children, but everything else might still work."

I bent and let my kiss be my response to that. She opened for me eagerly. Being with her wasn't normal or predictable, but man, I felt so alive. Nothing was impossible when she was in my arms. Bellerwood? I had renewed faith I could keep him in check. Ashlee's potential health issues? We'd figure them out.

The van came to a sudden halt. I pulled back the curtain and confirmed that we'd arrived at our destination. "We're here."

She adjusted her skirt and her hair. "Where?"

"Have you been to Sturbridge Village? It's a re-creation of an 1830s colonial town. There are actors in costumes of the period."

"I came here on a field trip for school a long time ago. I've been planning to bring Sage, but I was waiting for her to be a little older." She smiled as she searched my face. "What an interesting choice for our first date."

Interesting? My goal was to leave her a whole lot more impressed than that, but to be fair, so far she'd only seen my van. The door slid open. I got out of the vehicle then turned to help Ashlee out as well. "I've arranged for a private tour and some additional things that I'm sure weren't on your class trip."

"This may have been where I threatened to throw Timmy Stevens off the bridge if he said one more thing to Phil about choosing to sit near the teacher on the ride over. I didn't blame Phil. Shit goes down on buses."

"I wouldn't know, but I'll take your word for that."

Her mouth rounded. "Have you never been on a school bus?"

"Never."

"How does that happen?" Of all the things we'd shared, from my job to the fact that Jesse and I had twins popping up everywhere, this was what she seemed most shocked by.

"Private schools and chauffeurs."

"Wait." She waved her hands in the air. "Have you ever been bowling?"

"No."

"Camping?"

"Not once."

She raised a finger. "Do you know what a New York wiener is and have you ever eaten one made by a sweaty man in a white tank top who prepares them on his bare arm right in front of you?"

"I can't say that I ever have."

She hopped in excitement, took one of my hands in hers, and announced cheerfully, "I'm planning our second date. I know the perfect place to take you."

None of the above options she'd listed sounded tempting to me, but had she asked me for a kidney right then I would have handed mine to her. Still, I teased, "Should I be afraid?"

She pinched the air with her free hand. "A little, but I guarantee you'll have fun. You might go home nauseous, but you'll definitely have a story to tell your family."

I pulled her to me, gave her a quick kiss on the lips, and murmured, "We may have differing ideas on how a date should leave us feeling."

She laughed against my lips. "Where's your sense of adventure? I won't even tell you where we're going. Just like this, it'll be a surprise."

Oh, boy.

CHAPTER TWENTY-ONE

Ashlee

A YOUNG MAN'S voice interrupted my gleeful planning. "Excuse me. Mr. Rehoboth? I was sent out to tell you that everything is ready for you."

Thane brushed his lips over mine briefly, then straightened, and turned toward the man. "Thank you. This is Ashlee Pryer."

"Welcome," the man said, and his voice shook a little. It was only then that I realized he was nervous. I looked from him to Thane. There was nothing about Thane's expression or stance that should have been intimidating.

Hand in hand we followed the young man into the building where staff circled around him like he was a celebrity. He shook hands with each of them and answered their questions patiently. When one of the staff members asked if he could take a photo with Thane, I saw him through their eyes for the first time.

Thane Rehoboth wasn't just a man I'd met in an unconventional way who'd asked me out on a date. He was also all over the news for his involvement in a space station project. Without stopping to think if I should, I adjusted Thane's tie so it would be straight for the photo. The smile he beamed at me warmed me straight to my toes.

He stepped away to take the photos. Watching him with others gave me time to appreciate his complexity. He was successful beyond what most people would ever achieve but had also somehow remained grounded. He held the attention of all in the room and my guess was it had as much to do with his physical presence as his recent fame.

If the way the women were fawning over him was anything to go by he didn't lack for hookup opportunities. I tried not to think about how much I'd overshared on the drive over. With so many healthy, potentially saner, possibilities . . . what was he doing with me?

Please don't let it be about Sage.

I shook my head. He could be part of her life without having to pretend to be interested in me. In fact, that situation would have made all of this less confusing. Why would he bother to take me out if he wasn't really interested?

Thane looked up, met my gaze, and walked away from the people who were talking to him as if they weren't there. "Are you okay?" he asked just loud enough for me to hear.

"Of course."

"What's wrong?"

Pinned down by those intense eyes of his, I blurted, "Sorry. I forgot you're a big deal."

Surprise followed by amusement shone in his eyes. "I'm not. They recognize me because a story about me hit social media. Next week I could probably walk in here and no one would notice."

"I doubt that." But I loved that he'd said it. "I'd be surprised if some of those women didn't slip their phone numbers into your pocket while they were hanging on you."

"Ooooh," he said, looking amused enough that I wanted to smack him. "Is someone jealous?"

I looked away. "You can do whatever you want with whomever you want. We don't have any commitment to each other."

"Yet," he growled into my ear and I snapped my head around to meet his gaze. We stood there for a moment, simply breathing each other in, then he said, "It's okay to feel a little territorial. In fact, I like it because I'm beginning to feel the same about you."

I opened my mouth to say something, couldn't come up with anything that came close to expressing how much I wished we were alone, and decided it might be better to keep some of my thoughts to myself.

"Ready to start the tour?" he asked.

Of his body? Yes. Of the village. Sure. I guess. I nodded and together we made our way to the young man who'd greeted us at the van. He was waving to us from next to a door leading into the village.

During our short walk through to one of the main

streets, Thane took my hand again. Our guide explained that we would come across many costumed historians. Although they'd be dressed in period-appropriate attire, they weren't actors. They were simply people who knew a lot about the history of New England and enjoyed sharing that with visitors. Some were paid, some were volunteers.

Our guide led us to another man who was wearing loose-fitting colonial-style work clothing and standing beside an old-fashioned horse-drawn carriage. He tipped his straw hat at us and my smile couldn't have been wider. I asked if I could pet one of the horses and as I tentatively did so, I said, "Sage would love this."

"We can come back," Thane answered so casually my breath caught in my throat.

This wasn't a one-and-done date. I'd already joked about a second and he'd implied we'd get to a place where we would be taking Sage out with us. On one hand that felt crazy fast, on the other, he'd cared for me after my accident. Who did that? His motivation might have been being Sage's uncle, but every time he looked at me, I knew she wasn't the only reason he was with me. Imagining the three of us becoming a family unit was painfully easy.

I gave myself a mental shake. Rushing in with unrealistic expectations was how people got their hearts broken. Sure Thane was everything I'd been holding out for—kind, patient, hardworking—all wrapped up in the body of a gladiator, but shouldn't that be enough to have me tapping the brakes? If things seem too good to be true . . .

I should try harder to look less like I want to octopus-style wrap myself around him.

Not that he seems to mind.

A moment later we were seated side by side and being driven down the dirt roads of the village. We passed historically inspired buildings that lined a grass square where schoolchildren and their chaperones gathered. The sound of the horses clip-clopping as we passed old-time banks and workshops gave the ride a feel that it was transporting us back in time. When I saw a man in a top hat and black suit with long tails I grabbed Thane's thigh spontaneously, "Hey, that would have been you back then."

As soon as I realized how high on his leg my hand was, I began to withdraw it, but his hand settled on mine, holding it where it was. He leaned toward the window on my side, his warm breath a tickle on my cheek. "I do appreciate a good suit."

"Me too," I said in a strangled voice. The muscles of his thigh bunched beneath my touch and I pretended to still care about the view outside. It was impossible to breathe normally when he was so close that if I turned my head my lips would likely graze his cheek.

"I have no desire to go back in time, though," he said. "For me it's all about moving forward."

With me? I barely stopped myself from asking the question. *I need to calm down.* I struggled to clear my head enough to maintain a coherent conversation. "Forward sounds good." I inwardly groaned. Seriously? What is wrong with my ability to speak around him?

His fingers laced with mine. "Are you nervous?"

This time I did turn so I could meet his gaze. "So, so nervous. Like on a scale of one to ten, I'm about a thirty."

"I'm about a six."

My eyes rounded then narrowed. "You're saying that to make me feel better."

"Maybe." His smile was gentle. "But this is the first date I've planned that consisted of more than dinner and . . . after dinner."

After dinner? Oh. That wasn't how my dates normally ended, but it had also been a while. I blinked a few times as I processed that. I wanted to ask a follow-up question, but we'd arrived at our destination and the driver opened the door of the carriage.

Thane exited first, then helped me out. Placing my hand and my trust in him felt natural. We were met by a middle-aged man in a red vest over a long-sleeved blue shirt and loose tan pants. He led us to a working replica of an 1800s wooden gristmill. As he walked he told us the history of the mill, pointing out the parts that had been taken from mills that had closed. The millstones, he said, had come from a mill in Connecticut. Listening to Thane ask questions about the process of turning wheat into flour was fascinating. I would have expected him to be curious about the waterwheel and how it produced the power to move the millstones, but instead he seemed curious about combustible dust.

"I've never heard of combustible dust. I'd ask you what it is, but something tells me it's all in the name," I said.

Thane answered, "It is. I know in the modern production of flour or any substance that produces small, flammable particles that accumulate, there can be a risk of fire."

Our historical guide nodded. "Modern isn't always better. We process and store less grain here than you'd find in a modern mill. We have significantly better ventilation. Also, since we are water-powered, which necessitates a location on a river, a natural solution to the problem of a fire was readily available." After a moment, he asked, "Would you like to see the waterwheel?"

"I'd love that," I said with enthusiasm that brought a smile to Thane's face.

When we stepped through a side door on the building, our guide brought us first to see the large, still-functioning waterwheel then pointed toward a grassy area off to the side of it. My hand flew to my mouth. A simply built, wooden pergola was closed off on three sides by floor-length white curtains for privacy. Thane took my hand in his as we made our way toward it. Beneath the shade of the pergola was a wooden table with a linen tablecloth, two chairs and a beautiful bouquet of wildflowers. "Is that for us?" I asked in a hushed voice.

His head dipped in acknowledgment and his hand settled on my lower back. "You like it?"

Like it? I was ready to burst into happy tears. Instead I looked from his face to the romantic setting and back, then threw my arms around his neck, pulled his face down to mine and expressed my feelings with a kiss. Okay, several kisses. More than I probably should have given him in front of our guide. I couldn't help myself, though. No man had ever done anything so thoughtful for me. Against his lips, I murmured, "I love it." Had we been alone I would have stayed right as I was, plastered against his chest, but we were still very much in a public place.

We stood there, both breathing unevenly, unable to look away from each other. Ever since I'd decided to become a mother, Sage had been the filter I saw everything through. She was always at the forefront of my thoughts and my life revolved around making hers as good as it could be. I'd sought Thane out for Sage, but this was no longer about her. At least, to me it wasn't. Something Joanie had said came back to me then: *It's good to see you honoring your needs for once and not just Sage's. I love how you put her first, but motherhood shouldn't be all sacrifice. You deserve a little something for yourself.*

I smiled. My "little something" was off to a good start.

"What's so amusing?" Thane asked in that low, sexy tone of his.

I shook my head. Nope, I wasn't about to say a single thing to diminish the romance of the setting. "Us. Careful.

You know how they say if you feed a stray cat, it'll keep coming back? This is the kind of first-date vibe that gets you a second."

"That's the point." The wink he gave me sent the most delicious tingles straight through me. He took me by the hand again and guided me to the table where he held out a chair for me before taking the seat across. It was old-fashioned and my soul was eating it up.

Our guide filled our water glasses and explained the courses we'd be served. They were all historically accurate and I was sure they'd be delicious, but I couldn't focus on anything beyond Thane. The food came quickly and we were alone again. With the light sound of moving water as well as children laughing in the distance, it was the perfect romantic backdrop.

"What makes you happy, Ashley Pryer?" Thane prompted as he cut into his chicken.

I used the excuse of chewing my food to give myself time to consider that. Joanie, Mike, and I loved to debate such questions. Often we did so over a couple of beers or wine. This was a date though, and I hadn't been on one in so long I was unsure of how to best proceed. Was I supposed to come up with something flirtatious in response? *God, I'm awful at that.* "I do," I answered, then added, "Happiness comes from within. The choices I make, the people I choose to surround myself with, even the way I allow myself to interpret situations—all of that determines my mood."

He nodded.

"And you?" I countered.

After wiping the corner of his mouth with his napkin, he said, "Your answer has me questioning if my own requires tweaking."

"I love that feeling." I leaned forward. He arched an eyebrow so I continued, "Joanie, Mike, and I debate everything. They're my safe zone—the place I can voice potentially faulty beliefs without judgment. We agree about a lot, disagree about enough, but hear each other out. My parents encouraged us to be open with each other like that, and I believe it's why we're as close as we are. Being able to have real conversations with people is how we grow."

"Ashlee, how are you still single?"

That made me laugh. "It's been remarkably easy." I sobered somewhat and held his gaze. "I'm not willing to settle."

When Thane didn't immediately respond to that, I gave myself a mental kick. Was I trying to scare him off? *Hi, I potentially have brain damage that might affect my sex drive. I can't have children. Oh, and why am I still single? Rigid high standards. Bask in the glory of how sexy all of that sounds.*

I lowered my eyes and rubbed my thumb across my forehead. Thane took my hand in his. I didn't fight it, nor did I raise my eyes to his. He'd gone all out on this date. All I had to do was not sabotage it.

"How are you interpreting this situation that has you

frowning?" he asked.

"I'm not frowning."

"You are." He chuckled then cleared his throat. "Having high standards is not a bad thing. I've ended dates early because a woman has eaten from my plate without asking."

My eyes flew to his. "Seriously?" I wasn't sure how I felt about that.

"It's rude."

"Maybe, but enough to end a date over?"

He raised and lowered a shoulder. "In my experience familiarity doesn't tend to bring out better behavior in people. In fact, it's often the reverse. First dates are when people are still figuring each other out. It's when they present themselves at their best. Therefore, if someone is disrespect-ful straight out the gate, the likelihood that they'll only become more so over time is high enough for me to lose interest."

"Wow." How would someone like that handle being around a child? It also struck an odd chord in me that had me asking, "So, if I took something off your plate right now, I'd never see you again?"

His eyes darkened. "I didn't take you for the type who challenges rules."

"Then you have a lot left to learn about me. I don't know how I feel about you being the type who makes rules."

"Every civil society has them."

"I'm not interested in dating a civil society."

"You said you're unwilling to settle. It sounds like you have a set of your own rules."

I sat back at that. "You're right. I do."

"And those are?"

I hesitated. How much honesty was too much? "I don't want a drinker. A few drinks now and then are fine, but I don't want Sage to grow up around someone with an alcohol problem."

"And?"

"I don't want someone who'd smoke around Sage or have habits that might drastically change our lives for the worse—like gambling."

"And?"

"Okay, I get the point."

"No, don't stop. I want to hear your nonnegotiables."

The lack of sarcasm in his voice was the only reason why I was willing to continue to share. "I won't put up with someone with a temper. Respect is the foundation of any relationship. He'd need to be willing to move to where I am because I'm very close to my family and I wouldn't want that to change."

"And?"

My voice thickened. "He'd need to be able to love Sage. She's not just my priority, she's my heart. I couldn't be with anyone who felt threatened by that. I want what my parents have, what Joanie and Mike have—a love that makes everyone around them feel loved as well."

He held my gaze with an expression I struggled to decipher. "All I want is someone who'll ask before scarfing my food."

I smiled at that. "I highly doubt that's the extent of your criteria."

He took a moment, then said, "I wasn't raised the way you were. Until recently I had zero faith that women were capable of loyalty."

"Ouch." It was a harsh outlook, but from what little I knew about his life I could see how he'd come to that conclusion. "And now?"

"I've seen first-hand that some can be. Crystal is not only devoted to my brother Jesse, but she brings out a good side of him. I wouldn't want to be the person who tried to come between Monica and Scott. I have a feeling her wrath would be legendary."

I looked around at the effort he'd put into our date and thought about what he'd said about how he didn't normally do more than take a woman to dinner. I'd wondered what he was doing with me and even questioned if it had to do with wanting to be in Sage's life. He was answering those questions with such honesty it was heartbreaking. Here was a man who'd been abandoned, not just by one mother, but by two. Of course, he had trust issues. I'd never known what it was like to have a parent walk away from me and couldn't imagine how that affected a child. Still, he was able to own that side of himself with a dignity that was inspiring. "You're looking for the same."

"No."

I was gutted by his response. *And here I am thinking I'm special.*

He gave my hand a squeeze and said, "Why would I keep looking when I've found what I want?"

"Found?" My mouth opened and closed like a fish out of water gasping for air. "Me?"

"Is that so impossible to believe?"

"Are you . . . are you saying . . . what are you saying?"

He leaned toward me, holding my gaze, damn near looking into my soul as he said, "That this . . . whatever this is between us . . . feels important. I don't know how to do this right. I never imagined I'd want to. I can tell you, though, that I don't drink, smoke, gamble, or have much of a temper. I would never resent your devotion to your child."

"Because she's your niece?"

"Because I don't do anything halfway. Know that before you decide to plan that second date. I work a lot. If I make a promise, I keep it. The women I've dated have understood that I wasn't looking for anything permanent. I made that clear up front."

I was confused. At first it had sounded like he was saying he wanted something serious with me. Was he saying the opposite now? "I don't understand."

He frowned and ran a hand through his hair. "Like I said, I'm not used to this."

"This?"

Straightening in his chair, he pinned me with a look. "I don't want to wake up in the morning and wonder if you'll be there."

My chest tightened as the proud man before me revealed a vulnerable side to him and I had to blink back tears. It was my turn to give his hand a squeeze. "No one wants that. I'm afraid of letting someone into my life and discovering I chose wrong. It's why I have those nonnegotiables, not because I'm judgmental, but because Sage will have to live with my decision and I don't take that lightly."

With a self-deprecating smile, he said, "I keep telling myself to take things slowly with you."

"But I'm irresistible, I get it."

"You are."

His words hung in the air, upping the sexual tension between us. I was no longer in doubt that he wanted me. It was a heady realization. A little scary, as well. It sure sounded like he was looking for more than a one-night stand. Did I dare let myself start to believe again? "If we did this, you'd probably wake up alone a lot for a while."

He blinked a few times.

I rushed to clarify, "Because I have Sage. I'm sorry, I wouldn't want to sleep over and I couldn't have a man in our house until . . ."

He swooped in with a light kiss that took all the awkwardness out of the moment. When he sat back, he linked his hand with mine again. "Never apologize for being a good mother."

Tears filled my eyes again. "Thank you."

His free hand caressed the side of my face. "No, thank *you.*" With amusement in his eyes, he said, "You know what? Take something off my plate. I doubt I'll care."

I tipped my head to one side. "Oh, no. If this is your way of weaseling out of trying New York wieners, it won't work."

"It's not." *God, I love his smile.* "I'm serious. Take something."

Was he testing himself or me? I wasn't sure. I pointed to his plate. "A wedge of potato?"

"Sure."

Seriously, how was this a big deal to him? The imp in me made me ask, "With my fingers?"

"If you'd like." His eyes widened as if the thought was slightly horrifying to him though, and I choked back a laugh. How bad am I at dating if I give a guy a stroke?

I sat back and folded my arms across my chest. "Before I touch anything on your plate I need to know why it bothers you so much when someone does."

His expression closed. "I told you why."

I searched his face. "The problem is . . . I don't believe you. If it was only about respect, you wouldn't care at all if I touched your food because you asked me to. It's more than that."

He held my gaze, neither admitting nor denying that I

was correct.

I continued, "What was mealtime like at your home?"

"Formal. We had a cook and staff."

"So, your father wouldn't have approved of you eating off each other's plates."

"He would have been horrified if we had."

"And his opinion matters to you."

"More than almost anyone else's."

I was beginning to understand. "And his wife. The one who adopted you. How would he describe her?"

"Lately his opinion of her has softened."

I took a guess. "What was it that he didn't like about her?"

"He knew she was only with him because he was successful. At least, that's what he believed at the time."

"So beyond their lack of ability to be loyal, you also see women as takers."

His rejection of that idea shone in his eyes and the way he tensed, then he inhaled deeply. "I suppose I do."

Had any other man said that, I would have been offended, but he wasn't trying to be insulting. In fact, there was a compliment in his honesty. He wasn't trying to impress me—he was letting me in.

A thought came to me that had me sitting forward again. I spoke softly because he needed to hear the truth, but it didn't need to sting. "You asked me to take food off your plate not to give me a chance to prove to you that I'm not with you for material things . . . you were testing if you could be okay with me even if I was. I deserve better than that."

He appeared about to deny it, but didn't. He'd been kind to me when I'd stumbled through how to express myself. I couldn't do less for him.

"Hey," I said in the gentle tone he'd used with me. "So do you. You and I may be too different to make it past this date, but even if we are, we could be friends. My parents like you. I'm sure you could come around and have dinner with my family. I think you need to see how little a healthy relationship has to do with things. My parents are comfortable now, but they started off with nothing. They say they could be just as happy living in a small apartment on a tiny income as long as they still had each other and us. You need to find someone who makes you feel the same way."

CHAPTER TWENTY-TWO

Thane

THERE'S NOTHING MORE unsettling than when someone pierces through a narrative you've told yourself, uncovers something ugly, then holds it up for you to face. I'd always been the even-tempered, cool-headed one in my family. The fixer doesn't have problems.

I should have immediately told her that we weren't too different for that second date. Part of me wanted to drag her out of this far too public place, make love to her all night long, and let everything else sort itself out.

None of that sounded like me, and that had my stomach churning. I'd never been impulsive, but I also didn't hedge and waver. Decisiveness. Action. Achievement. Those were my values.

I thought back to when Jesse had first met Crystal. He'd said time on Scott's farm had allowed him to step outside of his life and discover not only who he was but who he wanted to be. I'd dismissed that as the impaired ramblings of a love-drunk man.

Everything he'd said then was beginning to make sense. My father's jaded view of women had kept him closed off to the opportunity of having a real partner. Had his ex-wife not adopted Jesse and me, our father would be alone.

It wasn't what Jesse wanted for himself.

It wasn't what I wanted either.

In fact, every time Ashlee described her family, a part of me yearned for more than my empty apartment. I wanted to come home from work to laughter instead of silence. Jesse's decision to marry, buy a small farm, and start a family suddenly made sense.

Not the farm part but a life with a little chaos.

Ashlee waved a napkin at me. "It's been a while since I've been on a date, but I don't remember being this bad at it. I didn't mean to offend you."

"You didn't." I laid a hand over one of hers. "What you did was give me a lot to think about."

She made a raspberry sound with pursed lips. "Now if that isn't a nice way to say we should end this date early, I don't know what is. I'm sorry—"

"Don't. You said nothing that wasn't true. And don't assume silence is a bad thing. Sometimes a person requires a moment to think."

"And your impatient tone? I should take that as a sign that things are going fabulously?"

I sat back and took a breath. It was disconcerting how often she was correct. Especially as I became more successful, fewer and fewer people dared to correct me. Ashlee was sweet, but certainly no pushover, and I liked that. "Any frustration I have is with myself, not you. I can't say I've enjoyed the last few minutes of our conversation, but they were things I needed to hear. Apparently, I have some issues I need to work on."

"Thank God," she said.

My eyes flew to hers. "How is that a good thing?"

"Because we now have something in common. I love my life, but I'm flying by the seat of my pants most days. It's a relief to know you don't have it all worked out."

We took a moment, simply staring into each other's eyes. A smile spread across my face. "I've been a mess since the day I met you. I don't know if I'm losing my mind or waking up from a slumber. All I know is I want to get nauseous on wieners with you."

Her eyes shone with emotion even as she flashed me a bright smile. "I promise to bring a supply of antacids. Wait until you see the place. They have a life-size animatronic Santa they leave up year-round. The tables still have jukeboxes you play by putting quarters in them. If you can eat ten orders of the wieners and not throw up they give you a coupon for a free year of wieners. No one I know has ever won that coupon."

"You scare me a little, Ashlee Pryer, but in the best way."

She laughed. "So, we're good?"

I leaned over, cupped her chin, and kissed her before saying, "We're more than good. I knew the moment I saw you in your car, all bloodied and beaten up, that my life would never be the same."

"That's so . . . *romantic*?" She chuckled.

"You definitely turned my life upside down. Some for the better, some—"

She placed a finger over my lips. "Stop while you're ahead. Honesty is good, but we can spread it out a little."

I laughed and kissed her finger. "Good point." I stood. "I scheduled a boat ride to where they say ducks are always looking to be fed. Then I thought it would be fun to make an old-fashioned toy for Sage so I arranged for us to do that with one of the woodworkers here."

She stood, walked to me, and hugged me so tightly I didn't need to ask if she approved of my plans. I tucked her head beneath my chin and simply held her, breathing her in. Our connection was so intense I could have stayed there all day. "Ashlee?"

"Yes?"

I kissed the side of her head. "I do want to be your friend." She tensed a little in my arms before I added, "I also want to be your lover, your discussion partner, and whatever else this leads to."

She shuddered against me. "That sounds good to me."

I closed my eyes and held her closer. Being with Ashlee was a series of complicated, emotional, confusing events and discoveries—everything I normally would have avoided.

The problem, if it was indeed a problem, was that I could no longer imagine my life without her in it.

CHAPTER TWENTY-THREE

Ashlee

THE NEXT MORNING, still in my pajamas, I was enjoying a tea while Sage played quietly with the wooden puzzle Thane and I had made for her. The front door of my house opened and my three nephews tossed greetings my way as they ran past me in search of Sage.

"Don't run in the house," Joanie called out from the doorway, but the boys were already down the hall and likely beyond hearing range.

My mother walked into my house behind Joanie, holding a plate of homemade muffins. "I hope we're not intruding. I told Joanie we should call first, now that you have a man in your life."

I closed the door behind them. "We've only had one date, Mom."

"One?" Her eyes rounded. "I thought—"

I accepted the plate from her, then turned to Joanie. "You didn't tell her?"

Joanie raised both hands. "You say that like I can't be

252

trusted with secrets. I like Thane. I'm not about to do anything to mess that up."

My mother's hands went to her hips and her eyebrows arched. She didn't need to say more. I said, "I would have told you earlier, but first you were sick and then I didn't know if I'd see him again. It's a long story, but if you have time, I'll spill everything."

Joanie said, "Start without me. I'll check on the boys. Mom and I were thinking about taking them to the zoo today. You could come with us."

I ran my hand over my still mussed from sleep hair. "I'd need to shower and change."

"No rush." She wiggled her eyebrows. "Unless you want to see what Thane is up to this fine Saturday morning. We could take Sage without you, right Mom?"

Ever the practical one, my mother said, "I'll need to hear this *long story* first before I can give an opinion on that one."

Joanie mouthed, "Good luck," to me, then disappeared down the hallway.

I waved for my mother to follow me to the kitchen. After placing the plate of muffins on the table, I made her a cup of coffee. I checked that no little ears were anywhere nearby, lowered my voice, and started with my decision to seek out Sage's biological father.

I kept going, leaving very little out, and slowing only for the speed bumps of my mother's reactions:

"I wish you'd told me you were considering that."

"That wasn't a safe choice."

"Oh, Ashlee, tell me you didn't."

"So, when we met him the two of you were still strangers?"

"He's not? Then who is?"

"That's so odd. Imagine adopting two boys and not knowing they both have twins."

"I understand why you didn't believe him."

"I'm glad you gave yourself time to heal."

"Oh, my goodness, that sounds like the perfect first date."

"You said that? Oh, Lord."

"I don't know if I like that."

"Good for you. He'll respect you more for speaking up."

"I'm surprised you didn't have sex with him."

That last line had my mouth rounding. "Mom! I have Sage."

"Of course. I just know it's been a long time for you."

I took a deep breath and tried not to be mortified. This was the price I paid for telling my mother everything.

She continued, "And it's probably better to wait. Men like a bit of a challenge."

"I'm not trying to be a challenge, Mom. This is Sage's uncle we're talking about. That alone is confusing."

My mother nodded. "Are you holding out until after you meet his twin—to make sure you've chosen the right one?"

"No." I hadn't even thought of that.

Wrinkling her nose, my mother said, "I've never dated a twin. I don't know how that works. Would you be attracted to both of them?"

I rubbed a hand over my eyes. "God, I hope not. Can we stop talking about the twin. This is about Thane."

"You're not the least bit curious? I mean, he was the one you went looking for."

"Thane told me some things about him. His name is Zachary. He moved around a lot. His last name was changed a few times when his mother remarried. Thane said something about all of them being adopted out of the same agency . . . for an experiment? It was all overwhelming at the time so I didn't ask many questions. I guess I should have brought it up on our date, but I didn't think about it." Amazing what a person could push out of their thoughts when they wanted something to work out.

My mother took a long sip of her coffee, before saying, "I had a good impression of Thane. I'm not saying this has changed that, but it is complicated."

"Exactly."

"And possibly dangerous. If someone separated twins on purpose as part of an experiment what else are they capable of? The world is full of crazy people we shouldn't invite into our lives."

It was an interesting stand to take for someone who fed strangers daily at our truck wash. "What are you afraid of, Mom?"

"I'm not sure yet. What does Joanie think of the situation?"

"She thinks the whole thing is awful and that if it's still going on it needs to be shut down."

"And you agree?"

"Of course."

My mother's expression turned pained. "Your father wouldn't be able to sit back and do nothing either."

"That's part of why I didn't say anything."

"This is serious, Ashlee. We shouldn't say anything to your father yet." She placed her cup on the counter beside her and met my gaze. "And you—you were always the impulsive one. Joanie stayed right at our side and if we told her not to do something she didn't do it. You, on the other hand . . . if you thought someone was in need . . . there was no stopping you. My gray hairs? They're all from you. So, I know you probably won't take my advice, but we need to address this with caution. We don't know who we're dealing with."

"What are you saying, Mom?"

"Maybe you shouldn't see Thane again."

"Because something horrible happened to him as a child? That doesn't sound like you."

She looked away and said, "I was living in California when I met your father. I got involved with some shady people. I was barely twenty and sporting a black eye when your father found me crying in an alley. I'm not proud of some of the things I did back then, but the experience taught me to be careful about who we let into our lives."

"That's how you met Dad? I thought—"

"It's not a time of my life I like to remember. Your father pulled me out of there and took me back to meet his family." Her eyes filled with tears. "The Pryers took me in, cleaned me up, and showed me what a healthy family was supposed to be like. I lived with them for a year before your father asked me out, and I was so afraid of losing his friendship I almost said no."

"I had no idea," I said in a hushed tone. Some of the details matched the story they'd always told us. I knew they'd met when my father was still a trucker. My father's parents were both deceased, but they'd always said they'd loved my mother from the first time they'd met her. That meant even more, now that I knew the circumstances. "You don't have to tell me, Mom. I'm glad Dad got you out of there."

Her eyes were full of pain and memories. "It wasn't that easy. People like that, people who have something to lose, they're dangerous. They didn't want me free. After I'd been with Grandma and Grampa Pryer for about a month, one of them showed up here. Your father dealt with him and sent a message back with him."

My eyes rounded at that. "What kind of message?"

"I don't know. Your father wasn't always a trucker. He spent some time in the military and through that he always had unexpected connections. I was just happy to be free.

Honestly, I didn't ask because I didn't want to know." She inhaled deeply and met my gaze. "I made sure you had a better life than I did. A sane one. A safer one. Sage deserves the same. Please don't invite danger into our lives."

"I won't." I was still reeling from all she'd shared. There was no way Joanie knew or she would have told me. My mother had sheltered us from the ugly in not just the world but in her own history and I wasn't sure how I felt about that. "Mom, I'll be careful."

"If you keep seeing Thane, you won't be able to help yourself—you'll get us all involved."

"I'm not a child anymore. I would never do anything to endanger the family."

She gave me a long look. "You waited for a man in a dark parking lot."

"For Sage."

"Exactly. I'm not confident that you won't do something that puts us all at risk *for Thane* next. It'd be better if you ended things with him now before you get to that point."

"Thane isn't mixed up in any trouble."

"You don't know that."

"You said you liked Thane."

"That was before you told me about experiments and adoption agencies and crazy brothers. Is this really what you want to get involved in?"

"Thane would never hurt me . . . or Sage."

"It's not him I'm worried about. He'd be what invites

danger into our lives."

I wrapped my arms around my waist. Part of me could understand why my mother would be concerned. If someone had hurt her, scared her . . . enough that she hadn't even felt safe on the opposite coast . . . that would make it hard to trust people. Looking at the situation through her eyes, there were some red flags, but when I thought about never seeing Thane again my stomach twisted painfully.

Joanie bounded into the kitchen. "So, zoo or Thane?"

I held my mother's gaze. "I'll come to the zoo with you guys."

Joanie looked surprised. My mother looked grateful. I hastily retreated to take a shower because I needed time to think.

CHAPTER TWENTY-FOUR

Thane

I T WASN'T EASY, but I didn't text Ashlee first thing the next morning. I responded to work emails, went for a long swim, checked the time more than I cared to admit, then finally sat down in my home office and stopped fighting back memories from the night before.

I wasn't accustomed to women distracting me from my work, but Ashlee had charged in, set up camp in my head, and was making it damn near impossible to get anything done.

We'd ended our date early enough for her to be home to have dinner with Sage. I smiled as I thought back over what a perfect day it had been . . . right down to the heated kiss we'd shared on the doorstep of her house. I'd been tempted to stay and spend the rest of the day exploring the beauty of her but I'd forced myself to end the kiss with a promise to call her and walked away.

Would she have let me inside? If the way she'd clung to me was anything to go by—yes. With women in the past, the outcome of the date wouldn't have been in question. Sex was sex. If they were willing and I was interested—why not?

Ashlee was different. I was different with her.

I'd meant what I'd said about wanting to be her friend, her lover, and more. It was unsettling how easily I could imagine what "more" would entail. I wanted Ashlee in my life, in my bed, questioning me, exciting me, pushing me out of my comfort zone with her gentle challenges. The more time I spent with her, the more I wanted to be the man she brought out in me.

I sent her a text: **How is it that you're all I can think about this morning?**

She answered a moment later. **I did warn you that I'm irresistible.**

You did. And you are. What does your day look like today?

Sage and I are at the zoo with Joanie, her kids, and my mother.

That sounds like the perfect Saturday. It did. I loved that she was so close to her family.

It is.

How difficult would it be for you to slip away for a little tomorrow?

It's a school night.

We could do lunch again.

When she didn't answer immediately, I placed my phone on my desk and ran my hands over my face. Not only had I never been the type to chase a woman, but Ashlee was reducing me to adolescent-like yearning. I couldn't remember the last time I'd wanted anything as much as I wanted to see her again.

The space station? What space station?

Bellerwood? Bellerwood who?

The delay in Ashlee's response gave me time to consider what I'd do if she said she couldn't see me the next day. It was unsettling to realize there wasn't a damn meeting on my schedule I wouldn't cancel if she suggested an alternate time.

Joanie said she can watch Sage if we're not gone too long.

What time?

Eleven? She sent me a link to the wiener place she'd told me about. **Let's meet at the restaurant.**

Okay. The ease with which I'd agreed to go somewhere I would previously have had no interest in was a testament to how much I cared for Ashlee. I smiled as I imagined one of our future children asking me when I'd known she was the one for me.

I'd say: *This moment. Right here.*

She could have asked me for anything and I doubted I could have denied her. I wanted to have her, protect her, see the world through her eyes—but more than anything else, I wanted Ashlee to be happy.

Sage wants me to push her on a swing. I'll see you tomorrow. Oh, and don't wear a suit or the owners will think you're a health inspector.

I had to read that last part again because I was certain I'd misunderstood. **If you change your mind there are several**

amazing restaurants where I could get us a good table.

You'll survive and, who knows, you may even like wieners.

I laughed. **See you at eleven.**

I was still smiling a few minutes later when Jesse called me. "Scott invited us to dinner at his place tomorrow. Crystal is feeling good enough to go and Dad is in. Can you make it?"

"I'm free."

"Crystal wanted me to tell you that you're welcome to bring Ashlee."

"We're not at that stage yet, but I appreciate the offer."

"How did yesterday go?"

"Are you asking or is this for Crystal?" Jesse had never asked me about anyone I'd dated.

"Mostly Crystal, but since I have a feeling Ashlee will be sticking around, I'll admit I'm mildly curious."

"It went well. I took her to Sturbridge Village."

"Interesting first date choice." Jesse's tone became amused. "And thoughtful. How unlike you."

"Why did you call again?" I asked, his jab rolling off my back.

"Prepare to be grilled by Crystal and Monica at dinner."

I shook my head, but smiled. "By then we will have had two dates, so perhaps I'll have more to say."

"Lunch again? Working your way up to adult mealtime?"

I rolled my eyes. "She has Sage. Apparently children are a time-consuming responsibility. You'll understand that soon enough."

Jesse countered with, "You say that like you'd know. Name a child you've spent any time with."

"Sage," I said. The memory of that meeting came back and brought a smile to my face. "She was actually quite pleasant. Who knows, if you raise your spawn right, I might even end up liking it as well."

Jesse laughed. "You'd better. I'd hate to see you lose the title of favorite uncle to Scott."

"Never going to happen." I chuckled because Jesse's swipe had landed as intended. Brothers had inside intel on how to build you up or tear you down. Jesse was the first person I'd call if there was trouble, but he also knew how and when to push my buttons to get a reaction.

"Seriously, Thane, it's good to see you with someone you care if you see again."

I took a moment before responding because our conversation had taken a hard left into real. "Thank you. Ashlee and I still have a lot to figure out, but she's important to me."

"We all figured that out at the hospital."

"I can't believe I'm going to say this, but she feels like *the one.*"

"Then don't screw it up."

"That's it? Where's the lecture on taking this slowly? Thinking things through?"

"Thane, you have the two of us confused. If you want

that lecture you'd be better off talking to the man in your mirror. Like me, you've put all of your time and energy into goals that are now paying off. It took stepping into Scott's life for me to see that I wanted more in my own. I thought I had everything, but it was nothing compared to how good it feels to come home to Crystal. We could lose everything and we'd build a new life for us without missing a step because we have each other."

Jesse and I had never kept secrets from each other. I thought there was nothing I didn't know about him, but watching him embrace the role of husband and father was revealing whole new sides of him—and I approved of all of them.

Could I see myself going down the same path? Before Ashlee I would have said I had no interest in doing so. *Now?*

I wanted to see Ashlee with my family. I wanted to experience time with hers. All of that was uncharted territory for me, and I was surprised how appealing it was.

That night, I stayed in and completed some work remotely, but kept checking the time. Around nine, I gave in and sent Ashlee a text. **You awake?**

Yes

Sage asleep?

Finally. It was a five-book night.

I smiled at the wholesome image. **What are you doing now?**

I was cleaning up and considering taking a shower.

Now that's something I don't mind imagining.

Me doing dishes?

I joked, **Yes, you caught me. It's a kink, so please no judgment.** Instead of typing more, I decided to finish with a call.

She answered immediately, her voice in a hushed tone. "Hang on, I'm going to walk into the living room so I won't wake Sage." There was a rustle of movement, then she said, "Better. Now I can talk. What's up?"

"Just wanted to hear your voice." It was true. Completely out of character for me, but when it came to Ashlee so much was.

Her light laugh was a sheer joy. "Really? You're not calling to suggest an alternate place for lunch?"

It was my turn to laugh. "No. I've resigned myself to my fate."

"It won't be that bad. I promise."

Taking the conversation on a serious tangent, I said, "I don't even care if it is, Ashlee. I've discovered that, with you, things don't have to be good."

"Is that a compliment?"

I groaned. "It is. I probably could have said that better. What I'm trying to say is that although we've only been on one date, that's not how it feels."

The pause before she spoke was long enough for me to question my sanity. If a "man card" was a thing, meeting her had shredded mine. When had I become someone who didn't know how to talk to a woman?

When I'd started to care.

When I'd realized I wanted to come home to not just anyone, but to Ashlee.

"I feel the same." Her tone was soft and tentative. "May I ask you a question?"

"Absolutely."

"What are you afraid of?"

"I'm not sure I understand what you're asking."

"Day to day. In life. What scares you?"

With anyone else I would have chosen a surface concern to share. Not that anyone outside of Scott would likely have asked me such a question. This was Ashlee, though, and I wanted her to know the real me. "Failing—my family mostly. My father has never once let me or Jesse down, and that set the bar high for us. You?"

"Same. I don't want to brag, but I'm pretty sure I have the world's best parents. I'm not saying we never argued, but they made sure I always knew I was safe and loved. That's what I want for Sage."

"Every child should have that." Ashlee's words spoke to a part of me I'd spent a lifetime denying, and filled me with a tsunami of unexpected emotion. As a child, I'd wondered what was so unlovable about me that not one, but two mothers had walked away from me. Over time, I'd built a thick callus over that question, but I was beginning to see how much of my personality had been shaped by the experience.

"Oh, Thane, you must think I'm so insensitive. I don't think of you as someone who—"

"Stop. There's nothing wrong with celebrating what you had or wanting that for your child. If anything, it gives me hope. I landed well when I became a Rehoboth, but I see how it has shaped some of my views. It's good for me to also see things through your eyes."

"You mean that."

"I do. In fact, the only point of contention I have with you is that you waited so long to come into my life." God, that felt good to say aloud.

"Thane." Had I said too much? Her tone implied I may have. "There's something I need to tell you."

The world around me froze. I reminded myself I was born a survivor and if her next words were that she didn't want to see me again, I'd be fine. The successful businessman in me cringed at the shit-fest I was if I allowed myself to feel anything. "Say it."

"I want to be with you . . ."

"But?" *And this is why I don't fucking open my heart to anyone . . .*

"I need to know that you'll help me keep my family safe."

What? That wasn't where I'd thought this was going. "Ashlee, did something happen?"

"Not yet, but sometimes I get ideas in my head that sound good at the time, but are risky. I truly believe they're worth the risk because everything important is. But I have Sage now. I can't put my family in danger."

"Help me understand what you're talking about."

"If you and I do this . . . if we move forward with whatever this is . . . do you see any way this could hurt my family?"

"Ashlee, I would never let anything or anyone hurt you or your family. You have my promise on that."

She cleared her throat. "When I told my mother about why you weren't raised with your twin and how you may have been part of an experiment—it scared her. She's afraid being with you will somehow bring those people into our life."

"I won't let that happen."

"Are they dangerous? The people who ran the adoption agency?"

"I don't know, but I can tell you, for their sake I hope they stay hidden. I was raised to never go looking for a fight, but if one comes to me, I don't lose. You're safe, Ashlee."

There was a break in her voice when she said, "I'm sorry. I'm not usually so worried about everything. I don't know what's wrong with me."

I did. Or at least, I had a good guess. "You had a near-death experience. I've heard that can shake a person up."

"How long can I milk that?" she asked with light humor.

"As long as you need to. Don't apologize for who you are, Ashlee. Anyone who tells you they don't have demons they're battling is either lying to you or themselves."

"Thank you." After a pause she said, "I should probably go take a shower. Sage will be up early and I'll need to get her to my sister's. I have a lunch date tomorrow."

"You do?" She was so damn adorable. "Tell me about this man. I need to know if I approve of him."

"Oh, he comes across as arrogant and stuffy at first, but beneath that, he's all heart. I may have mentioned him to you already. He's the one who helped me after my accident. He sat with me, read a story to my daughter, and even brought me the most considerate little gifts while I was in the hospital."

"Arrogant and stuffy?"

She laughed. "Don't tell him I said that. I wouldn't want to hurt his feelings."

"I'll keep your secret as long as you keep mine."

"And that is?"

"I know this guy. He's always had a jaded opinion of relationships, but I suspect that's changing. I've heard a rumor that he hasn't stopped smiling since he met you."

"This guy . . . you don't think he'd make something up like that?"

"No, he's many things, but dishonest is not one of them."

"This is really good news, because I've been called ridiculously picky when it comes to men, but I have a feeling that's because I was waiting for him."

Neither of us said anything for a moment after that.

"Ashlee?"

"Yes?" Her voice was a little strangled.

"I can't wait to see you tomorrow. If it weren't for Sage, I'd be at your door tonight."

"If it weren't for Sage, I'd let you in."

I closed my eyes and told my dick that no matter how excited it became at the thought of it, we weren't headed over there. "I'm not going to sleep well tonight."

"Me neither," she said with a laugh.

"I could help you with that," I offered in a purr.

"It's too late for me to ask Joanie to watch Sage . . ."

"I don't have to be there to make you come, Ashlee. But if you're not ready for that step, just tell me."

The sound of something crashing to the floor was followed by her saying, "*Oh, I'm ready.* I mean, what do you have in mind?"

CHAPTER TWENTY-FIVE

Ashlee

H IS LAUGH WAS deep and so sexy it was impossible to be embarrassed. Not wasting any time, I rushed to my room, locked my door, and put jazz music on in the background. "Should I dim the lights?"

"You want to be on FaceTime?" he asked in a surprised tone.

"God no," I said so emphatically, he laughed again.

"Then set your lighting to whatever makes you comfortable."

I dimmed the lighting then sat on the edge of my bed. In a rush, I asked, "I've never done this before. Am I supposed to still have my clothes on?"

"There are no rules, Ashlee, and there's no rush. I'm fine with us talking all night, but it would also be wonderful to come to the sound of you giving yourself pleasure over and over."

"The second option does sound better." I blushed from head to toe at the enthusiasm I heard in my own voice. The last man I'd been with was the one I'd broken up with because he'd said he could never love someone else's child. Sex with Nate had been good, but not great. Before him, my only experience was with my high school boyfriend, Eric. Although we'd had a lot of sex in the beginning, and it had made me feel close to him, the only reason I'd thought it was good was because I'd had nothing to compare it to. "I'm sorry. Am I killing the mood?"

"Ashlee, I'm in my bedroom. Where are you?"

"Same. Mine, I mean, not yours. Of course not yours." I put a hand over my mouth to stop more from coming out.

"I'm taking off my shirt. Why don't you do the same?"

"Okay," I said, feeling a little silly. I placed the phone on the bed beside me then pulled my shirt up and over my head. I unsnapped my bra and tossed it as well. "Done."

He sucked in a breath. "Good. Now take off the rest. I'm settling on my bed with my cock in my hand."

That was quite an image and it had me shedding the rest of my clothing. "Should I get my—" Unsure if I should have mentioned it, I stopped there.

"Absolutely. What do you have?"

I swallowed hard and headed to the drawer beside my bed to retrieve it. "The bullet type. Small. Quiet. Just enough to keep me from going homicidal."

"I've never quite heard them described that way before, but I approve." His voice deepened. "And I can't wait to use it on you."

Breathing heavily, toy in hand, I crawled beneath the comforter on my bed. "Some men hate them."

"Some men are uneducated, selfish pricks."

He wasn't wrong, and it was a relief to know that wasn't him. "I didn't know if you'd be open to them."

His tone remained serious. "Within reason, I'm open to whatever excites you. Everyone has different kinks and boundaries, but isn't half the fun in the discovery of what they are?"

Kinks? Eyes wide, I said, "You're so—so . . . *honest.* I'm not used to talking about sex."

"Not even with lovers? No discussion?"

"It's been a while, but especially not them."

"What if it's not good?"

"I hope for better the next time?"

"Interesting."

"You?"

"I want it to fucking rock both of our worlds. If it's not amazing, why bother?"

"Why indeed."

"I don't hear the hum of a bullet."

I settled deeper onto the bed, placed it over my clit and turned it on low. "And I don't hear . . . what am I supposed to hear?"

"Just my voice. Place your phone next to your head on the pillow. You're going to help me touch you. Close your eyes."

I did.

"I want you to trace the features of your face—softly. Run a finger along the line of your jaw, over those delicious lips of yours, up your cheek and across your forehead. Each light touch is a kiss from me. Can you feel it? Each little tickle is the caress of my breath across your skin."

The reality of the moment fell away as my imagination filled my senses until I could almost feel his lips brushing over mine. His voice was doing for my brain what the bullet was doing for my sex and the combination was heady.

He commanded my hand to trace my ear, caress my neck, tease its way across my collarbone and down my other arm. Each place I touched felt more alive and primed. When I brushed a finger lightly across the tip of one breast, it was no surprise that my nipple was already puckered with excitement.

When I licked my fingertip then traced a wet circle around that nipple, it was his tongue I felt. When I moved my hand to my other breast as instructed, I imagined the heat of his breath warming my chest.

"Move your hand slowly down your stomach," he said in a tight voice that implied he was bringing himself as much pleasure as he was bringing me. "If I were there I would be kissing my way lower. Can you feel me there? Spread your legs wider for me."

I kicked the comforter off and brought my feet up higher and let my knees drop outward. At the same time, I turned up the bullet.

"If I were there," he growled, "part of me would be inside you. Which part do you want right now? A finger? My tongue? My cock?"

"Oh, your tongue. Yes."

"Then take your finger, Ashlee, and stick it deep inside you. Get it nice and wet. Now trace your pussy the way you traced your face. Imagine me using my tongue, my teeth, my lips. I can't get enough of your taste. Where do you want that tongue? Tell me."

"Right here," I said, letting the bullet fall aside as I began to circle my clit with my finger. I stroked faster and faster over my nub, all the time vividly imagining it was him bringing me that pleasure, until all I could do was moan out his name and beg him to not stop.

"Are you close, Ashlee? Because I am."

"I'm close. So close."

"Then come, Ash. Let yourself go."

A wave of heat rose within me, lifting me with it to a place where nothing mattered beyond the intensity of the rush. I called out, "Yes. Oh, that's it." And came.

He swore and made a guttural sound.

Neither of us said anything for a moment. His heavy breathing echoed my own. I reached over and turned the bullet off.

"Not as good as being there," he murmured, "but I do love the sounds you make when you're excited."

I pulled the comforter back over my body and smiled. "Me too. You know what I mean."

"I do. God, I wish I were there with you. I want you tucked to my side tonight."

"If it weren't for Sage—"

"I know."

"Hey, on a good note, I've resolved the question of if my bits and pieces are fully functioning."

"I'm glad," he said with a chuckle. Then in a serious tone, added, "Either way, we would have figured it out, Ashlee. I would have found a way to make it good for you."

Tears clouded my vision. "You're a good man, Thane Rehoboth."

"Don't build me up into someone I never was, Ashlee. I've been with a fair share of women and most of them would say that although the sex was good, I didn't invest anything beyond that. I was always clear from the beginning, but that doesn't mean I haven't been called a coldhearted bastard more than once."

"So, you've never been serious about anyone?"

"Depends what you consider being serious. I've been monogamous, mostly because it was easier. But I never made promises and they always went home."

"Always? You never let someone sleep over?"

"Once or twice when I was young and drunk. Eventually, I chose clarity over chaos. It's a lot easier to get a woman to understand that things are not progressing anywhere if she doesn't wake up next to you."

"Wow."

"And you? Have you ever been serious about someone?"

"I've only been with two men besides you. Neither one of them ever sent me home, and I was with each for more than a year. They made all kinds of promises, but none that their actions lived up to. I don't wish ill on either of them, nor do I miss them."

"Good, now unless you want to take me in the shower with you, I'll say good night. Don't want you to forget about your date tomorrow."

"Thane?" I didn't want the night to end, not yet.

"Yes?"

"If I take a quick shower, will you talk to me until I fall asleep? I'm a little nervous about tomorrow and . . . is it weird that you're both what I'm nervous about as well as who I know can calm me?"

"No, that's actually beautiful. Go take a shower, Ashlee. Then call me."

CHAPTER TWENTY-SIX

Ashlee

THANE HAD OFFERED to pick me up from my house, but since I needed to drop Sage off at Joanie's, it was easier to meet him at the diner that was practically a landmark in my town. Anyone passing through might have driven right past it. It was tucked between a smoke shop and a liquor store on a main street that had lost its luster generations ago.

As I parked on the street, a herd of loud teenagers exited the diner and I smiled. *Some things never change.* Back in college, I'd tried to introduce some of my classmates to this hometown gem. They'd been far from impressed. If I remembered correctly, they'd labeled the whole downtown a "double-check that you locked your car" area.

That wasn't at all how I saw my hometown. It was difficult to be friends with people who couldn't see past the worn exterior of the buildings—or the limited income of the people who frequented them. A pang of guilt hit me as I realized that whether I'd planned it consciously or subconsciously, bringing Thane there was a test.

My family wasn't fancy. In fact, when Joanie and I had been young and money had been tight for my parents, coming downtown for wieners had been a treat. Even Sage knew the place well, because taking her and her cousins there once a month was how Joanie and I were continuing that tradition. Realistically, how well could Thane's life and mine mesh? I was falling hard and fast for him, but that didn't mean I wasn't worried about our differences.

Thane parked and stepped onto the sidewalk. I froze as I took in how his jeans clung to his muscular thighs. The black T-shirt he'd chosen wasn't tight fitting, but it accentuated his wide shoulders and strong arms. He could easily have appeared in an ad for a gym . . . or anything, really. I doubted there was a woman under the age of dead who wouldn't buy whatever he was selling.

The fact that his high-priced car appeared out of place behind my modest one ceased to matter when I met him on the sidewalk and he shot me the sexiest smile just before pulling me in for a kiss. I threw my arms around his neck and melted into the bliss of his embrace.

The scent and feel of him enveloped me. Memories from the night before did, as well. He dug his hands into my hair and I writhed against him, moving back and forth over the hard evidence of his arousal. Sure, we were different, but he'd have to be another species for me to not want to give in to how he made me feel.

Lordy.

When he raised his head and smiled down at me, all I could do was let out a sigh of pleasure. *Why did I think lunch was a good idea? Would it be wrong to ask him how far he lives from here and suggest we go there instead?*

His voice was husky when he said, "After last night—"

"Yes?" I murmured. *Is he thinking what I'm thinking?*

"I'm looking forward to trying a wiener. It's good for me to expand my palate."

I blinked a few times. He sounded sincere and not at all judgmental of the backdrop to our date. "This is one of my favorite places. My parents used to take Joanie and me when we were little. We still come here with the kids."

He held my gaze. "I see. Ashlee Pryer, you are as bad as I am when it comes to testing people, aren't you?"

I wasn't proud of my motivation for bringing him there, but I couldn't look away, nor could I lie. "It does appear that way."

He smiled. "Good. It's a relief to know you don't have it all worked out."

His callback to our earlier conversation removed the awkwardness from the moment. "I'm not a sophisticated person, Thane. I not only don't own diamonds, but I also don't care much for jewelry. Brand names don't impress me. I've never cared much about what other people think of me. You need to know that up front."

He nodded slowly and sarcastically replied, "You're right. I definitely wouldn't want to be with a woman who isn't

281

with me for my money."

I playfully pushed on his chest. "I'm serious."

"So am I." He caught my hand and held it to him. "I'm not offended at all that you're asking logistical questions about us. It's smart. I approach major decisions the same way. I need to understand the variables first before moving forward." The question those words birthed in me must have shown in my eyes, because he added, "As far as we're concerned, I'm already onto the *how* part."

"How?"

"How do I get you into my bed? How do I keep you there? How sick will this wiener make me and will it postpone how I'd like to spend the second half of this date?"

"Second half?" My cheeks flushed and warmth spread through me. "Oh."

"If there's time. I know you need to get back."

I flicked my tongue across my bottom lip and swallowed hard. "As long as we don't linger too long here . . ."

"Understood." He linked his hand with mine and gave me a tug toward the diner. "No lingering." He threw open the glass door and motioned for me to enter hastily. We were both laughing as he closed the door behind us.

"Ah, Ashlee," a generously tattooed mountain of a man in a white tank top and red apron said from behind a steaming grill. "It's about time you brought a man around again."

"Monny, this is Thane. Be nice. Thane, Monny can be a

ballbuster, but he's harmless."

As they shook hands, Monny said, "If I make you cry, I'll give you extra ketchup for your fries."

Not appearing at all intimidated, Thane asked, "Is this where we arm wrestle for condiments?"

Monny flexed like a body builder would on stage. Although he was a good thirty years older than Thane, he had an impressive build. Without missing a beat, Thane mirrored him. They looked at each other for a moment, then burst out laughing, which was a good thing, because I couldn't contain my own amusement. "Really?" I asked with an eye roll.

With a shrug, Monny said, "You always were a tough one to impress, Ashlee." To Thane, he added, "Be good to her. She's the kind you'll spend the rest of your life thinking about if you mess it up."

Thane placed his hand on my lower back. "I will be and I don't doubt that at all."

Seemingly satisfied, Monny turned his attention back to me. "Your usual?"

"Yes, please," I said.

"And you?" he asked Thane.

Thane looked from me to the menu and shrugged. "The same, I suppose."

"You got it." Monny began placing sliced buns on the grill, then a matching number of wieners. After removing the buns from the grill he placed them on paper towels briefly then began to stack them on his forearm.

"Right on the arm? No gloves or anything. Okay, then," Thane murmured.

I shot him a look that he responded to with a nod. That he hadn't turned on his heel and left was impressive, considering what he'd shared about how he'd been raised. I doubted he'd experienced Monny's style of service. In a hushed tone, I said, "You're going to love it. I wouldn't have brought you here if these weren't the best wieners on the East Coast."

"I'm open to trying new things," Thane assured me even though his eyes widened when Monny expertly popped the wieners on the buns, then slapped a thick meat sauce, his special seasoning, mustard and a generous amount of diced onions on each. "That's a lot of onion."

"I know," I said as my mouth began to water. "Monny makes them exactly the way I love them. The sauce recipe was his father's. Right Monny?"

"It sure was," Monny said. "Is this for here or to go?"

I exchanged a look with Thane. In unison we said, "To go."

He packaged the wieners in pairs, put them in a brown paper bag then poured an unhealthy number of French fries on top. As if reading Thane's mind, Monny said, "I used to put a little cup in there, but it always overflows anyway. Besides, if you tear the bag correctly it doubles as a plate."

"Practical. I like it," Thane said. I couldn't tell if he was being sarcastic or not and I respected that.

I thumbed toward a hallway on the other side of the diner. "Monny, I'd like to show Thane around if that's okay."

"Go. Stay. You know you're always welcome. Grab your own drinks while you're back there."

I reached for my wallet to pay and realized Thane was doing the same thing. The decision of which of us would pay was resolved when Monny said, "This time it's on me."

"You don't have to do that, Monny," I said quickly.

"Put your money away. You know no one wins an argument with me," Monny said, his chest puffing.

I linked hands with Thane. "It's true, no one messes with Monny. This is where kids in school would come when someone was picking on them. No matter what was happening out there, everyone knew if they came here, they'd be safe. Monny doesn't talk about it, but he's probably saved more people from danger than the police. Monny, do you remember that woman who was on the run from the guy she'd dated and he tracked her down here?"

"I taught him a thing or two about respect," Monny said.

Thane's hand tightened on mine and a quick look at his expression revealed he was moved by the story. "Sounds like that woman chose the right place to hide."

"He threatened her in front of the wrong person. You don't hurt women or children. It's that simple. When I began to explain that to him with my fists, he took out his phone and tried to film me, so I smashed that too."

I couldn't help but add, "Then he threatened to return with the police."

Monny nodded. "Damn fool. Word travels fast in a town like this. No one was going to help someone like him. He's lucky he didn't end up in my meat sauce."

Thane's eyebrows rose.

I leaned against him and chuckled. "He's joking."

After nodding, Thane said, "How about that tour you were going to give me?"

"Oh, yes." I retrieved the bag from Monny, then leaned over the counter and gave Monny a kiss on the cheek. "Thank you."

Thane shook his hand again. "I can see why this is one of Ashlee's favorite places."

Monny flashed a toothy smile. "You're welcome back any time. I could even put your photo on the wall. Not every day we get a big, fancy space station designer guy in here."

Thane looked toward him in surprise.

Monny cackled. "What? You think I don't watch the news? I got a TV right there and your face has been all over it for months."

"I didn't design the station," Thane said with more humility than I would have expected from someone in his situation. "I'm just the lucky HVAC guy who was asked to determine how they'll breathe up there."

"I like that," Monny said. "You plan on moving there

when it's finished?"

"No thanks," Thane said without hesitation. "I prefer to keep my feet firmly planted on the ground."

"You think that station needs a diner?"

"I have no idea," Thane answered seriously. "I'll ask and get back to you." Then he added, "If these don't make me sick later."

"I can't guarantee that," Monny said with a laugh. "That's a lot of onions."

I took advantage of the break in conversation to lead Thane away. A short hallway led to a room of old-fashioned, shiny booths. "Every table has its own jukebox and they still work. The music is a little outdated, but Sage loves putting quarters in and choosing songs." Past the tables, I stopped beside an animatronic Santa that was almost as tall as Thane, then pointed to a bouquet of Easter eggs on sticks next to a leprechaun holding a pot of gold. "Monny loves the holidays, but hates decorating so he leaves all of it out year-round. Most of the things in here move and make noise if you press a button on them. Do you see the track on the ceiling? There's even a train that makes a loop around the room for a nickel. If you come here right after school every single booth will be full of teenagers. Come back at two a.m. and you'll find it full again with everyone sobering up after the bars close. It's an eclectic, chaotic place where people come to feel safe and accepted. Monny's philosophy has always been 'Start no trouble, take no shit.' I've seen him stand up to drug dealers, pimps, and even one loud-mouthed real estate developer. He would give his life to protect a stranger, and because of that he'll always have my business."

Thane tucked me to him and kissed the side of my head. "Just when I think I know you, and I couldn't like you more, you reveal another side of yourself, and I fall for you all over again."

I hugged him, fighting back a wave of emotion, then smiled. "Monny won you over too?"

"As long as the part about putting people in his meat sauce is a joke—yes."

"Eww, of course that was a joke." Just to tease Thane, I made a face. "Either way, it's a good meat sauce."

"What does it say about me that I'm less concerned with that and more about how much time we have before you need to pick up Sage?"

"How far away do you live?"

"There are at least ten hotels between here and my place, but I'll go wherever you want to."

I did want to see where he lived, but decided I'd rather spend more time in his arms than on the road. "How far is the nearest hotel?"

CHAPTER TWENTY-SEVEN

Ashlee

"THE DOOR," I said breathlessly as he slammed me up against the wall just inside the nearest hotel room we were able to find. My body was on fire for his. His mouth was hot and demanding on mine. I hated every layer of clothing between us.

He stepped back, whipped his shirt up and over his shoulders, and I sucked in a breath. A sprinkle of dark hair covered his muscular chest, leading downward, disappearing beneath the edge of his jeans. I couldn't get my own shirt off fast enough.

Between kisses we both kicked off our shoes and shed the rest of our clothing. The sexual tension was raw and all consuming. I could barely breathe as I stood there before him, waiting and yearning, fighting a need stronger than I'd ever felt.

"You're so damn beautiful," he growled.

"So are you," I whispered, allowing my gaze to stray to his large cock before blushing and locking my eyes on his again. "All of you. Not just . . ."

He traced one of my cheeks gently. "You're welcome to compliment any part of me you'd like. He actually likes the attention."

I laughed at that. "He? You say that like he's not part of you."

"Oh, he's definitely part of me." Leaning closer, he licked my bottom lip then asked, "Why are we talking?"

My hand possessively closed around his erect cock. "I have no idea." He filled my hand and I began to pump up and down while he claimed my mouth again, running his hands over my breasts, my hips, my ass. As his excitement grew, so did his girth. He was so big.

He fucked my mouth completely with his tongue, then moved on to my neck. Thane did nothing halfway. He took his time, explored behind my ear, along my collarbone and everywhere in between until he found the spot that drove me wild.

Oh, he's good.

Then he moved lower. His attention to detail was excruciatingly pleasurable. Before him I would have said my breasts were not that sensitive, but he was gifted with a tongue the devil must have lent him. And his teeth? They needed to be registered as deadly weapons because I was positive I'd die from the pleasure he brought with them as he nipped, tugged, and nibbled his way down my body.

I wasn't a small woman, but he lifted me as if I were. I

wrapped my legs around his waist and my arms around his neck as he carried me to the bed. I tensed, expecting to be tossed, but he laid me down gently as if I were precious and fragile.

There was no room for embarrassment as he stood beside the bed, devouring me with his gaze. "Open yourself for me," he ordered. "I want to see you."

I shifted on the bed so my sex was facing him and parted my legs slightly. He reached forward, hooked his hands behind my knees and hauled me closer to the edge of the bed, and planted my feet far apart on the edge of it. I met his gaze between my bent knees.

He slipped a finger inside me and rolled it. My breath caught in my throat and I gripped the bedding on either side of me. His thumb settled on my clit and began to move back and forth over it. I clenched around him. He thrust a second, longer finger inside me and moved it rhythmically deeper and deeper until I gasped and bucked against his hand.

"Oh, God, that's good."

Kissing his way from my ankles to my inner thighs, he sank to his knees and blew on my throbbing nub. Parting me with his fingers, he used that talented tongue of his to thrust into me. In and out. Dashing over, now and then, to tease my clit in an unbearably erotic dance that had me mindlessly begging him not to stop. A cascade of fire rolled through me, but it wasn't enough. I wanted more of him . . . more of this.

He held up a hand and my devastation was deep when

he walked out of the room, but in a heartbeat he was back—this time with a condom that he rolled onto his thick cock. Taking me by the hips, he raised my ass off the bed and drove that huge dick of his deep into me.

I called out his name. My sex stretched to accommodate his size and for a moment I thought he might be too much for me. Pleasure quickly replaced discomfort and I knew no man would ever be enough after him.

His hands tightened on my hips, holding me in place as he pounded into me. There was no reprieve, this was a claiming and I was down for it. I gripped my legs around his back, moving to meet him, thrust for thrust. I was rising . . . rising . . . so close . . .

When he withdrew I nearly wept.

"Get on your knees," he growled.

I scrambled to flip over onto my knees before him, offering myself to him wantonly. His first thrust sent me onto my elbows and tossed my hair up over my head. "Harder," I whispered.

"What?" he asked. "Don't be shy, Ashlee."

"Fuck me harder," I said between pants. "I love it."

He didn't need to hear that twice. Thrust after powerful thrust, he pounded into me. A second orgasm rose within me. I rode out a confusing burst of pleasure and tears while he continued to take his own pleasure. He reached forward, buried a hand in my hair, arching me before him as he continued to fuck me.

When he pulled out again, I was still dazed from my climax but more than willing for whatever he wanted. I spun to face him and in response to his prompting I climbed on him, poising my wet sex above the tip of him.

He took two steps toward the wall, slammed me against it, and thrust inside me again. Oh, God, there was no way I could orgasm again, could I? I'd always been happy enough to get one release, but when he took one of my breasts into his mouth while pounding into me, I discovered I was capable of so much more than I'd thought. He teased me right back to the very edge of losing it, then drove me right back into bliss with one powerful thrust after another.

He came with a growl and a swear, then stood there, holding me as we both fought to breathe normally again. Slowly, he lowered me to my feet. He stepped away to dispose of his condom, then was back, kissing me gently.

When he raised his head, I snuggled into his chest. "I'd lay down with you, but I'm afraid I'll fall asleep and I can't stay."

"Then we'll just have to stand here for a while," he said, holding me closer. "Because I'm in no rush to let you go."

Understanding that feeling, I smiled and kissed his neck. "I have a little time. I just respect that Joanie has had Sage a lot recently."

"We'll make it up to her."

My heart melted at that. Thane wasn't the kind of person to say anything he didn't mean. Who would have thought I could find the man of my dreams by confusing him with his twin and chasing him around a parking lot?

Another thought occurred to me. "Hey, Thane?"

"Mm-hmm?" he murmured into my hair.

"I dropped the bag of wieners near the door. You should try one while they're still warm."

He groaned. "Woman, you're heartless, but for you, I suppose I'll risk heartburn and whatever bacterial infection a person can get from an old man's sweat."

I laughed, bouncing my chest lightly against his. "I've been eating there since I was a child and I'm fine."

"You are." His hand slid up between us to cup one of my breasts. "But just remember, if you kill me off, I can't ask you to marry me."

I nearly swooned at that. Marry him? He really was serious about me. That confidence allowed me to answer with a joke, "I'm willing to risk it. Man up, get your ass over there and get our lunch."

"Yes, ma'am." He raised his head, locked eyes with me. "Should I give you my insurance card now or after you call the ambulance?"

I put my hands on my hips and pointed toward the bag near the door.

"One last kiss in case it's my last."

That made me laugh. He was chuckling when he returned to my side with the paper bag. I put a towel out on the bed and motioned for him to put the bag on top of it.

When I tore the bag open so it lay flat on the towel, Thane joked, "Look at that, just like fine china."

I sat on the bed, unwrapped one of the wieners, and held it up. He crawled onto the bed next to me, placed his hand around mine, and took a bite of the wiener while I was still holding it.

He sat back and chewed.

I waited.

"It's not bad," he said.

A smile spread across my face. "Really?"

He picked up the second wiener and looked it over. "Maybe too many onions, but overall, pretty good."

"I love extra onions. Monny says it's better without them. Try it that way."

He pushed some of the onions off and took another bite. "Okay, I see the appeal of it."

I took a big bite of the one I was still holding, savoring it, onions and all. "To me it tastes like childhood and good memories."

He took another bite of his, chewed it well, and said, "I could get used to it, as long as I never find a fingernail in it."

I spit out a bite of my wiener at that and burst out laughing. "You're an ass."

"But I'm not wrong." He started laughing as well and that was the moment I knew we belonged together. The connection I'd felt the first time I'd looked into his eyes was still there, stronger than ever. Something that intense had to be what happily-ever-afters were made of.

I took the rest of his wiener away from him. "I do want you to live."

"Too late," he said with a somber expression and collapsed onto his back, making a dramatic throes-of-death groan.

We laughed.

Hugged.

And parted much earlier than either of us wanted to.

CHAPTER TWENTY-EIGHT

Thane

THE NEXT MORNING I found no joy in waking in my bed alone, eating the breakfast my housekeeper had prepared for me, or starting my day with a solitary swim. Before Ashlee, the quiet had been comfortable.

Now it feels empty.

I called her as I dressed for work. "Morning, sunshine."

"Hey," she said quickly. "I can talk as long as you don't mind that I need to get Sage ready while I do."

"Who's that, Mommy?" Sage asked in the background.

"It's my friend, Thane. Do you remember him from the hospital?"

"Oh, yes," Sage said, "I love Freddy."

"Freddy?" I asked.

Ashlee chuckled. "The stuffed frog you gave her."

"Oh, Freddy. I'm glad she likes him."

When Ashlee told her daughter what I'd said, Sage responded, "I don't like Freddy, I love him. If he turns into a prince, I may marry him. Unless he's not a nice prince. No one needs a mean prince. And I don't know if I want to be a princess anyway. They always have to wear dresses, and I like to ride my bike and play in the sandbox."

Somehow Ashlee had made a child who was as adorable as she was. "I have a feeling your little girl is going to run her own country when she's older."

Sounding pleased with that, Ashlee said, "I do want her to know that anything is possible if she works hard enough for it. Sage, do you know what Thane is working on? A space station so people can live up in the sky."

"Freddy doesn't want to talk about that right now," Sage said. "He lost my backpack."

"Wow," I said. "Tough crowd."

"Kids will humble you," Ashlee assured me. "Sage, where did Freddy last see your backpack?"

"Maybe in my toybox?"

"Why don't you and Freddy go look for it while I make your breakfast?"

As Ashlee fielded Sage's requests that she should look instead, I walked into my living room and imagined the two of them in my apartment. My place was immaculate. Outside of a few photos, most of the décor hadn't been moved in years. My living room looked staged for a photo shoot for a modern lifestyle magazine. As it was, my apartment wouldn't be welcoming to a child, but was that the way I wanted to live?

I thought back to what my father's house had been like

when Jesse and I had lived there. My father had strict standards for how his children would behave in public, but when we were in our own home we'd made forts out of blankets, wrestled, fought, played hide-and-seek in the many bedrooms and only been chastised when we'd gotten truly unruly.

One of Ashlee's concerns was that the man she chose to be with would need to be capable of loving her child as well. Of all the things I needed to think through, that wasn't a concern. There was room in my life and my heart for a little chaos.

"Sorry," Ashlee said. "Mornings are always a little crazy here. Joanie says one should be easier, but I'm not sure that's true. Sometimes I wish . . ."

"What do you wish?"

"That Sage had a sister too. I know it's not possible, but I can't imagine my life without Joanie. Sage has her cousins, but there's something special about sisters."

"I wouldn't know about that last part, but nothing is impossible, Ashlee. Remember that. There's always a way."

She cleared her throat. "Are you saying . . . would you want . . . what are you saying?"

What *was* I saying? I had to stop and ask myself that question before answering. "This is a journey for me, Ashlee. I'm not going to lie and say I thought about much of this before I met you, so I'm still working through some of it. What I do know is that I want to be with you and that you come as a package deal, so when I say that, I'm including Sage. We should probably start there before we ask ourselves if we'd want to add more, but I would be open to looking into options for expansion. If there's something I've always known, it's that family comes to us in many ways."

She let out a shaky breath. "Do you think it's too early for us to be talking like this?"

"I'm a planner. I visualize then make things happen, so for me, no." Her silence was unsettling. "Ashlee, is it too early for you?"

"I guess not. You're right. It's important to talk about these things up front. I've read articles about couples who wait too long to have these conversations."

When she didn't appear to want to say more on the subject, I let it drop. Sage returned and was chatting away in the background as she ate her breakfast. "Today's your first day back at work," I said.

"It is."

"How long are you allowed for lunch?"

"Since I work for my parents, they're pretty flexible, but I'd say an hour at the most."

"Would you like to have lunch with me? My choice of place this time."

Her voice lowered. "Lunch? Or lunch lunch?"

"Mommy, what is lunch lunch?" Sage asked.

"Don't worry about it, Sage," Ashlee said quickly.

"I'm not sure." I chuckled. "How about today I feed you

something nice to celebrate your first day back at work? Then tomorrow or the next day, we can have the kind of meal we had yesterday . . . minus the wieners."

"I'd love . . . all of that. Where is your office? Will the drive be long with all the traffic?"

"Let me worry about that part." We weren't yet ready for what she'd coined my sex-mobile, but I could see that in our future.

Sage said, "Mommy, Freddy is done with breakfast."

"Did Freddy find your backpack?"

"Yup. Right here," Sage said with pride.

To me, Ashlee said, "I have to go, Thane. I usually take my break at noon if that works for you."

"I'll be there."

"Bye, Thane!" Sage said in the background right before Ashlee ended the call.

I smiled as I dropped my phone into a pocket in my jacket. Talking to Ashlee always puts me in a good mood. She was right about the drive, though. With traffic, her job was about forty minutes from my office. I'd need to find a solution to that issue, but thankfully I was in a position to do that easily.

My morning took a quick downward turn when Bellerwood summoned me to his office for an unplanned meeting. I could have refused to go, but he was taking steps to move the project forward and I didn't want to derail that. After a tense back and forth about the timetable for launching segments of the space station, we settled on a schedule that worked for both of us. Normally, I would have left then, but I thought about what my father had said about Bellerwood being family now. One consequence of what was likely an undiagnosed condition that kept him mostly trapped in his thoughts, Bellerwood was a difficult man to feel any attachment to. Monica had shared with me the struggle it still was for her to connect with him at times.

"Walt," I said, "would you like to come to dinner at my father's this week? We're planning on Thursday evening."

He'd frowned and said, "If Monica wants to dine with me, she'll invite me."

"She loves you," I said, knowing how that one word always caught his attention. "And family doesn't require an invite. I would enjoy having you there as well."

For the first time in all of our exchanges, he seemed not only present, but emotional. "My wife used to say, '*Family doesn't wait for an invitation.*'" He'd looked me right in the eye and said, "I'm sorry about your twin. I looked into him more. I wish I had good news for you, but he's nothing like you or Scott. I wouldn't contact him."

"I know, not until the space station is finished."

He shook his head. "I wouldn't ever contact him. He's a very troubled man. You don't want that in your life. Especially if you're thinking about raising his child as yours."

I inhaled sharply. Bellerwood was nothing if not blunt. "He has no attachment to either of them. He and Ashlee have never even met."

"In my experience, the most dangerous people are the ones who have nothing left to lose. Do you think your twin will be able to be happy for you when he hears that you had a good childhood, never wanted for anything, are now well respected and wealthy while he is living the opposite experience? Then tell him that you'll also be raising his child . . . leaving him without even that . . . and see if he doesn't try to end you in your sleep."

"Wow, that went dark fast." I pocketed my hands. "I was intent on tracking him down in the beginning, but that's on hold for now. If he is as miserable as it appears he may be, I do want to help him. You're correct, though; it's something that will need to be done in a way that leaves him feeling better about himself rather than worse."

"I don't see that happening."

"I do because it's what I would want someone to do for me if our situations were reversed."

He nodded. "I'll be there on Thursday."

"Great. I'll tell everyone."

He called my name when I turned to leave.

I glanced back.

He said, "Jesse believes I'm moving forward with the project without the bean fuel because he threatened me. I'm actually doing it because you didn't. There aren't many people I trust, Thane, but I've watched how you navigate people and problems. You keep your brother in check and your business thriving. With or without a new fuel source, this station will succeed because people like you won't allow it to fail. I hope your twin doesn't turn homicidal when he hears about you."

"Me too." *Me too.*

CHAPTER TWENTY-NINE

Ashlee

ONE PERK OF working for my family was instantly apparent as soon as I was back at my desk in the office of the truck wash and looking through my emails. Everything that had been urgent had been professionally handled and the work waiting for me was well organized.

I would have been much more productive had my thoughts been in such good order. My body still did a head-to-toe flush every time a steamy memory from the day before flitted through my thoughts.

Three orgasms? Was that from me bottling them up for years or due to his talented appendages? It was a question that had me indulging in X-rated fantasies as well as looking forward to some in-person theory testing.

My mother stopped by my desk often enough to catch me being less than my usual attentive self. She asked me if I had a headache or was tired. She reminded me to take it easy until I was fully myself again.

"I'm fine, Mom," I assured her.

She pulled up a chair next to mine, saw how little I'd accomplished, and said, "You seem distracted. Is there something you want to talk about?"

I took a deep breath before answering. She'd essentially asked me to stop seeing Thane. It didn't feel like a good time to tell her I'd not only slept with him but that things were quickly progressing between us. "Thane is taking me out for lunch," I said, keeping my eyes glued to my keyboard.

"Oh."

Had she confronted me about it, I might have gotten defensive and said something, but that gentle expression of disappointment cut deep enough that I didn't know what to say. I couldn't regret meeting Thane, even if she assumed nothing good would come from it.

My mother touched my arm. "So, you're still seeing him."

I pressed my lips together before saying, "Yes."

"Does Joanie know?"

Anywhere but there was where I wished I could be. "Yes."

Her hand dropped away. "I still think it's a mistake."

"I know you do."

"There's nothing I can say that would change your mind, is there?"

Fiddling with a pencil, I answered, "Probably not. I really care about him, Mom. I know it's early, but I think he's the one."

"The one?" her voice rose an octave. "Oh, hon, men like him—"

"Don't say it. You don't know him. If you want to get to know him, I'll bring him around. If you don't, I'd appreciate if you allow me to decide for myself what kind of man he is or isn't."

"Of course." My mother stood and I instantly regretted how I'd spoken to her. She was all heart and if she had a fault at all, it was that her feelings were easy to hurt because she cared so much.

"Mom."

She raised a hand. "No, you're right. You're a grown woman. It's not my place to tell you who you should or shouldn't be with."

My eyes locked with hers and I pleaded, "All I'm asking is that you give him a chance. That's it. We talked about his twin and he said he'd never let anything happen to any of us. I believe him."

She clearly didn't, but she didn't say it.

I asked, "How much did you tell Dad?"

"What could I tell him? Your father is like you . . . if he sees a problem he can't help but jump in. You may be willing to put our family in danger, but I won't help you do it." She turned and began to walk away.

"Mom—"

For the first time in my life my mother ignored my call and closed a door between us. Tears filled my eyes and I almost ran after her, but stopped myself. I couldn't make the promise she wanted me to.

Was she right? Everything in me said no, but that didn't change how guilty I felt. She and my father had always made Joanie and me their priority. Didn't I owe them the same?

But at what cost?

Thane wasn't just some man I'd met and hooked up with. I couldn't simply replace him by choosing someone off a dating app. I could imagine growing old with Thane.

I love him.

He talked like he felt the same for me. Would a man discuss the future and raising kids with someone he didn't love?

Thane had to love me. I couldn't be as certain as I was about him and be wrong about that.

Mom just needs time to get to know Thane.

I'd talked myself into a better frame of mind until noon came and went without Thane showing up. Twelve fifteen. He might be stuck in traffic. Twelve thirty. No call. No text.

I pushed back the negative thoughts that began to circle.

He'd be there. Thane didn't say anything he didn't mean. All I had to do was have a little faith and things would work out.

CHAPTER THIRTY

Thane

I'D ARRIVED AT the Pryer's Truck Wash a few minutes before noon and was about to text Ashlee when her father stepped out of the building and motioned for me to join him. "Mr. Pryer," I said in greeting.

He looked me over then shook my hand and said, "It's Kit. We're not real formal around here."

"It's nice to see you again."

He made a sound deep in his chest. "What are you doing here?"

"I'm taking Ashlee out to lunch."

His eyes narrowed. "I don't know what to think of you, Thane. You've been very kind to my daughter and to my family, but I'd like to know why my wife tenses whenever I bring your name up."

What could I say to that? "That sounds like a question you'd have to ask her."

He pinned me with a look. "I have no patience for liars, so choose your next words with care. How long have you been dating my daughter?"

"We met the night of her accident."

His eyebrows shot up. "Explain to me then why you paid for her medical bills, why you sat at her bedside. I'm all ears. Speak."

Had Kit been anyone but Ashlee's father, I might have told him it was none of his business, but I understood that his demand stemmed from his concern for her. "If you don't know any of the story, it's a long one."

"I'm not going anywhere."

Understood. I started from the beginning, making sure to paint Ashlee's appearance at my job site in the best light I could. I explained how she'd felt Sage needed something from her father and how she'd confused me with my twin . . . the one I hadn't known really existed. None of the story would have made sense had I left off the part where Zachary and I were separated before adoption. I ended by simply saying that Ashlee and I were dating and that things appeared to be getting serious.

Eyes narrowed, he said, "You're either the most prolific bullshitter I've ever met or the world is even more messed up than I thought."

I raised and lowered a shoulder. "Everything I've said is true."

"Diane didn't tell me any of this."

"It is a crazy story that doesn't necessarily paint my family in the best light. She may have wanted you to get to know me before tainting your opinion of me."

"How would it make you look bad that you were a victim of some sick bastard's experiment?"

"Ashlee said your wife is concerned that the man who founded the agency or someone who was involved in it might become dangerous if their secrets are uncovered."

"Are you digging up their crimes?"

"Not at this time."

"I wouldn't judge you if you were."

"I'm sure I will look into it in the future, but right now there's too much going on for me to put energy into it. And, even later, before I'd go looking for some old kook, I'd focus on helping my twin. He wasn't placed as well as I was, and I hear he's struggling."

"Okay," Kit said before giving me a clap on the back. "I believe you. Just be good to my daughter." His hand gripped my shoulder tightly. "Because if you're not, you won't be alive to help that twin of yours." He dropped his hand and shot me a smile that was more of a baring of teeth.

I smiled back awkwardly. *Good talk.* "Where can I find Ashlee?"

"Her office is—" He looked down at his phone. "I have to take this. Go in the main door and ask for her."

"Will do."

As he strode off, I let out a breath. Despite the threat, I liked Kit. He was a straight shooter and fair. That he was also protective of his daughter only made me respect him more.

"Thane," a male voice said from the parking lot.

I recognized the man from one of the photos I'd seen at Ashlee's house. "Mike."

"Joanie said you'd be here. Have a minute?"

I glanced down at my watch and realized I was late. "I really should—"

"Good." He stopped only when he was nose-to-nose with me. "You and I need to talk."

"Sure."

"I didn't grow up with a sister . . ."

Here we go.

Mike continued, "But I love Ashlee like she's one. I need to know what your intentions are with her. She's not the kind who dates one man after the next. She's looking for a husband."

"I know."

"I'm a nice guy. I don't go looking for trouble. I don't even get speeding tickets. But I'd risk jail time if anyone ever hurt my family. I say risk, because I've got a lot of friends who are skilled when it comes to disposing of bodies."

"Please don't say they put them in meat sauces."

"What the fuck? No. That's sick. All I'm saying is you fuck around with Ashlee, and you'll find out that no amount of money is enough protection."

"I'm almost certain I'll be proposing to her within a month."

"A month?" Mike's face transformed with a smile. "No shit. Really? I heard things were going well."

I threw up my hands in confusion. "Then why the death threat?"

His smile was wide and friendly. "Ashlee gave me this talk on my wedding day. All I'm doing is paying it forward."

That piqued my interest. "Ashlee threatened you?"

He laughed. "She sure did. You mess with one of those sisters, you earn yourself the wrath of both." His expression turned more serious. "I love that about them." His gaze locked with mine. "All joking aside, don't join this family if you're not willing to be that level of loyal. Joanie told me about the situation with you and your twin. It sounds like a plot for a thriller movie. I don't know if the people who did that to you are as dangerous as they are mentally fucked up, but don't bring them to Ashlee's door. The Pryers are good people. They don't need that kind of shit."

"I agree."

"And don't talk too much about it. Joanie's already half-convinced we should look into the adoption agency to make sure they haven't done this to other children."

"Assure her that if they have, they will be brought to justice for it. It's a complicated situation that needs to be addressed methodically—in a systematic manner."

"I know what methodically means." Mike sighed. "I'll tell Joanie what you said and you can do whatever you want with my advice, but I wouldn't talk much about that twin of yours. I don't like to get involved in other people's business, but even I want to check in on him to make sure he's okay."

I did as well, but I'd promised Ashlee that I'd keep her safe, and promised Jesse that I'd wait before contacting Zachary. I would seek him out and help him, just not until Crystal had her baby and I had more information about Zachary, the agency, and anything that might put Ashely or her family at risk.

My phone buzzed with a message from Ashley. **Are you still coming?**

Yes. Already here. Still in parking lot. It sounded lame, but better than passing the blame to her father and brother-in-law.

Awesome. I'll be right out.

To Mike, I said, "That was Ashlee. She's coming out."

Mike winked. "Quick, look afraid of me."

He correctly interpreted the look I gave him.

His smile widened. "Or don't. Your choice, but then I'll only have to do this again for effect. I can't let Ashlee go around thinking I would do less for her than she did for Joanie. Pick a side. Are you one of us or not?"

"Right." Out of the corner of my eye I caught Ashlee heading toward us. I had zero fear of the man before me, but if he was family to Ashlee, he would end up as family to me as well. I considered how I would respond to him if I actually was intimidated. Standing taller, I growled, "You can threaten to do all of that and worse, but there's nothing that will stop me from taking Ashlee to lunch today. She's not just important to me, she *mine*."

Laughter sparked in Mike's eyes, before he leaned closer and mock snarled back, "Be good to her, Thane, or forever watch your back."

We stared each other down, doing our best to look serious as Ashlee approached. She put a hand on my arm. "Everything okay?"

I didn't look away from Mike. Between gritted teeth, I said, "For now."

Mike was the first to break our standoff. The smile he shot Ashlee was lopsided and almost goofy enough to out us. "Thane and I are good. We just needed to come to an understanding." He looked at his watch. "I should get back to work. Don't forget what I said, Thane."

I nodded once and kept my expression composed as he walked away.

"I'm sorry about that," Ashlee said in a rush. "My family can be a little overprotective."

"It's okay. I respect them more for it." As soon as our eyes met the little game I was playing fell away. Never before had I been so certain I was where I was meant to be. She and I belonged together. "I know that things are complicated right now, but we'll figure it all out. I promise you that."

She stepped closer and when her body came to rest fully against mine, I wrapped my arms around her and expressed everything I was feeling with a kiss that lasted longer than any parking lot kiss should. It was more than a dance, more than a caress—sexual tension, intense emotions, and frustration. She clung to me, the fervor of her response matching mine.

When I finally raised my head, we were both panting. I rested my forehead on hers and closed my eyes. Although I'd said it partially as part of the game with Mike, it hit me that I had meant it when I'd announced that she was mine.

Straightening, I met her gaze and asked, "Ready for lunch?"

Her smile started in her eyes. "Lunch or lunch lunch?"

That's all it took for me to forget where I'd made reservations. "I'm open to both. We could also have something delivered."

Cupping my face with both hands, she said, "My house is empty and less than a mile away."

CHAPTER THIRTY-ONE

Ashlee

TWO WEEKS LATER, dressed only in one of Thane's shirts, sated from a tantalizing romp that had started on the table and ended on the floor, I used chopsticks to feed him a noodle from a takeout box. Bare chested, but in boxer shorts, he offered me a bite of his sushi. There was a rightness to being together and weekday lunch breaks at my house had become our intimate escape.

We also went on "real" dates. On a few evenings, Mike and Joanie had watched Sage so we could go out. Thane surprised me with an extravagant dinner on a yacht one night. He flew me to Disney on a private plane when I told him there was a new ride there that sounded wonderful. I was still getting used to the reality that there was no restaurant that wouldn't put aside a table for him, no show that was sold out if I wanted to see it. If I didn't have something to wear, a gown arrived. I wondered if he realized, though, that of all the places we went, all the things we did, the days we spent at my house were the ones I treasured the most.

The sex was amazing. Better than amazing, but that wasn't all that made our lunch breaks special. Had sex been all we did, that would have been enough to keep me satisfied, but we also laughed, played board games, ate off each other's plates, and talked about everything. He was a different person at my house and I loved how relaxed he'd become. The arrogance I'd seen in him at our first encounter was gone—replaced by a man who was so considerate there were times it made me teary.

For me, he bought a helicopter so he could spend more time in my arms and less on the road. He flexed his engineering skills by fixing my garbage disposal and a kitchen drawer that I'd had difficulty closing since I moved into the house. He came to my house early one day and replaced the sagging roof of Sage's playground. They were simple things, but each was about taking care of me or making things safer for Sage. To me that all meant so much more than his offer to take me to Venice whenever I'd like to see it.

"Would you like to come to the zoo with Sage and me this weekend?" I asked between bites of stir fry chicken. It was time.

He paused and met my gaze. "I'd love to."

"I'd imagined her getting to know you while at dinners with my family, but my mother is still a little . . ."

He took my hand in his. "She'll come around."

"I hope so. I understand why she's afraid, but she doesn't

know you." The sadness in me was reflected in his eyes. "And I want her to. She's making me choose between the two of you and I hate it."

"Is there anything I can do? Would it help if I spoke to her?"

"I appreciate that, but I don't think she could handle that." I sighed and gave his hand a squeeze. "She's upset with Joanie too, and that's not like her." He searched my face. "I tried to talk to my father. He told me to give her time."

"That sounds like all you can do."

"So, I just accept that? This is how we are until we aren't? I don't think I can do that."

"I know it's hard," he said, putting his food aside and pulling me close. "When it comes to people, what we want and what we get are often not the same."

I frowned. "You would never take that passive track with your business."

"That's true."

There'd been something in his voice that in the passion of my argument, I'd missed, but it gave me pause. "This is also difficult for you, isn't it? You don't talk about your twin anymore. Is that because of me?"

His eyes darkened. "I love you, Ashlee."

"I love you too," I said, laying my head on his shoulder. Choosing this moment to say those words for the first time felt more powerful than if he'd said it while we sipped champagne. Better even than an after-orgasm declaration. At my house, while simply enjoying the presence of each other and talking our way through the awkwardness of life . . . that was when love was the most beautiful. "You shouldn't have to choose me over your twin."

His arms tightened around me. "It's not the same as you and your mother. I don't know him. If I never have a relationship with him . . ."

"You'll just put him in the same pocket as your biological mother and your father's ex-wife? Tell yourself you don't care?"

He kissed the side of my head. "I'll seek him out one day, just not now. Crystal is due to have her baby anytime. I can wait."

I placed my hand over the steady beat of his heart. "You do so much for others. It's okay to say what you need now and then."

His chest rose and fell beneath my hand. "Marry me, Ashlee."

I froze. Had I heard him correctly? "What did you say?"

"You heard me," he murmured as he tipped my face toward him. There was such emotion in his eyes; I fell in love with him all over again.

"I did," I said breathlessly. "Are you sure?"

He stretched to reach into a pocket of his jacket, which was draped across the back of the couch. When he held a small black box out to me, my eyes filled with tears. With his thumb, he flipped it open, revealing a modestly sized round diamond—exactly what I would have chosen for myself. "We can have a long engagement or a short one. You can invite the world or just family. I love you, Ashlee Pryer, and I'm not going anywhere."

I held out my hand toward him. He slid the ring on my finger. "I'm not going anywhere either."

"Is that a yes?"

"No," I said, then quickly added, "it's a hell yes." Shifting my position, I rose onto my knees then straddled his lap. "We have ten minutes left before I need to leave. What would you like to do?"

With his hands on my hips, he moved me back and forth over his hardening cock. "Or you could be late, just this once."

I gripped his shoulders and answered him with a long, deep kiss that had me texting my father to ask for the rest of the afternoon off. When he asked me if everything was okay, I sent him a photo of the ring on my finger and told him Thane and I would stop in to see them that night with Sage.

CHAPTER THIRTY-TWO

Ashlee

THANE AND I decided the best way to tell Sage would be to make the news part of something she enjoyed doing. Over the past two weeks, I'd talked about him to her often and spoken with him via FaceTime while she was around so she could get used to him.

Although our engagement had come about quickly, I loved that Thane was willing to move forward at a speed that worked for all of us. The ring on my finger was a tangible sign that he was serious about us becoming a family. My hope was that Sage would be okay with the news that I was engaged. I texted Joanie to tell her not just that I was engaged, but that if Sage took it well we should all go over to our parents' house that evening. Her enthusiastic response to the news bolstered my confidence.

We picked Sage up from daycare and took her to the park near my house. My heart soared, seeing her greet him with a smile when she saw him standing by my car and handed him her backpack like there was nothing unusual about his presence there. "Hi, Thane."

"Hi, Sage." He took the backpack from her then gave me a surprised look and shrugged.

I mouthed for him to go with it.

Sage opened the back door to my car. "Thane, want to watch me buckle myself in? Mommy says I'm almost too big for the car seat. Then I get a booster seat. I like my car seat. It makes me tall."

"I imagine that it would," he said, moving so he could watch her settle herself in and snap the straps on. "You're very good at that. I bet you'll be driving before you know it."

"I don't want to drive," she said emphatically. "I like my iPad."

"Understood," Thane said then smiled at me. "Her instincts are spot-on. I get a lot more work done when I use a driver as well."

"Mommy's my driver," Sage announced.

"Yes, I am." I laughed. "Is it okay if Thane drives today?"

Sage picked up her iPad. "I don't care. Where are we going?"

"We thought we'd stop by the park and then go over to Grammie and Grampie's house. Your cousins might be there."

"Yes!" She air-pumped with joy.

We let Sage run off some of her energy at the park before taking her over to a picnic table for a drink and a snack. While we were all seated there, I said, "Sage, I have news I'm excited to share with you."

She smiled. "Did you get me a hamster?"

"No," I said with a chuckle. "Thane asked me to marry him and I said yes."

She looked from me to Thane and back. "What does that mean?"

"That means we would have a wedding and become a family."

I was hoping for more joy than showed on Sage's face, but, like Thane, she often needed the details before she agreed to something. "Like live together?"

"Not right away," I assured her. "But after the wedding, yes. How would you feel about that?"

She gave us each another long look. "What is a wedding?"

Wow, of all the things I thought I'd done to prepare her, I hadn't realized the big part I'd left out. "It's where two people stand up in front of everyone and they promise to be family to each other."

"Like a brother and sister?"

Thane coughed.

I held back my own smile. Sage was serious. "No. He would be my husband. Like Uncle Mike is to Auntie Joanie."

"Ooooooh," Sage said. "I like Uncle Mike." She looked at Thane. "He's a daddy. If you marry Mommy, would you be my daddy?"

He cleared his throat and seemed surprisingly moved by

her question. "If you want me to be."

She chewed her bottom lip. "I do want a daddy. Do you have a job?"

With a twinkle in his eyes, Thane nodded solemnly. "I do."

"A car?"

"Yes."

"How do you know you'll be a good daddy?"

Oh, my God, she's a hoot. She's interviewing him for the position.

Thane sat up taller. "I have an excellent father I love very much. I could use him for a reference if you require one."

"What's a reference?" Sage asked.

I supplied, "Someone you could ask about Thane if you didn't believe Thane."

"Do you have brothers and sisters?" She pinned him with a look.

"Brothers, no sisters."

"Cousins?"

"None that I know of."

"And no Mommy. I remember."

"Right, no Mommy," Thane said.

"Do you know how to make waffles?"

"No, but I could learn."

"I like them with blueberries."

"I would make them that way."

Sage reached across the table and pinched Thane's arm. I

gasped. Thane frowned.

"Sage," I said, taking her little hand in mine, "we don't pinch people. Why would you do that?"

Eyes locked with Thane's, Sage said, "I need to see him mad. I don't want a mean daddy."

My heart melted and I hugged her to my side. "Thane would never be mean to you, honey, because I'd never let that happen." Then I added, "Now, apologize to Thane because that wasn't very nice."

"Sorry, Thane," Sage said in a small voice.

Thane bent closer to her and said, "You and I have a lot in common, Sage. I wouldn't agree to anything before I looked into it either. You're one smart little girl. And although I can promise to never be mean to you, I can't promise I won't make mistakes. I've never been a daddy before."

"And I've never had one," Sage said with a sigh.

"Sounds like we'd have to figure out how to make it work together." He reached for my hand. "All of us."

"All of us," I repeated. "Now that sounds like the best kind of family planning."

"I'm sorry I pinched you, Thane," Sage said, her eyes filling with tears.

"Hey," he said in a soft tone. "You know those mistakes I said I'm going to make? You're going to make them too. And it's okay."

Sage sniffed and her face transformed with a smile. The

reassurance that things would be okay was one of my family's mottos.

Never had I thought I could love a man as much as I did Thane in that moment. Life wasn't a smooth ride and there would always be something unexpected popping up, but if we faced those situations together we'd make it.

"Sage, we were thinking about going to Grammie and Grampie's house to tell them our news. Does that sound like a good idea to you?" I asked.

"Can I tell them?" Sage jumped off the bench and ran over to take Thane's free hand in hers. "And can I also tell them that Thane likes hamsters? I think he does. *Do* you like hamsters Thane?"

He met my gaze. "Do I?"

I laughed. *Smart man.* "You like them enough to at least talk about the possibility of one when we all live together."

Sage stage whispered, "That means no, but we can ask again later."

Thane laughed out loud at that. "I see there's a learning curve to this parenting thing."

"And no instruction book," I added with a smile.

Sage gave Thane's hand a tug. "Come on. Let's go. I want to see my cousins."

We both laughed at that and stood. Sage walked ahead of us to the car. I said, "She took it well."

"She's a good kid, Ashlee. You've done well with her. And she's smart. I love that. I need someone to leave my half of our company to."

My eyes flew to his. "You mean that."

"Of course. Even if things didn't work out between you and me, strictly speaking, she's already family and always will be."

I won't cry. I won't cry. "I'm not sure there's anything you could say that would touch my heart more than that just did. I know I didn't find the right twin when I went looking, but I did find the right one, if that makes sense."

He bent and gave me a quick kiss. "It does." His phone buzzed. After checking it, he said, "Crystal is in labor and it's happening fast. Jesse said they have a suite and would like us to be there."

"Can I come?" Sage asked without likely understanding any part of that.

Thane met my gaze. "My family would love to meet Sage, but you did tell your parents we were coming over. I can't not be there for Jesse if he's asking me to be."

My hold on his hand tightened. "Of course you can't. My parents will understand. We can see them in the morning. I know how worried your brother has been about this pregnancy. You need to be there for him. And if you want me there, I'll be there as well."

"Me too," Sage said, taking Thane's other hand in hers.

He looked from me to her and back. "That's up to your mother, Sage. The suite would be similar to the one you were in, Ashlee. If you think that would upset Sage to see,

I'm fine with going alone."

I bent to look Sage in the eye. "Thane's sister-in-law is having a baby. That happens in the hospital like the one I was in. Are you okay with going to a hospital to wait for the baby to come?"

"How does a baby come?" Sage asked with wide eyes.

"Remember how you were in Auntie Joanie's belly and came out? Women go to the hospital to help that happen."

"Oh, yeah. Can I name the baby?"

"No," I said with confidence.

"Hold it?"

"Probably not."

"Why are we going?"

"Because Thane's brother Jesse doesn't want to be alone while he waits for the baby."

"Oh, okay." She looked up at Thane. "We should bring cookies."

Shaking my head, I laughed. "Ever the opportunist. That's my daughter."

Thane smiled. "Like I said, she has what it takes."

"I have what it takes," Sage chirped from his side.

"Okay, I'll text Joanie and my parents. They'll understand." *I hope.*

CHAPTER THIRTY-THREE

Thane

IT WAS PAST ten that night when Ashlee and I flopped side by side onto the couch in her living room. She cuddled to me and I turned my head to breathe her in. Despite being tired, I was smiling. "I thought for sure Sage would wake up when I carried her in from the car, but she was out."

"It's late," Ashlee said, cuddling closer. "Thank you for carrying her. She's getting heavy for me."

"Not a problem." My smile widened as I remembered how she'd worked her way around the room that night, winning over my family one after the other. "She's a charmer too. My family adores her already."

"She was a good icebreaker, that's for sure. I know to-night was an unusual way to meet them, but tell everyone I appreciated how welcoming they were to both of us. I was nervous at first, but they were all so nice."

"They know how much you mean to me." I lifted her left hand, loving how the ring I'd given her sparkled with promise. "And our news gave everyone something good to think about while waiting for Declan."

"Little Declan. He was so tiny. I remember thinking the same thing when I first saw Sage."

"How adorable was Sage when they let her put on a lab coat and mask so she could go in to see him?"

"It's something she'll never forget. In fact, when she tells the kids at daycare she'll probably say she delivered Declan herself."

"I won't correct her."

Ashlee chuckled. "You, sir, will spoil her if you're not careful."

"I'm sure you'll guide me through that."

Smiling, Ashlee gave me a brief kiss, before settling back against my side. "My father was always the softie. It was my mother who laid down the law in our house. As long as we keep a united front, we'll be fine."

I liked that. United was how my family always had been and how I hoped it always would be. "Speaking of united, when do you want to go see your parents tomorrow?"

"Late morning? It's the weekend and hopefully Sage will sleep late so she won't be cranky."

I tightened my arm around her. "I would love to stay, but that might be a lot to spring on Sage."

"It would be." She let out a relieved sigh. "I'm sorry. I know this sounds old-fashioned, but I'd like to hold off on that step until we're married—"

I kissed away the rest of her apology. When I raised my

head, I said, "I love you and the way you think. Text me in the morning when you're ready for me to come over."

It would have been easy to stay, but it wasn't difficult to leave because we would have forever together. Trust was something that didn't come easily for me, but Ashlee and I were solid in a way that went beyond the vows we would say to each other. Her ability to love her daughter told me she was capable of the kind of love I'd told myself I didn't need, but had always yearned for.

I was driving to where my helicopter and pilot would be waiting for me when my phone rang. I answered, letting it connect to my car's Bluetooth. "Speak."

The person on the other side let out a long breath. "I hope I'm not bothering you, but my husband gave me your number."

"You're always welcome to call me, Mrs. Pryer."

"Diane. Please. Congratulations on your new nephew. Ashlee sent us a photo of him."

"Thank you."

"This is awkward, so I'm just going to say it. I didn't want Ashlee to date you. It had nothing to do with you and everything to do with me not wanting to see my daughter get hurt."

"I understand, Diane. We've spoken a little about your reasons."

Her voice was thick when she said, "Then you understand that I'd die to keep my family safe."

"As would I."

"It's not that Ashlee and I haven't clashed before. I've always tried to convince her to take the safer path and she's always done things her way. I thought if I could convince her to not see you anymore, I could prevent her from doing something crazy like seeking out your brother for you."

"I've assured her that's not necessary. I'll handle that situation."

"You may love my daughter, Thane, but you have a lot to learn about her if you think that'll stop her. Joanie has already located your twin. I was so angry with her when she told me she'd tracked him down."

My hands tensed on the wheel. "They haven't contacted him, have they?"

"Not as far as I know, but they will if you don't. And, I'll be right there with them because I won't be able to let them go alone."

"That won't happen." Shit.

"Thane," Diane said.

"Yes?"

"No, I was telling my husband who I'm on the phone with." She added, "Hang on, Kit, I'll give you the phone, but I want to say something first."

I pulled into the lot where my helipad was and waited.

Diane said, "Not being the first person Ashlee called when you two got engaged was a wake-up call for me. I love my daughter and if she loves you, I'm sure I will too. I'm sorry that I didn't give you a chance. Nothing matters more to me than my family and now that it looks like you'll be joining it, I hope you'll allow us to have a fresh start."

I cleared my throat. "A fresh start sounds wonderful. My family argues, we mess up, but we always make up. I'm sorry I come with so much baggage. I promise, though, I will keep your family safe from it."

"I can see why my daughter loves you. Does Sage know you're engaged? How did she take it?"

"Sage was fine with it and my family adores her. Diane, call Ashlee. She needs you as much as you need her."

Sniffing, Diane said, "Okay. I will. Hold on, Kit wants to say something."

"Thane?"

"Yes, sir?"

"Marriage isn't a destination you get to and relax. It's a journey you take together. You'll have good days, bad days, things you should have told each other earlier, and things you should have kept to yourself. I've been with my wife more than thirty years, and I'm still discovering things about her. Like today, I just watched her put her hurt and pride aside and remind me why I fell in love with her all those years ago. Oh, man, now she's crying. I should go. You coming over tomorrow morning?"

"Probably closer to noon. Ashlee's going to let Sage sleep in and I'm heading home."

"Come hungry. It's not every day our little girl gets engaged. We'll gather and feast."

I chuckled. "I look forward to it." After explaining that the helicopter was powering up, we ended the call.

A short time later, back at my apartment, I'd stepped out of my shoes, stripped down to my boxers and was heading to my bedroom when Ashlee called. "Hey."

"Hey, sunshine."

"I just had the most wonderful conversation with my parents."

"I'm glad. Did your mother tell you she called me? We're good now."

"She told me. Thank you for accepting her apology so graciously."

"I understood why she was concerned. She also told me that Joanie located my twin."

"Don't be upset. Please. I was just as surprised to hear she'd done it as you probably were. I don't know what has gotten into those two. My mom said if I do anything crazy like go to find him without telling you, she's coming with me."

"Um, you're not going anywhere near him."

"Then you do it, Thane, because if you don't you'll always regret that you didn't. I know it's complicated and it'll be hard at first, but I believe in you. If your brother is suffering, I know you'll help him. If there are children out there with twins they don't know about, I believe you'll help them find each other. And you don't have to face any of that alone. I'm right here. We'll do it together. All of it. For better or worse, crazy or sane family, I'm all in."

There were defining moments in every man's life and that was one of mine. I chose to be the man the woman I loved believed I was. I'd talk to Jesse and explain that some things were more important than the Bellerwood contract. Somewhere out there, I had a brother and he needed me. "Okay, we'll do this. We'll contact him. But your mother isn't coming."

Ashlee laughed. "We can talk more about that tomorrow."

"Oh, my God, what am I getting myself into?" I asked with pained humor. "And why didn't I choose a woman who'd agree with everything I say?"

"Where would the fun be in that?" she asked with a chuckle.

Where, indeed. Ashlee had stormed into my life, turned it upside down, made me a father, and had me believing that things did work out the way they were supposed to.

Crystal and Declan were no longer at risk.

The space station was moving forward as scheduled.

It was time to find Zachary.

"Ashlee, promise me something."

"If I can."

"Don't ever change. The world needs more people like you."

"Mr. Rehoboth. If you're trying to win my heart, you

already have it."

"Good. Now onto a very important question."

"Yes?"

"Will we keep having lunch lunch after we're married?"

The joy in her answering laugh warmed me to my soul. "I'd be disappointed if we didn't. I love you, Thane."

"I love you too, sunshine. Go to bed before I start thinking of creative ways we could tire each other out."

"You say that like it's a bad thing," she teased.

And that's all it took for me to get significantly less sleep that night.

The End

"Don't want the story to end? Read on with Book 2 of The Twin Find: Out of Office

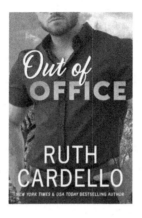

A recluse discovers that what he endured and survived was orchestrated by one evil man. With nothing left to lose, Zachary wakes up and chooses vengeance.

Charlotte Simmons may pretend to be innocent, but everything she has was bought with money made from my suffering.

I intend to uncover her family's sins and expose them to the world.

Lying about who I am? She doesn't deserve the truth.

Having sex with her to gain her trust . . . at least I'll make it good for her.

I'm going to rip everything away from her and her family . . .just like her grandfather took everything from me.

And I'm going to enjoy every moment of it.

Don't miss a release or a sale. Sign up for my newsletter today. Go here
ruthcardello.com/newsletter

About the Author

Ruth Cardello hit the New York Times and USA Today Bestsellers Lists for the first time in 2012. Millions of sales later, her books are compared to potato chips; addictive from the first one. Her multi-series billionaire world, with a combination of escapism and realism, has gained her a faithful following of readers.

Ruth was born the youngest of 11 children in a small city in northern Rhode Island. She spent her young adult years traveling and exploring. She lived in Boston, Paris, Orlando, New York then came full circle and moved back to New England. She now happily lives one town over from the one she was born in. For her, family trumped the warmer weather and international scene.

She was an educator for 20 plus years, the last 11 as a kindergarten teacher. When her school district began cutting jobs, Ruth turned a serious eye toward a love she's had for most of her life – writing. She's never been happier.

When she's not writing, you'll find Ruth spending quality time with her children, playing with her two grandbabies, connecting with her readers online, or running around her small farm with her husband, horses, and chickens.

Contact Ruth:

Website: RuthCardello.com

email: ruthcardello@gmail.com

FaceBook: Author Ruth Cardello

Instagram: authorruthcardello

TikTok: @author.ruthcardello

Bookbub: bookbub.com/authors/ruth-cardello

Made in the USA
Middletown, DE
16 May 2023